WREN JANE BEACON RUNS THE TIDEWAY

BOOK THREE

A NOVEL BY

DJ Lindsay

See also:
Book One, 'Wren Jane Beacon Goes to War'
Book Two, 'Wren Jane Beacon at War'

www.wrenjaneb.co.uk

A CIP catalogue record for this book is available from the British Library.

Book cover design: Alan Cooper, www.alancooperdesign.co.uk

Acknowledgements

In writing the third part of the saga of Wren Jane Beacon some familiar names crop up from the earlier two books, such as Peter Leppard and Glenda Whitley. But the research required for this book, largely set on the Thames, called for more extensive investigation. There was surprisingly little obviously available about the Thames during World War Two and it took some persistent digging to get hold of the story.

First and foremost I would like to record my thanks to Lotte and Chris Moore. Lotte, grand-daughter of the renowned A P Herbert whom she had known well during and after the war, was a fount of information about him and helped me considerably to get closer to him. Her husband Chris was equally helpful and their support has been much appreciated.

Three people were a great help in accessing archives. First, Vicky Holmes the archivist for the Port of London Authority records, now held at the London Museum, could not have been more helpful in finding material and in pointing to where more could be found. Second, Robert (Rob) Jefferies, curator of the Thames River Police Museum at Rotherhithe gave unstintingly of his time and knowledge in finding relevant material for my particular enquiries. And third, Jennifer Thorp, curator of the Alan P Herbert archive at New College Oxford, was a considerable help in extracting the river material which allowed me to get straight into the areas of interest to me.

And by no means least, my editor Wendy Yorke and designer Alan Cooper have worked their magic in taking my raw text and cover and turning them into a book. As ever, my thanks to them.

Dedication

To all you fine ladies

Looking back and forward

This third book in the Wren Jane Beacon series carries her story forward to the next major step, taking command of a launch on the Thames during the Blitz, with a full Wren crew. The first two books were dominated by her adventures at Dunkirk and the periods before and after when she became established as the first boat crew Wren.

Her fiery independence of spirit has meant that she has lived and worked just one step ahead of Naval authority and this pattern continues in this third book. Encouraged by her parents she has become more thoughtful about war and her place in it but her strong sense of duty is the other pillar of her view of the world.

One step behind these adventures and commitment, finding true love for the first time is an all-conquering force which sets her on an emotional journey as stormy as the seas she had survived on. The complex interweaving of her work as a Wren with her romantic life is an ever-growing thread through the books which finds a first fulfilment at the end of the second book and develops in this third volume.

Contents

Prologue

Apart from the intermittent shelling, Dover was having a relatively quiet time towards the end of 1940. There were still bombing attacks from time to time and a drifter was sunk alongside the jetty on 14th November, but the huge pressures of earlier in the year had gone. Although warships called in frequently there were no locally based vessels apart from the coastal forces boats which were becoming more common. This was largely because the Blitz had been shifted by the Luftwaffe to many other cities in Britain, mainly the industrial and communication centres. On 14th November the Germans launched a massive attack on Coventry, devastating the city centre and most famously destroying its cathedral. This was another event with long consequences. Air Chief Marshall Sir Arthur ('Bomber') Harris on surveying the damage remarked grimly that the Germans had sewn the wind. They were to reap the hurricane in the firestorm bombing of Hamburg and Dresden. In Britain, the Government had been exercising strict censorship on news about bombing raids. But the destruction of Coventry was so extensive that it could not be covered up, and it led to a change of policy allowing the media more or less to report as they chose. So these events appeared in the newspapers fairly immediately. There was a powerful groundswell of opinion among the British that the more retaliatory bombing Britain could do, the better, and there were some unfortunate incidents when baled out German aircrew were very badly treated by locals on the ground before authorities could get to them and remove them to the safety of a prisoner of war camp.

Outside their own little world in Dover, the war went on. London was being blitzed nightly, and chunks of the old city lost. The Navy was as busy as ever, with convoy duty in the Atlantic demanding more small ships than they had but the few carried on the grim battle with the U-boats as best they could. The main scene of action was the Mediterranean where Italy's entry into the war, and France's capitulation had radically changed the balance of power. The Italian Navy was large and well equipped but not well led with too much remote control from ashore. The British forces fought back as well as they could and refused to be dislodged from their powerful position in the area. A new development was increasing use of carrier-based air power to attack the Italian fleet wherever they could. This culminated in one of the seminal actions of the war. On the night of ten/eleventh November 1940 a group of twenty-one old Swordfish biplanes flying from HMS Illustrious attacked the Italian fleet lying at anchor in Taranto. They torpedoed and sank three battleships and damaged sundry other warships for the loss of two aircraft. The remarkable success of this raid was trumpeted far and wide by the Navy;

it was the first time that maritime air power had shown itself to be so devastating. This lesson was noted by other Navies including the Americans, but most of all by the Japanese who studied it very closely. The direct result was a change of plans and their imitation attack on Pearl Harbour. The law of unintended consequences meant that a raid carried out for local and tactical purposes in the Mediterranean was to be directly influential in bringing America into the war and hence to the Allies winning it.

In London the sorely tried citizenry got on with their lives as best they could. Despite the widespread damage it became clear even to Hitler that a city like London was too big and too amorphous to be destroyed. Equally, the morale of an entire population (British or German) could not be broken by bombing. But while it went on it gave a pretty miserable existence to those citizens who were directly underneath the bombs.

PART ONE:

INTERMEZZO

CHAPTER 1:
Is this progress?

Leading Wren Jane Beacon's exploits in the Navy's small boats had given her some notoriety to go with the rows of medals she was awarded. Despite all the orders to keep a low profile, her expedition to Dunkirk added to her other activities and misdemeanours had drawn a lot of attention to women working in boats, thereby upsetting and delighting the Royal Navy's top brass in equal measure. By late 1940 Wrens in boats was a serious topic in Naval circles.

For leading Wren Jane Beacon those few days in London at the end of September 1940 had been tumultuous. The investiture at Buckingham Palace, the enthusiasm of the French and Belgian legations, and her Director's friendly but demanding meeting, would have left her feeling emotionally drained afterwards had it not been for her suddenly finding love. Under the intense 'live for the day' pressure of wartime, meeting and falling for a man with an unexpected mutual background, and finding his feelings just as strong in return, had sent her spirits soaring in the two days they had together. On the long train ride down to Plymouth and home, joy in her heart more than made up for the draining of adrenalin as she came down off the high of the previous few days.

Her six days' award leave, back home in the snug womb of the Old Grange, had been very enjoyable. Jane got up late despite waking early, even had breakfast in bed. It was brought by old servant Agnes who brought news of her Italian husband, Pappa Gianni. He had been the family's outside man, but under the 'Collar the Lot' instruction from Churchill he had been somewhat brutally deported despite his long life in England. His letters reported that he had settled down well in Canada under a very light internment regime. Without any outside assistance, the Old Grange was starting to look a bit run down so Jane spent time doing odd jobs about the place, cleaning, weeding and even a little painting. She rowed up to the yacht *Osprey* and found her lying quietly like a gentle horse waiting for the next command. All was well, with a bit of water in the bilge which took twenty minutes to pump out and a couple of lashings to renew, but their original work was holding up well. The boat's topsides were getting rather faded but otherwise she was still in good order. Jane took her uniforms to the family dressmaker as soon as the medal ribbons arrived, and had them sewn on. They made quite a display.

While Jane was quietly enjoying this relaxation, several discussions went on about her with important consequences. The first was at the Admiralty, where a long planning meeting among a group of Admirals about policy in the Eastern Mediterranean had Wrens as boat crew tacked on to the end of the agenda. Two desk Admirals were there. They had met Jane during lunch at Bournemouth when their car journey had paused there. After her energetic talk about her life in the Wrens and what women could do, they had circulated a paper proposing the use of women more widely throughout the Service; this had had a very mixed reception. Both her Godfather Rear-Admiral Rodmayne and Vice-Admiral 'Black Joe' Penrose were at the meeting as they were shortly being posted East. The meeting, however, was chaired by the very senior admiral known as Buffy. Anyone from the WRNS was conspicuously absent.

The discussion was predictable. It was tabled that 'Use of Wrens as boat crew be given active consideration in the light of their demonstrated ability'. Buffy was having none of it. "Dammit, these bloody women will be taking over if you let them. So what if they can drive a boat. So can my dog if he's pointed in the right direction. I'll not have it, damn your eyes."

Admirals Rodmayne and Penrose looked at each other. "With all due respect, sir, the manning situation is getting so critical that we can't afford to overlook a resource like this. We have calculated that up to five hundred sailors could be released to the ships if we used Wrens on the boats now there's no doubt about their ability to handle them."

"That's not the point" roared Buffy. "Look at this bloody girl we've got – disobeying orders, cosying up to the Army, stealing and wrecking boats, going AWOL, arguing with anyone who comes near her, even pulling the wool over a tribunal's eyes. Is that what we want?"

"Well sir, she has had to fight her corner pretty strongly even to get this far. And I don't think you will find girls in general are so difficult. I'm told the other Wren doing it down at Dover is performing very well without any arguments at all."

"Yes but women will always be difficult one way or another. Have a fit of the vapours if you so much as look at them crossly."

"That's not been what we have found so far. They're proving tougher than we expected and you must know, sir, that in general they are being very well received wherever they have gone."

"Yes, but that's only to brighten the place up for the lads. I can't take them seriously."

"I rather think you're going to have to, sir. We don't have enough sailors to be able to leave them in easy billets ashore and that includes the boats."

"Do not threaten me, George. This discussion is closed. Next Item."

But was it co-incidence that a few weeks later a discreet memo came out from one of the desk Admirals, acting with authority, inviting the opinion of Port Admirals about whether they felt Wrens could make up boats' crews? Responses were mixed: Plymouth was positive but had been got at, Portsmouth doubtful and The Nore noncommittal until they had had a chance to see the pioneers in action. This was passed to the Director, WRNS and it sealed the plans for Jane's future. The Nore (and hence the Thames) it would be.

In a grand mansion on the North side of the Chilterns Lord Arthur Daubeny-Fowkes was at home for a weekend and got into conversation with his mother, the Marchioness, after dinner. She was a large lady, sitting upright without her back touching the chair, at ease in a purple velvet evening gown in front of a roaring log fire, a generous glass of brandy at her elbow and a dog at her feet. In passing he mentioned that his little brother had fallen head over heels in love with the Wren who had rescued him at Dunkirk. The Marchioness frowned. "Do we know anything about this Amazon?"

"Nice well educated intelligent middle class girl, Mater. Father a successful physician, I gather."

"Hmm. Is she in love with David?"

"Oh God yes, they couldn't keep away from each other. Dinner with them was a bit uncomfy, they were so deep into each others' eyes."

"Well, that is all very well and it will do David good to have an affair before he settles down. But they needn't entertain any thoughts of marriage – This filly doesn't sound as though she has the bloodlines at all and without the breeding how can you know what you're getting? David must marry a thoroughbred."

"She's stunningly good looking, if that helps."

"No it doesn't. It will simply warp his mind. No doctor's daughter need aspire to our level - they are service providers and mustn't be allowed to get above their station. We won't act against it yet – poor David needs some practise somewhere – but this will need watching and nipping in the bud if it looks like going too far. Kindly keep me informed."

Arthur felt saddened by this – his little brother had always struggled to survive at the bottom of the family heap and this sudden flowering had brought him out in a way Arthur had never seen before. But the Marchioness's commands were not be trifled with.

There was a curious mirror image conversation at the Old Grange. It hadn't taken her mother long to detect that Jane was on a dreamy cloud. "Is this a man, Jane?"

Jane nodded, happily. There was no point in trying to deny this one. "Yes, mummy. Do you remember I told you about rescuing some sailors from a burning destroyer at Dunkirk? Well, I met the officer involved at Buckingham Palace because he was up for a medal too. One thing has kind of led to another and we're so happy with each other."

Her mother gave Jane a quizzical look. "Do you know anything about his background?"

"A bit. He's Lieutenant-Commander Lord David Daubeny-Fowkes from some aristo family. And he's lovely, mummy."

"Jane dear, far be it from me to spoil your happiness but you don't want to be getting mixed up with the aristocracy. They're either degenerates or unthinking snobs who wouldn't consider us suitable for one minute. Be very careful where you put your heart because this particular love can only bring you heartache in the end."

"But mummy we love each other and he is the youngest in the family. He seems to think that gives him a bit more freedom to do what he wants."

"Just watch them close ranks if you get too close. Please, Jane, be very careful because I'd hate to see you hurt. You know I'd love to see you settled with your own partner but an aristo is taking a big chance."

Jane just smiled, the happy confident smile of youthful certainty.

The night before there had been a small celebration at dinner. It was exactly one year since Jane had gone through the gates at Devonport, becoming a Wren for the first time. The anniversary seemed worth marking, although it was hard to believe that a year had gone by already. Her father looked at his warrior daughter fondly. "Does your haul of medals make you feel more committed to the cause?"

"I suppose so. I know you tried to get me to think about what I was doing, but from day to day you just get on with it, y'know."

"Well, it does no harm to take stock here and there. At least you got some recognition for nearly dying."

"Thanks to the Army, yes. There are bits of the Navy who have not given up on wanting me out, so I'm told."

"Nothing unusual about that. The old curmudgeons won't ever take kindly to a girl standing out as you have."

"But father I had to, to make the point that girls can handle the boats."

Her father laughed gently.

What made Jane think much more about war and whether she should be supporting it was her visit to Horace's mother. Rescuing her childhood friend from his sinking, burning Hurricane and having him die in her arms had deeply disturbed Jane. But that was nothing compared with the wretchedness of his gently faded mother. She was struggling to suppress her tears from the moment Jane arrived and clearly had been hard hit by her son's demise. They took tea from fine bone china and nibbled on tiny cucumber sandwiches while Jane struggled to explain what had happened without making it more painful. A widowed mother's grief for her only child was so raw, so close to the surface that ordinary murmurs of comfort seemed almost insulting and Jane had difficulty finding anything appropriate to say. After a difficult half hour she rose to go, and on impulse gave Mrs Horan a hug. This austere lady was clearly startled by the gesture but it cracked the dam and the flood followed. She sat down with a thump. Jane sat down more sedately and held her hand, saying nothing as Mrs Horan sobbed helplessly. After some minutes she managed to get control of herself again and apologised. "Oh please, Mrs Horan, think nothing of it. I was pretty shattered at the time to find it was Horace we'd pulled out but that's nothing comparatively. I've seen quite a few deaths now and I suppose they all caused grief somewhere but it must be so different when it is your own. Horace's memory will live on, you know, and at least he died doing his best for Britain."

Mrs Horan gave Jane a wan half smile. "Yes, I can see that and it's some small comfort but I would still rather have him back."

"Well that's hardly surprising."

The distraught mother looked into some far away place. " He'd only been in combat three times."

Suddenly the lady got hold of herself, dried her eyes and stood up. "Thank you for coming to see me. I do appreciate it and I know I must stand up to my feelings."

And Jane found herself escorted to the door by a calm and composed lady.

Sitting looking out at the passing scene as the train chuffed slowly up to London, Jane reflected on her visit to Mrs Horan. In many ways that painful scene was a far greater indictment of war than all the poets, all the bitter memoirs, could ever be.

This was the real cost of war – sad solitary old ladies left with nothing but memories and a sense of waste, the purpose they had dedicated their lives to brought to nothing by a savagery they could barely comprehend let alone come to terms with. For what was left of their lives there was only emptiness. 'And I'm contributing to that?' thought Jane. 'But am I really? Isn't my role to help, to support and succour the system?' The moral voice at the back of her brain muttered 'Tell that to the Germans you shot.' The front replied 'But it was them or me.' And back came the answer: 'Precisely – at its simplest all war is them or me and you're actively a part of that brutal basic whether you like it or not.' Jane shook her head. Really there was no simple answer to this and it was easier not to go there. With a wry smile it occurred to her that she was sounding just like her mother. But a painful memory remained a hurt deep in her psyche.

Returning to the Wrennery of HMS *Lynx* at Dover had a sense of old familiarity to it by now, but there were changes in her cabin. Her former cabin mates Jo and Barbara had evidently gone. A picture of a Thames Barge in full sail with the bow wave foaming high round it was some indication, but the assorted movie star posters in the other bunk could have been any young female's.

Jane dumped her bags, gave Rufus the bear a pat, and headed down to the harbour. As she got close to the boat station there was something horribly wrong. The quayside was ripped up and broken, with a hole where the main embarkation steps had been. The boats office walls had holes in them. Worried, Jane looked over into the harbour. There was a large floating mat of timbers – some recognisably bits of boat, others just wood. The characteristic counter-stern of the picket boat stuck up vertically above the surface. Out at the pier ends one of the pulling whalers was rowing its way slowly round the corner. A quick check showed that neither of them was where they had lain, tucked up in the corner.

Appalled, she hurried in to the boats office. The old Chief Petty Officer was there, his head bandaged. "What on earth has happened here?" she cried.

"Welcome back, Jane. That's quite a chestful of ribbons you've got there. You were well out of this one – a shell from France got us last Wednesday. All the boats are gone –your *Amaryllis* is now matchwood, I'm afraid, as is *Titch*."

"And what about people?"

"Three dead, including your Nobby. Your Chief Roberts has lost a leg and is in hospital. Six others seriously injured. Not good."

"Oh dear. How is Chief Roberts?"

"Not too bad all things considered. Got some blast damage but mainly minus a leg."

"What will happen to him now?"

"Usually it would be medical discharge. Whether that will be the same now with our shortages, I just don't know."

"What a tragedy. And Wren Johnson? What about her?"

"Talk about joss. It was her day off and she was up in the Wrennery. She's out there now, pulling an oar."

"I suppose that's what will happen to me too?"

"If you're staying in boats here then yes, you'll be on an oar. We have a surplus of cox'ns for the moment."

Jane was dismayed at the step backwards. But something inside her said 'Don't give up. This is another test and you must not be defeated.' She just smiled and said "All right, when do I start?"

"Tomorrow morning 0630 as usual. We've got the two of you scheduled for the pinnace."

Just then Boats Officer looked out of his office and saw Jane. "Ah, Beacon, welcome back. Chief's told you what happened, I presume?"

Jane nodded. "Yes sir. Bit of a mess."

"That's an understatement. Fortunately we're not busy just now but my boat crews are finding muscles they didn't know they had and so will you. You are all right to go pulling, I assume?"

"Yes sir. I've been rowing all my life. These big sweeps will be a bit different but I'm sure I can cope. Does this mean an end to my being cox'n?"

"For the moment yes although it's been suggested that it will be interesting to see how you do as cox'n of oars once you get the hang of it."

"It'll be different, that's for sure."

Jane headed back to the Wrennery. She reported to Quarters Officer, collected her mail and settled down to read. Jane's Godfather had gone; his last contact with her a quick note of encouragement and farewell as he left Dover for the Eastern Mediterranean. Among the letters were two from Josef – impassioned pleadings to meet again mixed with wildly detailed memories of their last encounter. There was also a brief note from David. His command had been confirmed, in *HMS Bowman,* and he was off to work it up immediately. Apart from 'All my love' at the end, it was simply a quick business note and a marked contrast with Josef's outpourings. Jane checked in *'Jane's Fighting Ships'* and found *Bowman* was a 1930-built destroyer; just the sort of ship a dashing young officer might hope for, for a first command. But Josef's enthusiasms? This was something she would have to sort out very quickly, in fairness to him. Should she just write to Josef and say she loved another? That seemed a bit mean. But any meeting with him, even if she intended to keep it casual and chaste, was bound to carry baggage from last time and there was no doubt about what he wanted. His English seemed to be improving rapidly. The nearest David's note had come to anything closely personal was to remind her to send a picture, so she sorted out a couple, one in uniform with scar and white streak showing, the other in plain clothes and her other cheek. She wrote a quick loving note to go with them and posted them off.

Come five o'clock she was peacefully eating her cheesy oosh when Punch, her right-hand crew girl, plonked down beside her, closely followed by Sparrer, Punch's oppo. "Evenin' Jane. How was the Palace?"

"Not as scary as I feared and would you believe it, the King gave me an MBE as well at Churchill's behest. The French were hyper enthusiastic and I've met a bloke. Hope it works out. And you?"

"Oh, we were lucky to miss the shell and I can't say I am enjoying rowing again but I s'ppose it is nothing new. And look at this:" Punch twisted to show an oak leaf sewn onto her jacket.

"Oh good, it's come through. That's quick. Look what I got." On the end of her British medal ribbons Jane showed her Mentioned in Despatches oak leaf with a rosette sewn into the middle of it. There had been some doubt about whether this was correct procedure for a second MiD as regulations said only one oak leaf would be worn no matter how many times anyone got MiD, but for lack of clear guidance they had decided the rosette was as good an idea as any.

"I gather we're out at 0630. Is it you in my cabin now?"

Punch nodded "Yes, and Sparrer too. Quarters Officer decided to put all the boat Wrens together."

Jane was puzzled. "Sparrer? You're not boat crew are you?"

Sparrer nodded enthusiastically. "I am now. They wanted someone to do bowman in the pinnace and Punch persuaded them they wanted the lightest person possible. So I've been learning boat hook drill an' riding round in the bow of the pinnace."

Jane laughed. "And are you enjoying it?"

"Yeah I'm loving it. Me dad always said there was nothing like bein' out on the water and I see why now."

"Well, it will be interesting to get to know you better."

After supper Jane took herself off to the hospital in time for visiting hour. She found Stan lying on his back with a big cage over his legs. He was dozing so she sneaked up on him and kissed him gently on the forehead. He leapt about a foot in the air. "Jane! ForChrissake!" Then he collapsed back on the pillows.

"Hello Stan. I heard about your leg. How is it?"

"Well the missing bit hurts like hell but the surgeons tell me I should make a good recovery. It's gone below the knee which means I should get decent mobility and they've already measured me up for an artificial leg. Meantime It's a crutch." He then looked at Jane's jacket with its multiple medal strips. "Ee lass, that's quite a collection you've got there. Should scare any admiral."

"That's the trouble Stan, they don't like being scared. Have you any news of what will happen to you?"

"Some welfare person has been round to see me and my Divisional Officer reckons that I'll get a decent discharge but Jane I don't want a discharge. I only know the Andrew. Been in it since I was fourteen. I've told my Divisional Officer so, but he was a bit vague."

Jane remembered Stan sitting comfortably behind a desk. "Surely you could do the same sort of job as Chiefie does in the boats office? You don't need so much mobility for that."

"That would be champion."

"With the manpower shortages they're getting now I wouldn't have thought they could afford to do without you. Shall I make some enquiries for you?"

"By all means lass. You know what I'd like to do."

"What happened to Nobby?"

"He was right on the pier when the shell landed. A few bits of him were found and sent home to Essex."

"That's really sad – I liked Nobby and he was so helpful to me."

"Well lass, there's a war on and that happens. But yes, I'll miss him too. He'd been part of my crew for four years."

Jane nodded wistfully, and the two sat in silent contemplation for a minute.

She kissed his forehead again on leaving; walking down the corridor she met Sister Donaldson, bustling by. There was a moment's double-take. "Good heavens, Beacon! Nice to see you again. How are you?"

"Oh, fully recovered and back in harness. I've just been up to Buck House to collect my medals."

"Yes, I heard you'd been awarded a collection of them: very impressive. It was worth our while bringing you back from the brink." And with that the nurse who had done so much to bring Jane back to full health after Dunkirk, charged off leaving Jane to reflect that being impressed was a relative concept.

CHAPTER 2:
Bending her back

0600 next morning came soon enough. The prospect of having to go and row all day was not an enticing one but whether she liked it or not Jane had to obey military discipline and rolled out. Both Punch and Sparrer were sitting up but hardly hurrying themselves. "Jane, we've got five minutes yet before we have to be moving - relax." But Jane headed down to the harbour and the pinnace she was booked for, as soon as she was breakfasted and ready.

With eight oars a side the pinnace was demanding of manpower but with all the other boats gone Dover had a temporary surplus of boat crew so able to man it. Jane found herself assigned to the third thwart from forward beside Punch, on the starboard side although because she was facing aft she had to consciously think of orders the other way round. Starboard was now on her left hand. Punch gave quiet explanations. "When we get the order 'toss your oars' we all lift an oar up in a rippling motion starting from stroke. Right after the bloke in front of you, lift it vertical between your knees and remember to trim the blade fore and aft. 'Boat your oars' is the same process in reverse to stow them away. When Cox says 'out oars' you drop yours into the rowlock. The rest is pretty obvious. 'Give way' means pull on your oar. 'Oars' mean stop rowing and keep your oar exactly parallel with the water, blade feathered. You don't need to feather when we're rowing. " Jane smiled her thanks and concentrated. On the order, the oars went up although she was fractionally slow in lifting the long and heavy spar. The cox'n dropped the starboard oars, backwatered off the berth with Sparrer pushing with all her might on a boathook to get the bow off. Once off it was "Stand by together" and all sixteen oars went to the catch. "Give way together" and with some minimal clashing of oars they pulled away. The matelots had been doing this for a week now and had mostly got it right. Jane found the rhythm of the stroke odd at first – a long slow pull, leaning back on the oar with arms straight and letting her back and buttocks do the work, then a quick recovery to the catch, oar in again for another long slow pull. It made for easy rhythmic work but by lunch time her stomach muscles were grumbling a bit. By the end of the day her hands were raw despite their calluses. Flopping onto her bunk she groaned. Punch grinned at her, "Now you know what real work is. Don't worry I suffered for the first few days then you settle in." This was to be the pattern of work for the next couple of weeks. Jane found the second day painful in various bits of her anatomy but after that her muscles steadily hardened off and her calluses were shiny hard by any standards. Her stomach muscles tightened till they were firmer than any corset and her bell bottoms were hanging off round her waist.

The next thing to do was to make some enquiries about Stan. She started in the Boats Office which had some useful background information but could do nothing in executive terms. As far as they were concerned, Stan was gone. So she tracked down his Divisional Officer, a keen young lieutenant who was sympathetic but again could only tell her what the situation was. This was frustrating. Someone must have authority to decide and to tell her what the possibilities were. The breakthrough came when she met the Welfare Officer by chance, arriving at Stan's bedside at the same time as Jane. He was preparing a report with recommendations about Stan's future and the three of them got into a lively debate. The Welfare Officer had no idea that there were jobs a one-legged sailor could do in the Navy, and was simply making arrangements for Stan to be retired. "But that's ridiculous," exclaimed Jane. "Stan can still do a useful job, just not a mobile one. It's stupid to throw away all that accumulated experience."

"I'm sorry, I have no authority to do anything except arrange for his discharge."

"So who do I see to change this silly arrangement?"

"Commander Nixon is probably the best person. He has overall authority here for personnel matters."

"Can you arrange for me to see him?"

"Nothing to do with me, young lady. You'll have to arrange that yourself."

The light of battle was coming on in Jane's eyes. "Where do I find this gentleman?"

"He's based at *HMS Wasp.*"

"Right, that's where I will go then."

She had to wait till her next late watch before being able to go to Commander Nixon, but early the following week she was able to present herself at his office at 0930 sharp. He proved to be a mild-mannered balding desk officer, but she was careful to give him the full salute and report on arrival. He looked at her over his half-moon glasses. "Right, Miss Beacon, what is it you want to see me about?"

"It's about Chief Petty Officer Roberts, sir. Do you know he's lost his lower left leg in a shell blast? And the Welfare Officer is making arrangements to discharge him from the Navy?"

"I have seen the papers, and it seems correct procedure to me. What is your concern?"

"Sir, it's only his lower left leg, he will get perfectly mobile again and there's no reason why he shouldn't do a desk job, probably in a boats office. He's been in the Navy all his life and a boat cox'n for years, and desperately does not want to be discharged. Surely something can be done to allow him to stay in, given how short of senior staff we are and how useful he could still be?"

"You make an interesting case, young lady. Why are you so concerned about him?"

"Do you know I'm the experimental boat crew Wren?"

"Oh yes, I know about you."

"Well, Chief Roberts was my cox'n when I started and taught me most of what I know now. He has continued to act as a wise advisor to me and I am deeply worried that the Navy may be throwing away a useful chief with enormous experience and understanding. So his future is important to me."

"I see. You really think he can be mobile enough to hold down an office job?"

"Given the encouragement of staying in I'm sure he can be."

"I will consider it. Would it bother you if he was drafted elsewhere?"

"Not at all sir. My only interest is in seeing him treated properly and given the chance to stay in. I owe him that."

"Very well then, I will look at the medical reports and if they are encouraging we'll consider it. But no promises. He will have to pass a medical before being appointed to any active role."

Jane smiled, her happiest beam. "Thank you sir, I'm sure he will be delighted to be given the chance."

And she saluted, about turned and marched off, happier than for some time.

All the while, daily rowing went on. Jane rapidly learnt just how much they could squeeze into a rowing pinnace, piles of stores or mail distributed round under their feet, anything up to twenty liberty men in bow and stern, senior officers to be given full respects and get the stern sheets to themselves. In the pinnace their cox'n, who had been cox'n of the picket boat, was a twenty-seven year veteran Chief Petty Officer originally brought up in naval rowing craft. When put back in one, it did not take him long to polish up his old skills so that he could make the pinnace do anything a power-driven boat would, if a bit more slowly.

With a fortnight back at work gone by, Jane was caught by an unknown Chief Wren. "Beacon, it's Trafalgar night next week and we are having a joint mess dinner with the Chief Petty Officers' mess. Would you come in full regalia as our guest and reply to the immortal memory toast?" This startled Jane a bit as of all levels the Chief Petty Officers guarded their position most jealously and were least likely to welcome a very young junior rate. "Well, that's very kind and yes I'd be delighted to. What do I have to say?"

"Oh, just say some nice things about Nelson and some hopes for a victory in this war. Y'know, the Navy can't be beaten and that sort of thing."

So there was some quick research to do, then her best uniform was spruced up again, shoes polished, and medals pinned on. She was impressed to find herself placed next to the mess president who turned out to be chiefie from the boats office so an old friend, and her spirited response to the toast to the immortal memory went down very well. Once again Jane was struck by the immense solidity of this group, and she idly added up how many centuries of Naval service were in the mess. Passing five hundred, she gave up.

In the background Jane had settled in again at the Wrennery. It didn't take her long to sort out Sparrer who was inclined to leave clothes scattered about the cabin. Punch, sailor that she was, was always tidy and the three of them were left with the cabin to themselves. But Jane had noticed something odd about Punch's behaviour. She was being a bit mysterious and coy, not styles Jane associated with the big girl. Punch would go off into a reverie with a smile on her face and never more so than when she came back from the gym workouts she persisted with despite the rowing exercise. After a week or so of this, it all came out. "Jane, you know about this sort of thing. He wants me to do it but I'm not sure. Do you think I should?"

Jane guessed at the general drift of this but approached it cautiously. "He? Do it? First of all, who is He?"

"Eric, that's Taff the PTI. He trains me in the gym and we've taken a real liking to each other."

A horrible sense of *déjà vu* came over Jane. She wanted to say 'That useless chancer? Run a mile.' But clearly that wasn't the answer Punch wanted. "I know him and he's not my taste but you've been getting close to him?"

"Oh yes, he gives me a kiss and cuddle whenever I finish on the punch bag and now he's asked me to, y'know, do it with him." And Punch blushed a deep crimson. "Do you think I should?"

"It's your body, Punch. And what's this about the punch bag?"

Punch looked round but there was only Sparrer around and she clearly knew the story already. "Oi've kept quiet about it but there's another reason why I'm called Punch. Before the war I was the Eastern Area ladies heavyweight boxing champion and I'd have gone to the nationals if this bleeding war hadn't come along. I reckon I'd have won, too. So now I go to the gym to work out on the punch bag and Eric likes me very much."

"So that's why you are so fit and trim. Right from the start I suspected there was more to you than you were letting on about. It's just as well I didn't get stroppy with you on the pro course. You can punch?"

"Ooh yes, my left hook can knock men out. I've done that in the boxing booths at the fair."

"And now Eric wants to get intimate with you?"

Again, Punch had gone all coy. She sat, eyes downcast, her straight fair hair falling over her bright pink face, and nodded.

"Listen, Punch, you ought to know about his reputation as a ladies' man. I'm not sure how reliable a boyfriend he would be, and as for, er, doing it with him I'd be very careful. Do you love him?"

"Oi think so, he's so nice and encouraging."

'I'll bet' thought Jane but again kept it to herself.

"Well, Punch, far be it from me to put you off or encourage you 'cos whatever I say will be wrong. But remember that once you've done it you can't undo it. This would the first time?"

Punch, acutely embarrassed, could only nod.

"Ask yourself if you want to give it away to this bloke. If you don't mind, then go ahead. But if you want to save it for The One, then keep Eric at arm's length. But whatever you do, don't just accept him getting out at Fratton. You'll need more precautions than that to avoid getting pregnant. You have regular periods?"

This direct talk clearly bothered Punch a lot but she nodded. She was sitting there chewing her lower lip and looking frightened. "But Jane, doesn't it just happen?"

"Emotionally, yes. But you know the score enough to know that physically you need to know what's happening. Next time you see him, look at him and ask yourself if this is the bloke you want to give it away to. Then go away and think about it. Then take precautions because getting pregnant would be a big mistake. Please be careful – you could easily get hurt and I'd hate to see that happen. Has he said anything about me?"

"Not a lot Jane. He said something about he knew you and winked, but didn't explain any more; I think he was sort of implying that you didn't think much of each other."

"Well that would be right, for sure. You just concentrate on what you want to do. You don't have to do anything if you don't want."

"Well I know I shouldn't but Jane I want him. I've had a kiss and a cuddle with a fisher boy back home but boys don't get serious with girls like me very often. It's all right for you – there's always men round you. Someone like me has to take their chances when they come and if I have to do it with him to make that happen then maybe I should. With this blasted war on, who knows when I'd get another boy?"

There wasn't a lot Jane could say to that.

In the pinnace, the two girls had taken to swapping sides each day to even up the demands on their bodies. Once the physical adjustments had been made, life in a rowing pinnace proved to be rather pleasant. Keeping warm was never a problem and lost in the mass of men what any individual did was less obvious unless one clashed oars. At first, rowing at night was more challenging as the oar blades weren't visible and clashes more common. But by taking her timing from the back in front of her and concentrating on rhythm rather than trying to watch her blade, Jane got the hang of it. And rowing at night, with just the thump-thump of oars in rowlocks as guide in an otherwise silent boat, had an almost hypnotic magic.

The pinnace's work was largely inside the harbour, with the occasional foray to just outside the pier heads. On a filthy day of wind and rain they suddenly got orders to take a message out to a Corvette which seemed unwilling to close the harbour mouth. They rapidly discovered that rowing in a steep-faced choppy sea was not easy. Oars were knocked about, clashes almost continuous, and it was very difficult to get anything like a decent pull on an oar which was either up in the air or feet deep in the water according to how the boat was rolling. The most experienced of the rowers found themselves catching crabs, and bodies suddenly lurching backwards into the person ahead of them were frequent. But they battled on and managed to come up behind the stern of the Corvette which had turned head to wind and sea to heave to. This meant the pinnace was heading into the seas too and bouncing about all over the place making it impossible to come alongside. The envelope with the message was passed forward, they brought the boat's bow close in under the stern of the Corvette, and Sparrer had to stand right on the bow to try to hand the envelope up. By standing on tiptoe she had just got it into the hands of a matelot hanging over the ship's stern when the pinnace gave a lurch and with a squeak Sparrer overbalanced. Luckily for her, the second sailor on the ship's stern saw her go, reached down and grabbed her by the scruff of her oilskin as she tumbled towards the sea. Being a tiny lightweight, she gave the sailor no problems in hauling her inboard. But now she was on the wrong vessel. Getting her back was going to be difficult and dangerous. An officer appeared at the stern and bawled, "We'll have to take her with us to the Humber. Can't do a transfer in these conditions. We'll send her back in a few days." Which is how Sparrer came to have her first seagoing trip and loved every minute of it. "They were so nice to me," she reported some days later when back in Dover. "Gave me a little cabin in the officer's flat and let me spend me time on the bridge; I even learned a little navigation. I can take bearings now."

"Weren't you seasick?"

Sparrer considered this. "No, I wasn't, now I think of it. That just never occurred to me, I was enjoying meself too much."

Having lost Sparrer the pinnace crew had a grim battle to slog to windward back to the harbour with drenching spray driving over them on a whipping wind, and every foot forward was hard gained. Normally the half mile they had to go would have taken ten minutes at most. This day they were hard at it for over an hour before they finally crawled into the shelter of the pier ends with the whole crew utterly exhausted, soaked through to the skin and battered by the weather. Punch and Jane stumbled back to the Wrennery, peeled off their oilskins and collapsed on the deck, neither capable of more movement. But they recovered soon enough and next morning as they got the boat ready, Jane casually asked the cox'n if they had been in any real difficulties the day before. "Well, let's put it this way, Jane. You were all pretty near done in by the time we got into shelter. If we'd been out much longer and had to stop rowing, we'd have blown off to leeward and onto the Goodwin Sands quicker than you'd believe possible. So the answer is yes and no, but I wasn't sorry to see us in through the pier heads."

All through this time Jane was happily writing to David every day, and although his replies were shorter they grew much warmer as he got into the way of opening up about his own feelings. Jane could see that he struggled to get beyond the stiffness of his upbringing, and encouraged him in small steps to be more affectionate. His ship was still working-up somewhere in home waters. Although he couldn't say where she was, Jane sensed the Clyde from his descriptions of the mountains sweeping down to the sea.

With deep misgivings she had also written to Stefan, saying that she would meet him again but with no promise of a repeat of their last encounter. His wildly enthusiastic reply suggested that he hadn't really taken in the cautions in Jane's letter. So in the last weekend of October fit, strong, and with flat iron-hard stomach muscles from the rowing, Jane arranged a weekend off and met Stefan in London. If she was trying to show devoted love to David, this was not the way to do it. The powerful magnetism with Stefan rekindled and by the time she got back to base she was a throbbing sexual wreck after two days of non-stop passion. Now she really did have a problem.

There was a letter from David waiting for her. He was about to take his ship to sea on active service, and suddenly this pressure seemed to have opened a door in his mind. For the first time he wrote at length of his love for her, of how just looking at her pictures inspired him and gave him strength. This was when it hit her – here were two young men, both putting themselves in harm's way and both going into action bolstered by their belief that she was their one true love that they were fighting the war for. And she was deceiving them both. A sense of anguish, of despair at her own duplicity, ran through her. 'I didn't mean to do this, I didn't want to be untrue, really I didn't. Oh, David, I love you so much, why did I go back to Josef?' But the annoying answer was that she knew very well why she had gone back to Josef. He was getting more skilled by the minute and it had been the best sex she had known, loving every minute of it. 'Be honest' she thought to herself 'you went back to Josef knowing very well what would happen and you didn't complain at the time. And he's a nice guy who deserves better than being used and dumped. Now you're stuck with it. And my love for you, David? Where is that in this horrible tangle? I do love you, I really do, David. There was something magical around when we were together. Above all else, I want to be your one true love and to be committed to you. But that would mean dumping Josef which would be an awfully cruel thing to do. Can I be nice to you both? Probably, but that's hardly true love and commitment, is it? I don't know, I can't see a way out of this. Can I just accept that I am being true to David with my mind and true to Josef with my body? Well maybe but come on, that's a bit of a fudge, isn't it? God, what a mess.'

Jane had been sitting on her bunk, her body still with a warm buzz from the lovemaking, trying to make sense of it all; suddenly it all got too much for her. She pulled the counterpane over without even taking her shoes off and was asleep in seconds.

Crawling out the next morning she paid little attention to her cabin mates despite their ironic glances, and it was only when Punch sat on the pinnace thwart rather gingerly that Jane thought, 'Oy oy I bet I know what she's been doing.' She tried to catch Punch's eye but the big girl wasn't for being caught, looking down into the bilges rather fixedly. As they walked back to the Wrennery after a busy day, Jane asked "You decided yes, then?"

Punch blushed furiously, shrugged and tried to pass it off casually. "I couldn't keep him waiting any longer, impatient so-and-so."

Jane was tempted to ask Punch if she had enjoyed it but clearly she didn't want to talk about it so the subject passed. Back in quarters Punch shut herself in the heads for a long time and seemed very unwilling to join in any conversation. When she finally emerged Jane grinned at her. "Is there a big arrow over your head saying 'fallen woman'?"

"Oh Jane don't, please. The whole world must be able to see that."

"Not really, Punch. Believe me, you just have to behave as though nothing had happened and nobody will know. You don't look any different."

"D'you think so, Jane? I s'ppose I'll have to get used to it but it seems so obvious just now."

"Only to you. Sorry to disappoint you but it doesn't show."

"That's a relief I suppose. Especially as he wants to go on doing it."

'Why am I not surprised' Jane thought but just nodded sympathetically.

Punch clearly wanted to stop this conversation so Jane just patted her shoulder, and went out, thinking 'Punch, I just hope the rat doesn't hurt you too much'.

CHAPTER 3:

Aftermath

Next morning brought another surprise. A large lorry was parked under the harbour crane, with a motor cutter on its back. The girls went to inspect it and Jane squealed with surprise. It was P36, repaired and cleaned up and looking like new. Jane wasted no time in bounding into the boats office to ask if she could have it. "I'm afraid not, Jane. There's seniority here and brilliant you might be, senior you are not. But take heart – there are more motor boats coming shortly. Meantime we are taking the pulling pinnace out of regular use as P36 can do the same job, and we're transferring you young ladies to a whaler. Good practise for you. But we have more to do with sixteen matelots in the middle of a war than have them pulling a big oar."

Jane felt a spasm of joy run through her. His statement meant he was counting the two Wrens as simply two more sailors, and the thought of what underlay that attitude secretly thrilled Jane. This was acceptance.

Boats Officer continued. "By the way, the boat repairers sent a little present back for you." And he produced a large wooden board. It proved to be the thwart on which Jane had written the number of people carried from the beaches on each trip, and her rough totalling up at the end. It had been neatly smoothed off and varnished. Did it ever bring back memories.

Delighted at this memento but mildly crestfallen by the news she took back, Jane passed on what was happening but Punch seemed unbothered. The main problem with them shifting to a whaler with just five oars was that Sparrer was going to have to row. Given how small she was, and that she had never rowed before, this looked a dubious prospect. But she shrugged her shoulders and pulled as best she could. The whaler rowing arrangement is of three oars on starboard, two on port; a couple of grinning matelots took the double side and Sparrer was given the bow oar. To begin with all she was asked to do was dip her oar in, in time with the other two. But after a couple of days she started to pull on it and although she collapsed in an aching heap each night on getting back to the Wrennery, she stuck at it. "I'm not going to let you down," was all she said to Jane's concern. Within a week she was showing a wiry strength and making a noticeable contribution to the rowing, which surprised Sparrer as much as the others.

A real camaraderie had grown up among the fourteen matelots and two (and a half) Wrens who had been rowing the pinnace, and when it was taken out of daily use they decided on a party to celebrate. First there was a sneaky sippers session at which Punch got more than a little lightheaded, then they all retired to a local hostelry where a rip-roaring party got going. Jane, pint in hand, circulated among them, noting how fit and tanned they all looked. She, not much given to doing more than pulling a comb through her mop so not a great user of the mirror, thought 'I suppose I must look the same'. She chatted to Lofty, the well-named killick who had been stroke oar and found that he had been a champion rower at *HMS Ganges*, the Naval boys' training establishment, before the war. "I tell you it was a bit of a jolt going back to it but on the whole I've enjoyed it." Jane agreed; not that she would mind returning to a motor boat. Then she moved on to a group of half a dozen all ribbing each other about their rowing abilities and debating the best way of rowing. "Here's someone who can tell us how to do it. Come on Jane, would we be better with a shorter quicker stroke?"

"I don't think so. Consider it: momentum is everything in keeping a big boat like the pinnace going. You don't want it starting and stopping all the time, so the more power you can put through the oars, and the more continuously, the better. That means having the oar blade in the water for maximum time. Think how horrible it was the day we had the struggle outside because we couldn't keep up a steady momentum." They mulled this over and nodded in agreement.

Jane had been aware that among the rowers was the two badge AB she had had the groping incident with in the skimmer. He was standing rather on his own so Jane decided to see if there was any way of making peace. "Hello Willie, I hope you're all right these days."

He gave her a sour look but nodded. "Yes, I got over our little incident eventually."

Jane persisted despite his dour reticence. "I didn't like it but at least I could understand why you did what you did, but why on earth did you try to charge me with assault? If I'd chosen to make an issue of it you would have been deep in the rattle. So what possessed you to draw attention to it when I was content to let it be?"

"I was got at by my messmates who thought it demeaning that a girl could knock me about. They were all for me giving you a thumping but I really didn't want to do that." Suddenly he got animated. "I don't know what came over me that day; I'm not usually like that but your backside was so inviting stuck up like that. And I had no idea you packed a wallop like you do."

"Well I'm not exactly a little shrinking violet, am I?"

He nodded with a half laugh. "Then I was egged on by my messmates to do something and somehow it ended as me making a complaint. I don't mind telling you that was the stupidest thing I've ever done. I was laughed at right round Dover then got into trouble when the whole story came out. You've no idea how relieved

I was when you didn't press charges against me."

"Willie, there was no point. After it, they knew on the messdecks that I wasn't to be played with like that, and what else mattered? Listen, can we shake hands on it and forget about the whole business? I don't bear a grudge if you don't."

"I was angry about it for a long time but I suppose you can't go on like that forever."

Hesitantly he held his hand out and they shook on it. Jane looked him in the eye. "You're sure?"

With a sigh he nodded.

"All right, can I get you a drink?"

"I'll have a pint." Drinks secured they got to chatting more broadly and he turned out to be an interesting bloke, having served out East and been a flight deck hand in aircraft carriers. Like so many, he had drifted into the boats by chance. Eventually Jane moved on and got chatting with the pinnace's cox'n. "Boats Officer said something about giving me a trial as cox'n on the rowing boats. Do you know anything about that?"

"He mentioned it to me and I think the plan is to let you loose on a whaler first. Mind you, with the pinnace coming out of regular use you probably won't get that. Did you know I'm getting P36?"

"Well I didn't know it was you but obviously one of the seniors. Can you look after her better than I did?"

He laughed. "I'll try. Mind you conditions are bit easier here."

By closing time they were all fairly cheerful; Jane noted that Sparrer and Lofty seemed to have got very interested in each other; what was it about opposites attracting? Punch had a little group round her and Jane had chatted to everyone in the room. But it was interesting, she thought, that none of them had tried to get off with her.

Jane felt distinctly nervous the first time she took a whaler out as cox'n. The routines were familiar enough by now, but she still had to concentrate hard and think about what she was doing. Handling motor boats had largely become instinctive but getting the right commands out to the oarcrew at the right time called for a good deal more forethought and conscious planning of the next manoeuvre. But once past the initial nerves she found it fascinating and for a few weeks was very happy giving orders to matelots along with her two Wren boatmates. She chatted to Stan about this and again he was a well of experience and wisdom, having been brought up in rowing craft in his early days in the Navy. But none of that prepared her for the pinnace. A sudden rush of demand meant it was brought back into service for a few days and Jane found herself appointed cox'n. The orders were the same, the ways of doing things were the same allowing for its greater size and weight but somehow the pinnace was a much more intimidating presence. Perhaps it was sixteen attentive rowers all waiting for her to give the orders. Although she knew them all there was still a sense of demand coming from them. Or perhaps it was just the knowledge that she was very much on test, that the senior cox'n sitting quietly in the sternsheets saying nothing was nevertheless marking her card the whole time. So when they were assembled and ready to go, she took a very deep breath before shouting, "Toss your oars". But everyone behaved perfectly, and on several occasions her matelots helped by being quick on the order when she had been a little slow giving it. Back at the Wrennery she groaned at Punch, "God, that was terrifying. I'd rather have *Stukas* screaming down on me. Was I all right?"

"Yes of course Jane, you did fine. Just remember to keep your voice up, it was difficult sometimes to hear you in the bow."

"Believe you me, Punch, there were times when I had difficulty getting my voice to work at all, I was so nervous."

But over a few days she got into the swing of it and when the pinnace was taken out of service again after five days she was really quite disappointed. Again, Jane was unaware of it but reports had been fed back on her performance. They were highly complimentary and her first experience of commanding men had gone well.

A couple of days into coxing the pinnace, Jane got a memo from her OiC. Chief Officer Currie was passing on an instruction from Headquarters that Jane was to report to the naval auxiliary launch '*Water Gypsy*' at Lambeth pier on the Thames on 15th November for four days' evaluation with its skipper, Petty Officer Herbert. Thereafter she was to report to Superintendent Carpenter at Chatham to discuss progress and her impending permanent transfer to Nore Command. From there she would return to Dover to complete her time. Jane showed this to her two crew mates. "What's to happen to us, then?" queried Punch.

"I don't know. Would you like to come with me and see if we can make up an all Wren crew?"

"Ooh yes."

Sparrer looked worried. "Would we be rowing there too? Thames tides are awfully strong."

"I doubt it seriously, Sparrer. You'll have to learn to be a motor boat Wren. Can you throw a rope?"

"Well I've done a bit of that as bowman on the cutter, but not very well. Can you teach me how?"

"Oi'll do that" said Punch emphatically. Jane nodded approvingly but had a quiet word with Boats Chiefie and arranged for Sparrer to transfer to P36 while Jane was up in London, to double up and learn the skills she lacked.

A notice caught Jane's eye at the same time.
"Can you sing? Can you dance?
Do you play an instrument or give a recitation?
We're doing a sod's opera revue for Christmas
All talents welcome.
Contact Chief Wren Gibson at HMS Lynx."

So Jane did, offering dance, her accordion, and organisational skills. This led to her being asked to organise the dance group, play a couple of solos and help with scouting for other acts. This in turn led to an unexpected offer from Stan to do recitations, even if he was on a crutch. But his leg was healing up nicely, the Welfare Officer had disappeared, and the physiotherapist was talking about his trying out an artificial leg within a few weeks. Meantime he was getting quite good at getting around on his crutch and one leg. An offer of convalescent leave simply led to him staying in the chiefs' mess but without duties. It was very clear to Jane that he really did have no life outside the Navy which defined him. His sisters back in Lancashire were some sort of backstop but evidently not one he wanted to spend time with.

Meantime Jane wrote home for her tap dance shoes and consulted Jo to find a dressmaker to make her a short dancing outfit. As ever, Jo had a relative who proved to be very expert and got a lot of work preparing costumes for the show.

Back in the harbour, the sunken picket boat had been raised looking remarkably unharmed but close examination showed it to have blown its boiler, its electrics to be ruined and the hull to be holed and warped. Its unfortunate stoker had been closed up in his stokehold when the shell landed, and his badly damaged body was extracted when the boat was pulled out. But a cargo ship called by, delivered a replacement picket boat from Chatham, and took away the damaged one. It also delivered a replacement for *Amaryllis* and the port once more had boats with covered accommodation in them. This was sufficient and the whalers followed the pinnace back into reserve. But the rowing boats had truly shown their worth while nothing else was available.

Jane had arranged a make and mend for the day before she was due to head up to the Thames and spent it packing a kitbag. She had no real idea what to expect so squeezed in her best uniform, some plain clothes plus her boating kit. She wrote to David, full of love and affection, but decided against writing to Stefan in case he came down to London looking for her. By now she knew that he was based at an airfield just north of London and could get into Town very easily. She was still in a quandary over what to do about the two men she had such deep feelings for, knowing that trying to keep them both was honest to neither but scared of hurting either and equally scared at the thought of losing them. In some ways her life was really quite simple. In others, complicated beyond all common sense.

CHAPTER 4:
Meet the Tideway

It was a grey foggy day as Jane walked along the river bank from Waterloo East Station. Lambeth Bridge came and went through the tendrils of mist and the city had a hushed deadness to it under the clammy blanket. Arriving at Lambeth Pier Jane looked for a small warship, or even a recognisably Naval boat; there was only a rather scruffy cabin cruiser lying alongside. It was an odd looking craft with a tiny cockpit and steering position in the stern and a little open space in the bow – laid out very much like a leisure canal boat. But it was painted grey and flew a white ensign at its stern, so perhaps it would have some clue as to where she should go. There was no sign of life so she stopped alongside it and rather uncertainly called out, "Ahoy there".

Nothing happened for few moments then the boat rocked. A tall gangling Petty Officer emerged at the stern, took off his glasses, polished and restored them to quite the longest nose Jane had ever seen, and looked quizzically at her.

"Ah! A Wren is a Wren is a Wren. Careful where you wag your tail." And with this enigmatic comment he disappeared below again.

Now Jane had been given a briefing sheet about Petty Officer Herbert so knew he was an M P and a leading light of the London literary and theatre scene. Her notes were less clear about why he was a Petty Officer on a scruffy little cabin cruiser, other than to say it was part of the Royal Naval Auxiliary Patrol running on the river. 'Oh well,' thought Jane, 'At least he'll be able to tell me what is happening.' She tossed her kitbag into the cockpit and climbed on board. Descending into the cabin she saw him scribbling away furiously at what seemed to be a long and complex poem.

"Please excuse me. I've got to get this in the post this afternoon. I'll be with you in a trice. Do put the kettle on and make yourself a cup of tea."

Smiling, Jane pulled her kitbag in, put the kettle on the coal stove, and set about getting it to boil. The long thin Petty Officer was totally absorbed in his task and ignored her. As the kettle came to the boil she asked, "Would you like a cup too?"

"Ah! No-one's asked me that since yesterday. Yes please – milk and one sugar."

But none of this disturbed his concentration. Suddenly he put his pen down. "There. That should do them for now. I'll not let them get away with it, y'know." Creation completed, he suddenly relaxed, smiled and held his hand out. "You must be Leading Wren Beacon. I must say I hadn't expected such an impressive presence from a girl." He peered at her medal ribbons then the two stripes on her forearm. "Are those wound stripes?"

"Yes sir, I got them for Dunkirk."

"Two things young lady: I'm only a Petty Officer and you don't have to 'sir' me. And I thought wound stripes had been done away with?"

"More or less yes but there's some doubt about it so Wren headquarters managed to wangle them for me. It wasn't my idea."

He stood up and suddenly Jane saw why the boat was a tall angular shape: it fitted its skipper. "Right, young lady, I want to hear all about your exploits but for now let's deal with the practicalities. You have a little cabin arranged for you at Lambeth Palace, next to our rooms. That should give you somewhere to sleep undisturbed; our Nazi friends won't dare bomb His Grace. With your history I presume you've been bombed before?"

"Once or twice, sir."

"I told you, you don't have to 'sir' me."

"Yes, but you are an MP and terribly senior in every other way, so it just seems natural. I'll try not to."

He laughed, a short bark of the amusement always at the back of his eyes.

"So a young lady like you doesn't have any qualms about getting involved in the noisy stuff?"

Jane screwed her face up, considering the question.

"It's not that I mind or don't mind the violence. I've only shot someone twice. But somehow what I do seems to get rather close to the action. Really, I'm just doing my bit."

"But your bit seems to have been fairly extreme, judging by your medal collection. Why do you do it?"

She smiled. "You're sounding just like my father. He was in the Navy last time round same as you, and seemed to think I needed to do more than just rush blindly into action. But we've got a country to defend and I've seen enough of our enemy not to be very keen on them coming here. So I do my bit to keep them out."

"I see. And you're not bothered when your bit puts you in harm's way?"

"With this Blitz going on everyone is in harm's way so I don't see the distinction. At least I'm getting to do something I love doing."

"Ah yes. You've been in boats all along?"

"All my life, sir. But getting onto Naval boats has been special because it's a real job and badly needed. It's funny, you might not think running boats round a harbour was anything special but without us the whole place would come to a halt. Just getting the stores and the mail out, moving people around and taking messages, makes it all necessary and hence worthwhile."

"You can certainly make an eloquent case, Miss Beacon. Have you argued your point of view before?"

Jane winced. "I try not to argue but it does seem to happen somehow. I was President of the Debating Society at Leadown School and we had pretty lively sessions, which I suppose helped a bit. I won the debate on "This house believes women can do much more than simply supporting our men in any war.""

"Interesting that you should feel that. Do you still think so?"

"I'm living proof of it, sir. This war can either move women forward a long way or push us back to the stone age. I know which side of the debate I'm on."

"And where do you see us going now?"

"Well, if you mean the war generally, I think it will be a long hard slog and who knows? Perhaps a stalemate in the end. It'll need more than just us British pushing back to defeat Germany."

"That's a very perceptive comment, young lady."

Jane shrugged. "Last I heard the threat of invasion seemed to be receding; there's a feeling that Hitler is up to something else but we don't know what. Perhaps aerial invasion of England?"

"Perhaps. The word in the House is that we can relax a bit for now but that the threat has not gone away for good. Now, you will be coming with us for the next four days. We run from here right down to Canvey Island and back, delivering stores and mail and sometimes people as well. I am instructed to see how well you can cope with handling the boat, plus all the other things we have to do. Do you know the Thames?"

"I'm afraid not, sir. I come from near Plymouth and my boating has been there, plus down in the Mediterranean."

"Do not 'sir' me. It makes me feel very old. Well, you will learn the Thames soon enough and I'm happy to show you. Meantime, let's go over to Lambeth Palace and get you settled."

"It's rather grand staying there, isn't it?"

"Perhaps but also comfortable and convenient. Knowing His Grace helped me arrange it."

Which is how Jane came to stay at the Archbishop's residence and to have a grandstand view of that night's bombing, which seemed to be indiscriminate and as much up West as in the East End. This after an evening on the boat where by lamplight she told of the beaches of Dunkirk, of early days at Plymouth and of pulling downed airmen out of the oggin. She found Petty Officer Herbert to be entertaining company, quick on the uptake and with a lot of laughing comments.

Orders for next morning were to be on board by 0730, which was very relaxed by the standards she was used to, and she had been given instructions for how to find breakfast at the palace. The servants there treated her kindly and she left feeling well filled. On board she found two elderly sailors in naval uniform but it was obvious that they weren't really Naval ratings. Petty Officer Herbert introduced them as "Bill and Ben, good Lowestoft fishermen seconded to the Auxiliary Service. We're part of the Naval Patrol Service so my ratings come from there whenever I don't have my own people available." They both said hello and Jane recognised something about their accent and puzzled over it for a minute. Yes of course! It was just the same as Punch's way of speaking. "Do you know Violet Johnson, her father owns a spreetie?"

"You mean Punch? Yes of course – girl's well known round our area. Don't ever pick a fight with her if you want to stay alive. She flattened four fishermen not so long ago in a brawl outside a pub when one of them tried to get a bit fresh. You know her?"

"Oh yes, she's one of the other experimental boat crew Wrens and I work with her all the time."

"You'll be right then."

And somehow that sealed acceptance of her by the two older men.

There was a pungent smell of bacon from the cabin but with a good episcopal breakfast inside her Jane wasn't up to any more. So they cast off at eight o'clock and set off down the river. For the rest of the day Jane was in a daze. Berths and piers and ships on moorings came and went. Every one had a name which Petty Officer Herbert seemed to know off by heart. Each section of the river had its own name and the sluicing tides had all sorts of complex eddies and strong runs. They passed Gravesend and Jane thought 'So that's where Dora came from. Well well.' Pausing at an anti-aircraft battery to deliver ammunition the two sailors passed up the boxes onto the cabin roof. From there Jane picked each one up, lifted it over her head and dumped it on the quayside. The two old men looked at her wide-eyed. "Good God, girl, how on earth did you manage that? It takes two of us to lift them up."

Jane was puzzled.

"They weren't that heavy and I'm pretty fit. What's your problem?"

"Not a problem dearie, just amazement. No wonder you can work with Punch."

Jane smiled but the incident left her confused. The boxes were heavy but not that bad. Perhaps the old sailors had been swinging the lead a bit?

But evidently not: when she came aft to stand beside her skipper he said "You are quite something. You looked fit when you came aboard but I had no idea any girl could lift up boxes the way you did."

"Oh well, we've been rowing down at Dover for the last six weeks or so because our motor boats got shelled. Perhaps that has strengthened my shoulders a bit. You should see my number two, Punch. She really is strong.""

He shook his head in disbelief and said "My instructions are to let you handle the boat tomorrow. Have you any experience of that?"

"Plenty of general boat handling experience in a tideway but none of the Thames. If you'll show me where to go and point out the tidal eddies I should be able to manage. She's twin screw but single rudder?"

"Yes indeed. Come aft and watch with me as we head back up the river." They had a hasty sandwich lunch then set off again. Watching, Jane saw how much of the time he used the eddies to dodge the stronger currents and to put the boat alongside without having to fight it to get there. The boat handling was very impressive. 'I'll struggle to equal that' thought Jane. But that evening was another very pleasant interlude in the cabin's lamplight with the damp drizzly evening kept out by the cosy bogey stove. She talked too much and listened too little but he did seem fascinated by her stories of *Stukas* and shells and dead bodies at Dunkirk.

"We weren't allowed to go, y'know." He said sadly. "We were told we were needed here which was true up to a point but I still think we could have done useful things over there."

"It was the same at Dover; orders to stay put when our boats could have been so useful over there. That's why I stole a boat and went."

"It got you into trouble, didn't it?"

"Too right. Their Lordships wanted me put over the wall on principle and it was only the chance that I picked up some generals that got the Army onside. Those generals keep on trying to get me into the ATS and it's only to thwart them that the Navy keeps me in. I'm under orders from Wren HQ to keep a low profile and not annoy their Lordships for a bit. I suppose I might manage."

"I take it you don't want to join the ATS?"

"Do they have boats? I've really grown very fond of the Navy but it's the boats that keep me in. Goodness knows Authority has given me enough reasons to quit already. But I will not be defeated, do you understand?"

This last comment from Jane was a scowling shout.

Petty Officer Herbert backed off visibly.

"All right, all right, no need to shout at me."

Jane abruptly relaxed.

"I'm sorry. It has been a bit of a battle and that comes over me every now and then."

He smiled. "With determination like that I'm glad I am not a Sea Lord. Do you scare everyone?"

Jane frowned, a frown of puzzlement and frustration more than annoyance.

"I don't mean to scare anyone. I only want to do my job but I suppose I do get a bit short with people who get in my hair."

A P Herbert laughed. "With girls like you around Hitler doesn't stand a chance."

"You should see the senior Wren staff. Have you met our director?"

"Only socially but she was clearly a dynamic force. I've had my reservations about women in boats but if they're all like you then perhaps they can do some jobs."

"I'll do any job, never mind some. You've only seen ten percent of what we might be able to do. I'm looking forward to showing you tomorrow."

But on the controls the next day, Jane found it trickier than she had bargained for. *Amaryllis* had two twenty-five horsepower diesels and Jane was accustomed to using the power to chuck the boat about. *Water Gypsy*, much the same size of boat, had two Handy Billy engines of nine horsepower each. The boat could make about five and half knots at best. This was no problem when on the move, but coming alongside a jetty for the first time Jane ran up to it, put the offside engine astern, and expected the boat to stop. It didn't. Fortunately they were only going slowly anyway so the bump into the jetty was not major but a fender was lost and Petty Officer Herbert winced and coloured a bit.

"You'll have to get used to using the tide and wind a lot more, and remember that this boat only reacts slowly."

Jane, thoroughly shaken, nodded.

"Different, isn't it?"

"Let's keep trying."

During the morning he patiently showed her more about using the tide, and she started to get a grip of the boat's very different handling. The grey weather had passed and it was a bright day with blue sky and puffy cumulus clouds. But there was also noticeably more wind and, with her high slab sides and shallow draft, *Water Gipsy* felt the wind a lot. So berthing was much more of a challenge. Jane was shown how to balance wind against tide, how to spot the tidal eddies and how to spin the boat quickly relying on her manoeuvrability rather than raw power. It had never occurred to her that *Amaryllis'* power overcame most natural forces; now she was learning to work with the boat and nature in harmony. By the time they got back in the early evening Jane was a wrung-out bag of nerves, a mixture of thrill at what she was learning and fright at how close to the edge she had come at times. This was a whole new world to her.

That night the talk was of the River Thames, its people and activities. Jane had been fascinated to see close-to, the spritsail barges going by in silent stately progress. She had watched in amazement as one shot Lambeth bridge, dropping mast and sail together at the last moment as they ran under the bridge then a quick hoist for a touch of impetus before dropping everything again for Westminster Bridge. Given that there were only two people on board, it was quite a performance. That evening Petty Officer Herbert relented a bit.

"Call me Alan" he commanded and another little barrier was dropped.

He explained how the masts of spritsail barges are hinged in a mounting called a tabernacle on the deck, and counter-weighted so that it was relatively easy for a man on the winch to haul up the mainmast and sail again. Going through the bridges a light boat mast with one sail on it was rigged, hinged so that it could be dropped quickly, hauled up briefly between bridges then dropped again to shoot the next bridge. It was impressively slick seamanship and left Jane with a profound respect for the seamen who did it. No wonder Punch was at home with ropes and boat handling.

By day three she was getting more comfortable with the handling requirements and was going on and off ships and buoys and jetties and pierheads with some firmness, always tempered by the knowledge that she had no easy way out of trouble. Then, perhaps getting a little too confident, she got caught out badly. What looked like a solid and sheltered jetty proved to have the tide sluicing through it at four knots and as Jane ran in behind the jetty the boat took off in a wild spin, pirouetting and heading for disaster on the stone wall of the embankment rearing up black dripping and smelly ahead of her. She slammed the engines full astern and as the boat stopped in the water, put reverse rudder on to steer astern and – hopefully – out of trouble. As the boat gathered sternway it charged at the jetty but by varying the engine speeds she enhanced the steering and missed it by inches.

Back in the river Jane heaved an enormous sigh and looked at Alan.

"Do you want to take over?" She asked tremulously.

"Just for this once to show you how. I wondered how you'd do and it was interesting that you knew what to do to get out of trouble."

"Yes, but I shouldn't have been in trouble in the first place."

"Oh, that corner's notorious." He grinned and patted her shoulder.

"Well thanks."

But the rest of the day went well and by supper time Ben had cooked up a delicious corned beef hash with loads of onions potatoes and carrots in it. This, reflected Jane, was one huge advantage of boat set-ups like this. Instead of being tied to the meal routine of the Wrennery which meant living on sandwiches as they were out all day, here they could take their main meal when the day's work was done. A very acceptable bottle of wine washed it down and in the cosy lamp-light of the cabin, with ships hooting and rushing by, Jane felt a powerful sense of being at one with the world she loved. That night the talk was of the theatre and this gave Jane an opportunity to explore a half-formed idea she had in mind.

"At Dover we're putting on a revue for Christmas and I'm involved one way and another. I wondered if you would like to come and see it?"

"That might be fun if I can get away. What are you doing yourself?"

"Oh, dancing and playing my accordion and doing some of the organising."

"You play the accordion? That's a bit different."

Jane needed little encouragement to fetch her concertina and play a few tunes; one thing led to another and a lively little session followed. Bill and Ben sang in the cheerfully unselfconscious way of sailors, Alan grated along, in tune but not tunefully, and Jane warbled along the top. By late in the evening they were all very relaxed and Jane asked if he might write a ditty for the revue. The great songwriter A P Herbert considered it, laughed out loud and said, "Why not? I'll do it to the tune of 'What shall we do with a drunken sailor'. You'll need to give me a little scandal to put into it."

There was an intense air raid during the evening which seemed to blast at bits of London fairly indiscriminately but they ignored it. 'This is so like Dunkirk', thought Jane. 'If you get hit it's bye-bye world but here in a boat even a fairly near miss means nothing.' Later, as Jane went to bed, hoping that ecclesiastic invulnerability would protect her, the raid had been going on for four hours but it didn't stop her dropping straight off to sleep with a little smile on her face.

CHAPTER 5:

Dovering away

Her last day on *Water Gypsy* dawned bright but chilly and she was on board in good time. There was a variation in the day's routine; instead of heading down the river, *Water Gypsy's* bow was turned upstream. Once past Putney, early on the tide, she was sniffing the bottom in the much shallower water but managed to keep going and pass through Teddington Lock. Their destination proved to be a small Army depot where they shipped a lot of crates of ammunition, sinking *Water Gypsy* noticeably deeper in the water. Nearer high tide, the boat stayed afloat once back on the tideway and as they came to a line of rather fine terraced houses on the water's edge at Hammersmith, the skipper suddenly veered off course and stopped at one of them with a small mooring and a ladder over the wall which acted as a flood prevention barrier. Back in 1928 the area had been seriously flooded when the river burst its banks and higher walls followed.

"Welcome to my humble abode," APH said with a slight bow, inviting Jane to follow him up the steps. The humble abode proved to be rather better than that, and Jane was fascinated to see the river memorabilia dotted about the place.

"The Thames really does dominate your life, doesn't it?" She remarked.

"Yes and no, it's one of four equally dominant parts. My wife's out driving an ambulance and the children are all about their duties, but I needed to collect some papers so give me two minutes and we'll get going again."

With *Water Gipsy* fully loaded they pushed on down the river without the usual frequent stops, pausing only to collect a couple of Army gunners from Tower Pier before finally coming to a halt at an isolated ack-ack gun emplacement on Long Reach. The gunners and ammunition were all offloaded then the boat turned back. By the time they got back it was mid-afternoon and with no further orders for a couple of days, Bill and Ben were sent home. With Jane's assistance the boat was moved down to the Savoy moorings and her skipper settled down with every sign of doing some writing of his own. That being so, Jane also settled and wrote a long letter to David full of her doings and hopes and not least, her love for him. It was the first time in a week she had had time to write and there seemed a lot to tell.

Come early evening, her skipper enquired, "Do you cook?"

Jane had to shake her head and say, perhaps a little sadly, "No. Never needed to, going from school to a yacht to the Wrens. And we had a cook at home."

"Well, I can a little but I'm not promising you anything special."

Jane pondered for a minute.

"Tell you what, how about I stand you dinner at the Savoy? It's right next door."

"Oh, I know the place well but I don't think I need a girl to stand me dinner. But it's a good idea, let's do it."

Jane had brought her kitbag on board that morning; knowing that Bill and Ben were going on leave she had arranged to sleep on board the boat that night. So she pulled out her tiddley best uniform, smoothed some creases and popped her Dunkirk hat on. Her skipper had been markedly scruffy the whole time Jane had been on the boat, but he made a slight effort to smarten up, changing from his Pusser's wellington boots into leather shoes; they marched in looking not unreasonable. As they arrived at the Restaurant's door, Georges took a look at Jane, beamed and said "Good evening Miss Beacon. A pleasure to have you here again. Please come this way Mr Herbert."

Jane had noted that her skipper had started quite visibly when Georges greeted her by name, and as they settled in their booth he said, "You really are holding out on me, aren't you? The head waiter here knows you by name? You're not just some happy boat girl, are you?"

"In a way I am, Alan. Certainly being a happy boat girl is the main part of my life. But my boyfriend's family are regular customers so we tend to eat here and it's not surprising the head waiter should know me."

"Ah yes, the boyfriend. Who is that?"

"Lieutenant-Commander David Daubeny-Fowkes, if you want his full name. We met during Dunkirk."

"Oh, I know the Daubeny-Fowkes. Been in politics for generations. You move in exalted circles. But tell me more about how you met him."

This tale involved a long description of burning ships and rescuing people through the flames, and how his Report of Proceedings had helped in influencing the tribunal not to dismiss her.

"The Navy's medal was given mainly for that adventure."

From there he quizzed her at some length about her family background, her sailing and her musical abilities.

"You said also that you will be dancing at this revue you're doing. Are you good at that?"

"Well I was – not getting much practise now. I had hoped to do ballet but I got too big for that. Now it's just ballroom and tap and stuff."

"I'll have you on the stage one of these days. And I certainly will come to this revue of yours. Do you do chorus line?"

CHAPTER 5: Dovering away

"Well if mummy hadn't vetoed it I might have joined the Bluebell Girls – I was invited – and no doubt I could high kick but I haven't up till now."

The meal passed by in a pleasant haze and by its end they had exchanged a fair bit of biographical detail. He was intrigued by *Osprey's* Mediterranean expedition.

"Just the sort of thing I've always longed to do but never quite got round to."

Jane stayed on board that night and as she settled in the second cabin that sense of being at one with her element came over very strongly. The lapping and gurgling of water on the hull, just inches from her head, the sound of ships and boats and tugs passing by, propellers chunking in the water, the gentle rocking and tossing of the boat in ships' wakes, even the slightly raw smell of river water, all made up a whole which Jane loved with a passion. It almost seemed a shame to go to sleep, enjoying the sensations was so powerful. But suddenly it was seven o'clock in the morning and time to start again.

"Well young lady, I hope to see you again at some stage. I gather there's an idea afloat that you'll come back here in January with your Wren crew."

"Yes, that would be nice and thank you for being so tolerant with me."

He smiled and waved her off. Finding Chatham was easy enough; finding Superintendent Carpenter was more difficult. But eventually Jane tracked her down to be greeted by, "You're late, Beacon. Kindly explain that."

"I am? I wasn't aware of a set time. My orders were simply to report to you this morning."

Miss Carpenter scowled.

"My orders were for you to be here at 0930, not 1015."

"Well I'm very sorry Ma'am, but that never got passed on to me. And I lost half an hour trying to find you."

Miss Carpenter suddenly relented. She smiled and said "Yes, it is a bit a rabbit warren. Anyway, you are here now so let us consider the reasons. Your medal collection is very impressive but I have read your records and you must understand that I will not tolerate disobedience in my command."

'That's what they all say' thought Jane but kept it to herself.

"How have you fared with Mr Herbert?"

"So far as I know we got on really well. I made a few mistakes but nothing drastic and he seemed reasonably happy with my boathandling. I suspect he's not that keen on women pushing into areas that aren't their traditional ones but it wasn't anything he said, just a bit of a feeling."

"Right. I have been following this experiment with great interest and it certainly seems that you are showing how much women can do. The Navy is slowly relenting and especially on the Thames where a lot of the boat work is done by auxiliaries, we see no reason why there shouldn't be female crews. So we're arranging for you to come soon and your draft chit is for 27th December. We're not sure about accommodation yet but that will be sorted out. Any questions?"

"A couple, ma'am. Depending on the sort of boat it is, there may well be accommodation on board. Is there any reason why we shouldn't live on board the boat?"

"That seems a bit irregular and possibly unsafe but we'll look into it. It would certainly solve that problem as they're desperately short of quarters in London. And your second question?"

"What about Wrens Johnson and Jack, Ma'am? They've been with me and we make a good team, perhaps to crew a boat entirely with Wrens?"

"It is certainly in our mind for the three of you to work together. Whether that will make you fit to be an independent crew, I'm less sure about. But I like the idea and we'll see if it can be made to work. You are sure you're up to it?"

"I think so, ma'am. The Thames is very different but the principles are the same. I know it's dangerous to boast but I've not seen anything so far that was beyond me."

"Interesting. Your confidence is impressive: I only hope it's justified. You are aware that if this goes wrong you could set back the cause of Wrens on the boats by a long way?"

"That's been the case from the start, ma'am. When I went to Dunkirk it was on impulse and as you know I nearly got chucked out for it. But my doing it has brought our ability to the eyes of a lot of senior people now and the argument that we are not able to do it is fading away. Luckily it's something I know about and love doing, so the extra pressure from being an experiment isn't that terrible. I'd certainly be very keen to give it a go."

"All right Beacon, we'll see. Your draft chit will follow soon. Good bye for now."

So Jane, who had been left standing during this interview, came to attention, saluted smartly, and left turned. The train to Dover was packed and she ended up sitting on her kitbag in the corridor, but that seemed a small price to pay for a very enjoyable week. She reflected on the different styles of the three officers in charge that she had now encountered. Superintendent Welby, the widow of a four-ring RN captain, ran her Plymouth area like a ship with herself in command. Chief Officer Currie at Dover, somewhat younger, simply did it by force of personality and energetic clear-minded thinking. Superintendent Carpenter, with a great deal of pre-war management experience, came across as the manager she was and clearly set greater store by the system and doing things by the book.

But Jane also saw the possibility of a certain freedom. On the river there were other boats and she could see that they operated much like *Water Gipsy;* pick up your orders for the day and go and get on with it. That just might give the scope to do things their own way, which could be rather fun, especially if they were allowed to live on the boat. Jane saw a lot to look forward to.

By now the little cabin she shared with Punch and Sparrer was a second home. Although she'd only been away five days such a lot had been packed in that it seemed like longer. There was no-one about so she wandered down to the Boats Office which had been patched up. The rowing boats were all tucked up in the corner of the dock again which looked like good news – perhaps the other power boats they'd got would be enough. She strolled into the office.

"Hello Chiefie. What's happening?"

"Hello Jane. How was the Thames?"

"Fun actually. Do I gather we've stopped rowing?"

"Yup. We've got the picket steamer going, a standard launch and P36 and that's enough for our needs just now."

"Any idea what I'll be doing?"

"You are going cox'n in the launch for a few weeks. We've had an indent from Chief Wren Gibson to release you for a week before and during the revue, then it's Christmas when you are standby cox'n before you go on draft on 27th. We'll be sorry to lose you."

"Oh come off it Chiefie. You know very well you'll be glad to see me go."

"Nonsense Jane. The place will be a lot duller without you."

"Am I just entertainment value then?"

"Don't be difficult Jane. You know very well that's not what I mean."

"All right then, when do I start?"

"Tomorrow morning, 0630 as usual."

Back in her cabin Jane settled to read her mail. There was the usual wild outpouring from Stefan and a rather more measured letter from David, full of love and hope before setting off with another convoy. He was hoping his ship might be in port over Christmas and if so could they get together, but this was not sure. It looked very likely Jane was going to be on duty over the festive period so there was only limited prospect of seeing David again. A cheerful note from Alicia announced that she was being drafted to Liverpool which would be new territory for her and a long missive from Fiona about the joys of being a visual signaller. She reported that Dora continued to flourish as a regulator and was acquiring a reputation as a holy terror among miscreant Wrens. Fiona's letter enclosed one from Evadne, the

Rhodesian girl who had set the elephant stories going on pro course. She was well and happy to be doing her bit for the Old Country, but feeling stifled by being cooped up in a tunnel all the time acting as a messenger. Was there any chance of getting a transfer into the boats and some fresh air? She longed for open spaces again. Jane took note of this. Evadne had been quiet on the course but had had a self-confidence and sinewy physical strength to her that would be an asset on a boat. So she wrote an encouraging letter back promising to keep her in mind if there were any chances but sadly, not just now.

Chief Wren Gibson was in full flow when Jane caught up with her, organising costumes and backdrops and giving some girl a stiff bottle for offering a strip-tease. "It's not that kind of show, you silly girl."

'Oh dear', thought Jane with a vision of the skimpy dancing outfit she had commissioned, 'I hope I'm not showing too much.'

Chief Gibson turned to Jane.

"Ah, Beacon. I need two dance acts and some idea of what you're going to do. Can you organise a chorus line?"

"What, you mean a group of high-kicking girls?"

"Well, something like that."

"That depends on whether I can find them here. Have we any offers?"

"Three so far, and a couple that thought they might manage with some training."

"Add me in, that's six. We really need a couple more. I'll see what I can do. For the rest I'll do some tap dancing, a couple of medleys on my accordion and I can accompany others. Do we have a band?"

"We're very lucky – the Royal Marines have offered their services so we should have good music. As well as a chorus line I'm hoping the dance troupe can do a hornpipe and maybe a couple of novelty or backing acts."

"Hornpipe will be new to me but we'll give it a whirl."

"Good girl."

Next morning Jane was down on the dockside sharp to look at her new command. It had the usual layout of forward control space, main cabin with engine at its aft end and a passenger cuddy aft. But only one engine – a powerful enough Perkins but it was going to lack the raw power she had been used to. She had shouted at her crew before coming down and Punch and Sparrer arrived with thirty seconds to spare before Jane's wrath descended on them. But they polished the boat up well enough and what for Jane was a momentous day turned into a very routine one with stores to drifters, a destroyer's senior officers to run ashore and redeliver later, messages to take to a trawler waiting in the entrance and ammunition to run out to the detached mole batteries. All very humdrum stuff but for Jane this was welcome as it gave her time to settle into her new boat. It was a raw overcast day with brief showers of sleet as harbingers of winter coming very soon. But it was all a lot easier than commanding a rowing cutter, with only one snag: Punch was getting to the limits of her engineering knowledge and wasn't confident about running this altogether larger diesel engine. Determined to retain her all Wren crew, Jane quietly had a word with Chiefie who in turn spoke to the senior shoreside Tiffie and without any formal arrangement being made, a stoker was organised to come by the boat three times a week, check her over and give Punch a bit more briefing on what to do. Back in quarters at the end of her first day, Jane was equally exhausted and elated by the strains of running so much bigger a boat.

For the first couple of days Jane was too wrung out by the end of the day to think about much else, but a short sharp memo from Chief Wren Gibson reminded her she was supposed to be involved in the revue. So she went to the school gym which had been commandeered as rehearsal space, to find a lot of unknown faces all practising their own speciality. Chief Gibson seemed relieved to see her.

"Ah, Beacon, you've arrived. We've borrowed outfits from Ensa for some of your stuff."

In a wicker basket were ten chorus girl's spangly leotards and fishnet tights.

"So if you're able to, a high-kicking chorus line is possible. We've scrounged sailor's outfits for the hornpipe and there's a first rehearsal tomorrow night – now come and meet your fellow dancers."

They proved to be a mixed group, some tall and one tiny, some with the pasty faces of tunnel workers, others looking more like secretaries or domestic staff. Chief Gibson said, "This is Leading Wren Beacon, girls. She's in charge of the dancing so I hope you all get on."

'I am?' thought Jane, who hadn't really twigged that she was in overall charge of it. But Chief Gibson had already bustled off to her many other duties leaving Jane staring at this group and feeling a bit stupid. They were clearly expecting her to say something so she asked, "Right, how many of you can high kick?"

They all held their hands up so she started at one end and got them all to demonstrate.

"So you've all got dancing experience?"

Again a nodding chorus.

"That helps. Have any of you done chorus line before?"

A couple had so she put them in the middle, herself on an end, and assembled them. It was all a bit ragged at first, but clearly there was scope for something good.

"All right, who's done hornpipe?"

And again there was murmur of assent.

"That's more than I have, but we're getting instruction tomorrow night. See you then."

With a few days in the launch behind her Jane was relaxing a bit. The main problem now was the weather. With December well in, the cold was intense and snow and ice were making life difficult. Mercifully there was no call for buoy jumping but even doing ordinary work on and off ships was hard going. Her two boatmates remained remarkably cheerful in the grim circumstances although Punch slipped and went down with a massive thud on the dockside. She moved rather stiffly for some time afterwards. Jane casually remarked that she was looking for acts for the revue and to her surprise Sparrer piped up, "Could me 'n Lofty do a tango? We're ever so good."

"Are you really? I had no idea you were a dancer, Sparrer."

"Ooh Yeah, I was down the Palais every Saturday night an' I still do the grab 'n grope here. But Lofty's a lovely dancer an' we go on really well together."

"Tell you what, I'll play for you on my accordion. Can you both come tomorrow night and we'll try a rehearsal?"

"Yeah, love to."

And Jane was delighted to find that skinny little Sparrer was an excellent dancer, and the contrast with Lofty's six foot four made them an entertaining pair as she twirled and curled and wrapped herself round him. There was more than dancing going on here.

The mail brought Jane's new dance dress which met with general approval. It had a short pleated tennis skirt and a square-necked top cut the same way as their white front cottons, in white with navy blue borders and belt. She looked very nautical and in it was every matelot's dream of what a sexy female sailor should look like. Her only concern was that perhaps the skirt was too short but the others didn't think so, so she accepted it.

The chorus line was making great progress as Jane got to know them. There was Susan from Sutton Coldfield and the accounts department, Iris from Swindon and Bobby from Berwick, both teleprinter operators, Julie from Cardiff and coding, Olive from Hull and Edith from Coventry, both domestic services, and tiny Annie from Reading and the regulator's office. Annie was put in the middle and her partners reached across to each other for stability. Jane made up the eighth in the line. They had formed a strongly bonded team by performance night and Jane had been fascinated to get to know Wrens from other parts of the Service as she tended otherwise to live in her own little world.

CHAPTER 6:

Moving on

Well, the show was a huge success. It started with Jane leading the chorus line high kicking onto the stage to a tremendous roar and blast of whistles. She tap danced and played her accordion and took part in all the dance groups including being put out in front of the mixed team for the hornpipe. Her dance dress was a big hit, its 'sexy sailor' skimpiness and her long legs a winning combination despite her intense stage fright at showing them off. The male chorus sang A P Herbert's little ditty with plenty of sly digs including some Jane hadn't heard before, and Sparrer's tango brought the house down with her slinky black outfit, the skirt side split to the waist and her black stockings and suspenders indulging another male fantasy. Jane stood at the side of the stage playing her accordion for their music. Stan came on in uniform on a crutch and with a stuffed parrot on his shoulder. He gave them 'A lion has et oop our Albert' then two versions of 'the Death of Nelson', familiar routines that were well received. Jane, watching from the wings, was intrigued to see how Stan loved being in front of a big noisy audience. By the time the chorus line high-kicked on to form the backdrop to the finale the place was in a happy uproar. Ever so briefly, the war had gone away.

On the second night Jane spied A P Herbert sitting in the front row with a couple of friends. He came round backstage after the show and said, "Jane, that was marvellous. I could get most of you onto the professional stage in London if you wanted. Are you really all Service personnel?"

"Yes, Alan we are and only doing this for fun. But I'm glad you liked it – it's always nice to get approval from an expert. Can I introduce our tango expert? Meet Sparrer." Sparrer virtually curtsied to the Petty Officer, who smiled happily and congratulated her on a striking performance.

"When we come up to London in the new year Sparrer will be part of the boat crew, so you'll get to know her better. She's keen as anything."

"Oh really? A group of all the talents, obviously."

The wrap party after the third night was in full swing when Jane was called out. "There's someone here to see you."

Jane did an enormous doubletake. "David! I had no idea you were here!"

And she flew into his arms, still in her chorus line leotard and with heavy stage greasepaint on.

"I thought you weren't going to be getting in for a couple of days yet."

"Yes well, we developed condenseritis and had to come in early. We're tied up in Chatham now."

"Condenseritis? What's that? Sounds painful."

"Oh, it's when the main condenser starts getting leaky tubes and you get salt water into the feed. The boilers don't like that."

This explanation meant nothing to her but if it meant David getting off early that was fine by Jane.

The party went on late and Jane had to stay and do her duty, especially by her chorus line, but managed to sneak off with David a little after midnight. The cast all had unlimited late-night passes. The two of them sat looking out over the harbour, holding hands and catching up as much as anything, until the cold drove them away. Jane had her last day on the launch coming up and they arranged that David would ride round on it with her for the day. Jane felt distinctly nervous, showing off her boat handling skills to someone who was obviously a knowledgeable critic, but the day went well. From there it got complicated. The boats crewmen had arranged a farewell party for the three Wrens to follow on from their duty, but this would be a lower deck affair with a certain amount of pusser's rum to be drunk, and David as an officer couldn't join this. Besides, he had to go back to his ship briefly and was then under orders to go home for Christmas, and wouldn't be able to get away until 2nd January. It was likely his ship would not be ready until mid-January. So they decided that he would catch a train north when they finished on the boat, and make arrangements to meet in the New Year. By then Jane would have been drafted to London and although she knew little about what she would be doing, she had no doubt some time with David could be arranged.

Having seen David off, Jane headed back down to the harbour and met the others who were already in party mood. Sparrer concentrated on Lofty who wasn't showing any signs of backing off while Punch, who had been looking a bit glum for a few days, drank rather more than she should, turning giggly and a bit noisy. Back in quarters Punch, her tongue loosened by the rum, suddenly asked, "Is there any more to doing it? It doesn't seem much fun for the fuss that's made about it."

'Oh dear' thought Jane, 'this sounds familiar'.

"Punch, I know this bloke. Is he just jumping on, having a thrash then falling off?"

"I s'ppose you could call it that, yes."

"Doesn't seem to think about you much at all?"

Even full of rum Punch found this difficult and just nodded.

"You know I had a one-night stand with him?"

Punch nodded, finding it too difficult to speak.

"He was all for making it more but he was the same with me and I didn't half give him a flea in his ear. I had doubts for you when you first asked about it, but you obviously wanted him so I didn't say anything. Maybe I should have. And to answer your original question, no that isn't all there is to doing it. With a more considerate bloke who knows about women it can be quite marvellous, believe me."

Punch looked utterly desolate.

"I've given it away for nothing, haven't I?"

"Not necessarily for nothing. What's happening now?"

"Jane, there I was thinking that this was love and when I told him I was being drafted to The Nore he said 'well, there's no point in going on then, is there?' and that was it. I know I'm supposed to be tough an' all that but Jane I'm a girl and it hurts horribly."

And the big girl's lower lip trembled then she burst into floods of tears. Sparrer rarely said anything in these confessionals, but now she burst in, "Don't let the rat get the better of you, dearie. He's had his way with you then got rid of you – typical man. Why didn't you just punch his head in?"

Punch, through her tears, giggled. "Oi nearly did. Ooh I was tempted but it didn't seem like the right thing for a girl to do."

Sparrer erupted. "That's the trouble with us, always giving in and bein' nice to the rotten sods."

Jane couldn't resist giving Sparrer a quizzical look.

"What about Lofty?"

"Oh, Lofty's all right, he won't cheat me. And he knows he ain't getting nothing unless there's a ring on me finger. That's a valuable thing you've got there between your legs."

Jane had never talked that much with Sparrer and this was a whole new slant on her view of life. "You've got this worked out?"

"C'mon Jane, I come from Bermondsey. Everything's for sale there and if men want that thing they know they've got to pay for it one way or another. I've got two sisters on the game an' they make tons of money. For me, no-one's going near that valuable part before they pay, an' my price is a ring on me finger."

This was fascinating stuff for Jane who had never thought of her body or sex life in that way. She looked at Sparrer. "So where does that leave Punch?"

"Cheated, that's where. I know what I'd have done to the rotten fucker."

None of this was much consolation to Punch who sat there quietly weeping.

"All right, Sparrer, what can we do for her now?"

"Oh wipe her eyes and pick up the pieces. We're here to help but she's got to get through some of it herself. Haven't you, Punch?"

"Oi s'ppose. Will any other man want me now I'm used goods? I really shouldn't have done it, but it's too late now."

"Yes of course they will, Punch. What you want is a man that values you for yourself first and your parts second. The other sad thing about this is that with the right man sex can be physically terrific to the point that it's less important if that's all they want."

"Like your Pole?"

"You could say so but we're really quite fond of each other too."

Punch snorted. Sparrer whistled disbelievingly.

"Come on you two, it's not me that's got the problems tonight. Give me a break."

But this had taken Punch's mind off her own sadness. They all had a late pass that night to go to the midnight carol service. Jane and Punch were all for it, Sparrer much more doubtful.

"I've never been inside a church. Do you have to kneel an' do things?"

"No Sparrer this is just carol singing and a little sermon from the vicar. You'll enjoy it."

So they all went, Sparrer with deep misgivings but she did enjoy it and discovered that carols were really quite jolly things. She especially enjoyed 'Still the night, Holy the night' which despite its German origins, alluded to by the vicar, stirred some deep sense of peace in her. In the end they all turned in in a much better frame of mind.

There was a typical Naval Christmas Day dinner, all but a handful of watchkeepers gathered in the mess room where the Wrens were served by their officers in the old Naval tradition. Most of the officers were new to Jane who had very little to do with any of them and she found them quite cautious around her. But it was all great fun and later there was a dance in the junior rate's mess; a place that Wrens would normally have been dismissed for going near. In the midst of this there was a call for boat's crew and as Jane was standby cox'n the three of them hastily pulled on bell bottoms and trooped down to the harbour to find thirty rowdy matelots wanting to go back to their ship with their own motorboat broken down. So Jane got one final outing in P36, carting this noisy – but fortunately friendly – mob out to the trots, while towing their boat as well. Nothing would do but the Captain insisted on inviting the three girls on board and it was several gins later before they could get away. But it was lovely to be back in P36 again, even if briefly. Jane also had a date to visit the Poles on their motor gun boat. Since the first difficult encounter they had accepted Jane as a kind of mascot and treated her very well. By invitation she took her accordion along and played duets with one of their crew; the whole crew got together and sang sad songs of home and the families they had left behind. By the time it was finished a gentle sense of hungry longing had settled over them. With Jane going on draft it was also likely to be farewell to them so she left a couple of photographs and gave each one of them a little kiss in parting.

On Boxing Day a letter from Wren headquarters was passed to her. Opening it, Jane found a formal letter from Third Officer M Baker addressed to Leading Wren J Beacon. It advised Jane that, as her boat crew would be operating as a detached party, Third Officer Baker was appointed Divisional Officer to attend to their service and personal needs. She should contact Miss Baker at Wren HQ for all divisional matters. Beacon would be answerable for the performance of their duties in the usual fashion direct to the Naval officer in charge of Royal Naval Auxiliary Patrol vessels operating on the Thames and their pay and administrative matters would be provided by Nore command at Chatham. Their pay would be available to them at Tower Pier in the usual routine. It had been decided that as Wrens were not as strong as men, she would have a crew of five on her launch. Were there any particular Wrens Beacon was aware of, who would be suitable for this duty?

'Well well', thought Jane, 'Fancy Merle being my Divisional Officer. As for Wrens not being strong enough, they obviously haven't seen Punch. But a crew of five will suit me very well.' So she wrote back formally, suggesting Evadne Smith, the quiet Rhodesian girl from their Probationer Course who Jane suspected might adapt well to life on a launch despite her lack of marine background. For the other person, if they could find a Wren with mechanical aptitude able to care for the engine, that would be a major benefit.

The rest of Boxing Day was spent packing up and saying farewells. Chief Officer Currie had come to the Wrennery on other business and called Jane in to the office. "Well, Beacon, off on your travels again. Let me wish you good luck. It really has been a bumpy year, hasn't it? For your own sake I hope it doesn't go on at quite the pace you've set so far. It would do the cause of boat Wrens a lot of good if you quietly got on with your job for a while now. I shall follow your career with interest." And instead of putting her hat on for a salute the Chief Officer shook Jane's hand with a smile of farewell.

With the rest of the day free, Jane met up with Stan who was now out of hospital and getting around freely. He had a short wooden peg on his missing leg.

"Y'know, Jane, I find this easier than the proper artificial leg they've fitted me with. I know it makes me look a bit like a pirate but I'm finding I can play that up a bit."

The good news was that Stan had sailed through the medical and was being drafted to Pompey in the New Year. "Ee lass, I was right relieved when they told me I could stay in. I'm being lined up for a Boats Office somewhere around there but don't know which yet. "

Jane smiled gently, relieved that her intervention had gone well.

Punch and Sparrer both went on leave and Jane shifted her dunnage up to Lambeth Palace where she was back in the same little room as she had before. She was under orders to report to *Water Gipsy* but found it deserted so she was a free agent. This suited her very well as she had arranged to meet Stefan again and for two days they lost themselves in enjoying each other. Shattered but glowing, she popped down to *Water Gipsy* once Stefan had gone back to his base on the twenty-ninth and there waiting for her was Petty Officer Herbert.

"Hello, Jane, where have you been? I thought you were going to turn up yesterday."

This called for some quick thought; her draft chit had been clear enough.

"Oh, when I came on board you weren't here so I went for a bit of a look around. But here I am now. What are we doing?"

"There's only you and I on board so the answer's not a lot until the New Year. We're doing a bit of fire and mine watching whenever our friends come over, although it's been pretty quiet just lately. Let's hope it stays that way."

But at 2230 the drone of bomber engines could be heard and shortly afterwards the crump of exploding bombs started. *Water Gipsy* moved down to the Pool of London, watching for anything on or by the water. Quite deliberately the Germans had chosen one of the highest spring tides of the year; a high spring tide means one of the lowest ebbs. Out on the water there wasn't much *Water Gipsy's* crew could do but watch. The London Fire Brigade relied on the Thames for much of its water, but with the exceptionally low tide they were unable to get their suction hoses to the water's edge. The exposed mudbanks on both sides of the river glistened in the glow from the fires as the tide fell. Jane was puzzled.

"Why can't they go over them and stick their hoses in the water?"

Alan Herbert shook his head sadly.

"See those mudbanks? Some of them are firm but a lot are very soft mud –almost like quicksand and going onto them would be highly hazardous. So they can't get any water."

"How frustrating. Can't we do anything to help them?"

"Don't know what. The gap between the water's edge and their lines is too wide."

Jane looked at the fires. The *Luftwaffe* had deliberately selected the City business area as its target this night and commercial buildings were being demolished along with many wonderful old edifices, the Guildhall being a notable victim. Looking at them as the boat lay off in mid-river, Jane could see firemen on the shore waving furiously, then one, who must have been a seaman by the way he threw the heaving line, launched his line far out onto the mud. It was only twenty feet short of the water's edge.

"Surely we could get to that and pull a hose into the water?" she queried.

"It would be sheer chance whether you were on firm ground or disappeared into the mud which would be a waste of a life to my mind."

"Oh come on, let's give it a try."

"Well, be it on your own head."

They anchored the boat as close in as they dared, got into the dinghy and reversed to the bank. Jane hopped over, found firm footing and set off towards the rope when the inevitable happened. There was a sickening feeling of the ground disappearing beneath her feet and her heart lurched as she went down and down into the mud. This stopped when she was mid-thigh into the evil-smelling stuff. The rope was just six feet away but might as well have been six miles. Her gesture was over. But at least she hadn't disappeared entirely. She tried to move her legs but all that did was sink her deeper into the mud. The heat from the fires was intense and stuck as she was, she couldn't get away from it. Soot and cinders stung her face and eyes.

Alan called to her, "As the tide rises I'll bring the dinghy in to you and lift you out. You'll have to wait till then."

Jane had the most uncomfortable hour of her life. Her face was scorched, her lower body frozen. The sensation of the water slowly rising round her was terrifying and it was up to bosom level before Alan backed the dinghy in carefully until it bumped against her. She was facing the wrong way to be able to help herself into the dinghy so it was up to Alan to get arms round her and lift out. But he couldn't – the suction was too strong.

"Jane, we're in difficulties here. I'm going to tie you to the dinghy and hope that its natural flotation will lift you out."

"All right, but get it good and tight."

He passed several turns of rope under her armpits and bosom, led it inboard and lashed firmly to a thwart. For a while the dinghy sank deeper into the water, pulled down by Jane, until there were only a few inches of freeboard left. The water kept creeping up remorselessly and rose to Jane's chin; for about the first time in her life she was feeling overwhelming helpless panic. Alan, leaning over the stern of the dinghy and murmuring encouragement was at his wits' end. Then he had an idea; he abruptly ran forward, jumped on the bow and with a sucking noise that did the trick. Boat and Jane bobbed up clear of the mud. Her feet came out of her best pusser's Wellingtons which remained buried several feet deep in the mud. Rather than mess around where they were, Alan rowed out to *Water Gipsy*, tied up alongside it with Jane still hanging from the stern, then swapped the dinghy rope for one from the boat. By now Jane was virtually incapable of movement except a violent shaking, paralysed by cold and fright, so it was a case of hauling her into the dinghy where Alan washed her down with buckets of water to get rid of the mud clinging copiously to her. Jane sat there sobbing helplessly, the terror slowly dying down but still vivid in her mind.

Back at Lambeth Pier Alan looked at her and said, "I hope next time you'll listen to me. There's a fine line between bravery and foolishness and I hate to say it but you went over it tonight."

Jane was too shattered to do much more than nod. Her muddy outer clothing removed, she flaked out on the spare bunk still soaking wet and sank into a stupor of nervous exhaustion. Her ribs were raw from rope burn for days afterwards and her face was singed red with cinder burns about it, but these seemed a small price to pay for still being alive. Jane's focus had been very close to herself. Out there in the City the *Luftwaffe* inflicted one of the most devastating raids of the war on London. It took Jane twenty-four hours to recover; the City would never be quite the same again.

On the thirty-first they had the day off. Alan Herbert the great poet settled to writing something for Punch magazine. Jane was still getting fits of the shakes whenever the memory of the water rising up round her became overwhelming, but taking a deep grip of herself she settled as well and wrote a short but careful letter to David, conscious always of the hypocrisy of swearing undying love for him.

> *Water Gipsy*
> *Lambeth Pier.*
> *31st. December 1940.*
> *David my darling,*
> *I know it's only a few days till we meet again and I'm longing for it. But having almost been drowned I am still feeling pretty shattered by the experience and my sense of my own mortality is acute just now. My longing for you is made all the stronger by it. This beastly war hangs over us so totally that it's difficult to think about everyday things but underneath it I suppose life just goes on until war catches up with you. We really must try*

to find some normality in these strange times. My love for you might be heightened by the awareness of our mortality I have just had thrust on me but really we're just two young people happy to have found each other and hoping, longing, for the chance to be lovers.

We must not allow present times to spoil all the good things there are between us. David, my dear, we must live for each other, I know we must fight but also fight to be ourselves and with each other. Who knows what 1941 may bring? But whatever it is, my life has acquired a new light and meaning with you, and our hopes for a better life will come true, of that I'm sure. Meantime we must be defiant in the face of evil. I will not be defeated, we will not be defeated and whatever this ghastly war throws at us we will prevail. That we must believe and live by.

With all my love,
Jane.

PART TWO:

RUNNING THE RIVER

CHAPTER 7:

Pastures new

January 1941 came in raw and snowy, with a succession of westerly gales making life unpleasant on the water. On the second of January the peace on board *Water Gypsy* disappeared. Both Punch and Sparrer turned up, cautiously looking for their new workplace. Punch was pleased, Sparrer uncertain. "You mean we're going to live and work on this little boat for the next month?"

"That's right, we are now her crew and accommodation is so short in London I've arranged for us to live on board. I think you'll find it very convenient once you get used to the idea."

"What happens after that?"

"I'm hoping we will get our own boat to do much the same work and to live on that too."

"Oh, will Mr Herbert be coming to that one with us?"

"No Sparrer, he stays here. We are to be let loose on our own providing we shape up this month. So I'm looking for a brilliant show from you."

Sparrer pulled a scared face but said nothing. Punch laughed.

Alan Herbert had given a long look at the contrasting pair of deckhands who had just arrived.

"Well, at least you two have the background to be useful round here. We start work at 0730 tomorrow morning; I take it you're both ready to go?"

Sparrer nodded enthusiastically; Punch just smiled - she seemed very quiet and Jane made a mental note to check if she had any problems.

The evening meal was a joint effort; a large tin of brown stew was augmented by a modest amount of fresh beef, and loads of carrots. Punch made up a side dish of onions and potatoes.

"This is one of our regulars on the barge," she explained and with a bottle of wine provided by the skipper they ate well. After supper they were busily making up a food indent when the boat rocked to someone stepping aboard.

"David! I didn't expect you till tomorrow."

And Jane bounded into his arms, ignoring the ironic grins of her supper companions.

"Yes well, I'd had enough of Mater laying down the law so decided to escape today."

And he turned to Petty Officer Herbert "Good evening, sir. It is a pleasure to meet you. I hope you don't mind me barging on board like this."

"Not at all young man. Welcome aboard my humble boat – I presume it isn't actually me you have come to see?"

David laughed. "Not entirely sir, although it will be a pleasure to make your acquaintance." He turned to Jane, "Can I bear you off to supper?"

"Oh David, we've eaten already. But there's some left in the pot. Would you like that, then we can go ashore to somewhere?"

"All right, let's give it a try."

And he gave every appearance of enjoying the meal, with the last of the wine to wash it down. Meantime, Jane had been thinking.

"Alan, you know the little room across the road that I've stayed in? Do you suppose us girls might be able to have it as a changing room for our smart clothes and stuff? Getting on and off boats isn't going to be so easy in an evening gown."

"Women, eh?" But he laughed with it. "All right, I'll ask. It probably won't be a problem, as I don't think that room is used much for anything else. "

"I suppose I can go ashore in uniform tonight. But I really need to get some evening dresses. I wonder where I'd find them now? Must make enquiries. Where are we going, David?"

"Why don't we just sit in the bar at my canteen and catch up? I must say it's jolly convenient your being drafted to here."

David turned to the group and asked, "Do you mind if we disappear for a bit?"

And got smiling waves back.

Having walked over Lambeth Bridge and up the Embankment they settled with a beer in front of them and talked non-stop. It was after midnight before they walked back slowly and stopped at the pier.

"Jane, can I kiss you again?"

"Yes of course you can, you silly man. Come here."

And it was some time before they disentangled.

"David, I'd love to see the sort of suite you take at the canteen sometime."

"Yes of course, darling. I'm the only one staying there until the weekend when the parents come up to Town. See you tomorrow same time – and come for supper this time."

Jane simply smiled and hugged him again before turning and climbing on board the boat. She turned and waved to him then eased quietly into the saloon. For the moment she had a berth to herself so turned in and contentedly drifted off to the sound of water gently lapping against the hull.

Orders the following morning were to take mail to ships in the river, drop stores off at a battery then pick up a broken machine gun before collecting four naval ratings on their way to Tower Pier. As ever the river was bustling with traffic and several times Punch exclaimed as she recognised sailing barges working their way up river.

"That's the *Aeriel.*" She said as they dodged one heading in towards the south bank. "There's an eddy close in there, and she'll use that to tack. Old Sam knows his business."

Alan Herbert listened to this with interest. "You know the whole river like that?" He queried.

Punch nodded. "More or less. You have to know its funny little corners to work up river if the wind is against you an' I've watched me Dad do it so often that Oi suppose I know it too."

"Interesting – you'll be a real asset to any crew round here."

Jane couldn't resist butting in, "She'll have her own boat before long, you can bet on that."

"And then what do you do?"

"Learn the river from her – and you – then I have some ideas for other girls who are ever so keen to come on the boats so I can pick some good ones when I need them."

"Got it organised, haven't you?"

"Well, if we're going to make this girls in boats thing work, I need to be organ-ised. Have you thought of training any more after we move on?"

Alan Herbert smiled gently. "I'm beginning to wonder about that. I'm going to suspend judgement until you lot have had your month with me but it looks like there might be a useful resource there. The patrol service is struggling to provide enough male crews now."

Passing the Royal Docks on their way up Jane went forward to join Punch.

"Why so glum?"

Punch shook her head and said, "Not so much glum as worried. My period didn't come and didn't come and I was desperately worried I might be pregnant. But it finally turned up today so I can breathe again."

"They're normally regular?"

"Yes, more or less although they did get a bit funny when I was seriously training for the championships."

"Our mutual friend Taff actually got me pregnant. I had a miscarriage from a bomb blast at Dunkirk which solved the problem but didn't do anything for my peace of mind. It just goes to show, never trust getting out at Fratton as a method."

"You got pregnant? Wow. I bet you were glad it went away."

"Too right. You seem more relaxed in talking about this sort of thing now."

"Jane, the sense of relief is so overwhelming that it carries everything else before it."

Jane grinned and moved on, but it was good that Punch, normally so reticent in these matters, had felt able to speak openly to her about them.

They moored at Lambeth Pier again and Jane took her two crewmates to see the little room she had scrounged in Lambeth Palace. She organised passes for them both then promised that they could use it any time for changing, sleeping if nothing else was available and generally providing them with a forward base. Jane had brought her evening dresses ashore and hung them up.

Sparrer suddenly piped up. "Jane, I've been thinking. Y'know you said you needed more dresses but didn't know where you'd get them. Well, if you've got any money I probably know of people who could sell you some. Just don't ask where they came from."

"Well now, that's a thought. Are they good ones? "

"I ain't seen any but I'll tell 'em not offer you rubbish. Would you like me to ask?"

"Yes please, that sounds very interesting. I was wondering what I was going to do about it."

Meantime she changed into the black chiffon and wowed David when he picked her up. Over supper they debated how to make best use of their time till David had to sail again – estimates were mid-January.

"I've got to be on board during the day but there's no reason why I shouldn't slip up to Town each night. How will that work for you?"

"So far as I know we're only working days, although finishing time is always a bit uncertain. I hope that means we've got the evenings free. Our skipper seems happy to lock the boat up and leave it overnight which means we don't have to have a duty person stuck on board. I gather that sometimes he works down to the Sea Reaches then ties the boat up in Holehaven on Canvey Island overnight where there's some favourite pub of his. It's silly isn't it, Chatham to Canvey Island isn't very far in a straight line but miles away by land. I suppose we'll just have to miss those nights."

"Let's hope there aren't too many of them, then. Can you get off at all during the day?"

"Only if I formally have a day off, and I don't know yet how our skipper will be about that. But I can ask. Did you have anything in mind?"

He took her hand, looked longingly into her eyes and said "You shouldn't ask questions like that, Jane. I'm getting feelings I never knew existed and you don't want to know what is going on in my mind."

She cocked an eyebrow at him "Don't I? I love you David Daubeny-Fowkes and I want to know everything about you, including whatever dodgy thoughts you are having."

"Oh Jane stop it. You're too young and lovely to be knowing about those kinds of thought. I suppose all men get them but they shouldn't be projected onto anyone as innocent as you."

"What makes you think I'm innocent? People grow up pretty damn quickly in this blasted war y'know."

He laughed, "In some ways I suppose we do but even so I don't think that goes all ways."

Jane felt a cold grasp on her heart. Was this going to be Jamie all over again? She so much wanted to love this gorgeous man in every way possible, yet might that ultimate offer be a step too far? It certainly suggested to her that this was a path she would do well to venture down slowly and cautiously. She had an edgy feeling that actually it was her precious David who was the innocent in this relationship despite the gap in their ages and for a moment she felt heavy with knowingness. But she looked at him and the surge in her heart washed away that other dragging sense. Right now she loved what she saw in front of her; the future would have to sort itself out.

Disengaging from a final hug on the pier she said, "Remember you've offered to show me your suite some time – I'm ever so curious to see what a luxury suite looks like."

"Oh, it's nothing special. We always get one looking onto the river if we can which is supposed to be more dangerous as the river is the area the Nazis aim for, but we really like the view of the river and its traffic. Even Mater prefers that. But yes, I'll take you up sometime soon if you like."

"That would be nice. Sleep tight, my love."

And with a final peck of a kiss they parted.

CHAPTER 8:
Mind your manners

It proved to be a busy week. On Wednesday Evadne turned up, freshly drafted from Pompey. She stood on the pier looking very lost until someone looked out and saw her.

"Excuse me, is this the boat I'm supposed to be drafted to? I hadn't expected anything so small."

It was Punch, looking out the cabin door, who had spotted her.

"Are you Evadne or Susannah? We're expecting one of each."

"I'm Evadne – are you Punch? I remember you from Pro Course."

"Yes I am. You're the elephant girl, aren't you? Welcome on board."

Evadne looked doubtfully at the one foot gap between boat and pier and asked, "How do I do that?"

Punch was puzzled for a moment, regarding anything less than three feet off the same as being alongside and said, "Just step across. Pass me your bag." In the end she reached out a hand and yanked the hesitating land girl onto the boat. Evadne nearly fell over as the boat rocked gently with the movement. Then there were greetings and handshakes all round. The wakes from passing traffic meant that even tied up at Lambeth Pier, *Water Gypsy* rocked a bit most of the time and Evadne found herself stumbling about the cabin, constantly caught off balance. She turned a gentle shade of green, excused herself, shot up onto the after deck and was noisily sick.

"Have you never been on a boat before?" enquired Jane.

Evadne had gone pale beneath her sunbrowned skin.

"No, only the ship that brought me across from Durban and that was a lot bigger."

"Oh well, not worry. Lie down for now and believe me, you will very quickly get over this."

Jane had never been bothered by seasickness and Punch had got hardened off as a very young girl; they exchanged ironic smiles behind poor Evadne's back then saw her settled, clutching a hot water bottle. But Evadne was a physically tough free ranging soul and rapidly settled in to the ways of the boat. Within a week she was a full member of the crew, revelling in being in the open air and doing something usefully demanding again. Despite that, she never quite lived down being the girl who was seasick moored up alongside Lambeth Pier.

Thursday evening was a lot more worrying for Jane. At dinner David casually mentioned, "You know my parents are coming up to Town tomorrow? Mater has ordered that you are to join us for dinner at the canteen."

Jane was horrified. "What? David I barely know you let alone be introduced to your parents, a couple of senior aristocracy. How do I greet them? With a curtsey, a smile and a handshake, or what?"

"Oh, Pater's no problem. He's a kindly old soul more interested in his trees and anything to do with women is left to mater. Wait for her to indicate how she wants to be addressed – if she's the Marchioness of Hemel she's being fully formal and a small curtsey may be appropriate. But if she introduces herself as Marjory she's including you in the family set-up and the way you greeted Arthur will do very well. By the way, he'll be joining us."

Thinking of how she greeted Arthur she asked, "Will I tower over her? Her sort tend not to like that."

"Not a lot. She's about five foot six, I suppose, and is quite large round the way. Don't worry, no-one looks down on Mater."

If that was supposed to comfort Jane it did the opposite. The thought of encountering a formidable matron, the mother of the man she had such overwhelming feelings for, but who would expect not to be looked down on, was terrifying.

"What shall I wear? I've only got the two evening dresses."

"I'd have thought you would be better off in uniform. Pater at least will be impressed by your medal ribbons."

"Oh, was he in the last war?"

"Yes, he got to be Acting Brevet Colonel with the Welsh Guards before he was invalided out."

"Was he wounded?"

"No, got trench foot so badly he lost half of one foot and the other was never quite the same again. But then he'd been in a flooded trench for two months without a break before he had to be extracted. Still limps a bit, poor fellow."

"It must have been tough."

"No tougher than Dunkirk to my mind, but it's all relative I suppose."

"Yes my father's got a few scars from Jutland."

Next day she excused herself during a longish run down river, and spent some time sponging and pressing her best uniform, looking out new black silk stockings and polishing her shoes. "Oh for a steward to palm this off onto" she thought to herself then smiled at the way she had adapted to self-sufficiency. 'Why should anyone else do it for me?' she pondered, balancing that against the convenience of paying that someone else.

She was a bag of nerves when David collected her on Friday evening. Walking round to the Savoy she chattered incessantly while David simply grunted and smiled gently. His family were already assembled in the American Bar and arriving at their table Jane took in the Marchioness in a long silk gown in her favourite purple, the Marquis in a rather rumpled dinner jacket with bow tie slightly askew, and Arthur comfortable in a lounge suit. 'How convenient uniforms are' Jane thought, looking at this mixture of dress codes. David made the introductions, "Mater, this is Jane who I've told you about. Jane, meet my mother." The Marchioness smiled and inclined her head ever so slightly, but made no effort to get up and said nothing so Jane gave her the little bob of the knee that seemed to serve well when being introduced to very senior people and said, "How d'you do." The Marquis gave her a hearty handshake and looked at her medal ribbons. "Pleased to meet you, young lady. I see the Army also recognised your bravery."

Jane smiled. "It's very largely down to the Army that I'm still a Wren at all. The Navy were not enthusiastic."

"Yes, David told me about that."

Arthur, to her slight surprise, grabbed her very firmly and bussed both cheeks. "Lovely to see you again, Jane."

The Marchioness indicated the seat next to her and said to Jane, "Come here, child. Now tell me about the way you rescued David at Dunkirk."

With pink gin in hand and something specific to say, Jane was able to rattle on for ten minutes about driving her boat through the flames and collecting the scorched, wounded seamen from the ship's fore end. The Marchioness sat there impassively, nodding her head from time to time but listening intently, ignoring the rest of the chat going on around her. "So you thought this gave you license to get friendly with David?"

"Ma'am, it wasn't like that at all. At the time I had no idea who I had rescued; they were simply more people in trouble who I could help. And afterwards there was so much else going on in my life and near death that I rather forgot about them. But when I went before the King for my investiture, in the circulating afterwards this lieutenant-commander came up to me and introduced himself. I was totally stunned to discover he was the officer I'd rescued at Dunkirk. We got chatting about Dunkirk and he came with me to the French legation for my medals from them - and the Belgians." The Marchioness looked at Jane, her inscrutable expression relaxing a little. *"Vous parlez Francaise?"*

"Oui, bien sur, Madame."

"Ça, c'est bon." And the rest of the conversation went on in French. Jane decided to throw caution aside, "Then we just took to each other. I suppose it's wartime with that sense that we have no time to waste but within a couple of days we were

in love with each other. And I had saved his life."

"Have you been in love before?"

"Not like this, ma'am. I've had a couple of boyfriends but I've never felt like this about anyone."

Jane realised that the whole table had stopped chatting and were listening closely to the conversation. David contrived to look strained and happy all at once.

"Hmm. This will do David a lot of good."

At this point Georges himself came to tell them the table was ready and they filed downstairs to the heavily re-inforced basement where dining was going on. Jane was seated between Marchioness and the Marquis with him on her left. David and Arthur were directly across the table. Jane looked at the table settings with some dismay. She recognised six of the eating irons laid out on each side of her place setting but there was one, an oddly shaped spoon, which was new to her. It was teaspoon size, long and thin with a pointed end turned down - what on earth did she do with that one?

"Gosh, are we having eight courses?" she asked the assemblage. "Rationing doesn't count here?"

The Marchioness cut in, "A lot of it comes with us from our estate which is still an active farm. One is still permitted to eat one's own produce so we bring ours with us. But it has to be said that the Savoy chefs do miraculous things with the raw materials."

At this point the soup arrived, her sherry glass was filled, and they were off. In succession half a dozen quail's eggs, a small Dover sole – fortunately Jane knew how to eat it off the bone – a side of beef with vegetables and ample roast potatoes, a cheese board with stilton, cheddar and a Cornish soft cheese, and a savoury Scotch Woodcock came in turn, with the correct wine served with each course. The Claret with the beef and cheese was superb: old and silky but with the characteristic steely edge. Still, the odd-shaped spoon had not been used. Then, half a grapefruit was put in front of her, just as it was. At home Eunice the family cook would have segmented and sugared a grapefruit, but here it came as a bare simple half. Jane paused a moment to see what the others would do and all became clear – the odd-shaped spoon was designed to dig out the grapefruit segments. To her relief, Jane managed to use this strange implement without making too much mess. Finally, a single scoop of ice cream came, followed by a decanter of port, which was religiously passed to the left after the Marquis had drawn the stopper. Jane noted with amusement that nobody touched theirs until the Marchioness had taken hers, then the men stood briefly and the loyal toast was proposed. By now the Marchioness had relaxed quite visibly and chatted to Jane in a much more open way. Jane was curious, "Do you always eat to this standard?"

"At home it is usually just four courses according to what is available but when we come here we do like to do things properly. Whether we will be able to maintain standards throughout the war is another matter."

Over coffee and liqueurs Arthur claimed her attention.

"Jane, I have got it right that you're going to be operating on the Thames, haven't I?"

"Yes Arthur. All going well we do a month's trial and training then the all-Wren crew will be given their own boat to run as part of the Royal Naval Auxiliary Patrol. That might be quite fun."

"In that case I'd like to discuss a little activity with you some time. Nothing too demanding but an extra on your operations."

Jane looked doubtful. "I'm told we will be kept pretty busy but anything to oblige. What had you in mind?"

"We'll have to meet another time to discuss that; I can't really talk about it here."

"All right, we usually moor up at Lambeth Pier just now so call by some evening."

"I will."

With that they turned back to the general party which, with port and tobacco consumed was on the point of breaking up. The Marchioness frowned at Jane, meditative and calculating.

"Yes, you'll do for David for now. You have permission to go on seeing him."

Jane was startled by this, thinking 'He's twenty-seven, in command of a warship and still needs his mother's permission to have a girlfriend? No wonder he's a bit naive. And you just try stopping me seeing him.' But outwardly she simply smiled and said "That's good, ma'am."

As David walked Jane back to the boat, she asked, "Does your mother really rule you with an iron rod to that extent?"

"She likes to think she does but quietly we get on with our own lives away from her. You should hear about some of the hair-raising things my sister Arabella gets up to in New York. A new man every week; Mater would have a fit if she knew."

"And you only have me. Oh well, each to their own."

CHAPTER 9:
Different worlds

Alan Herbert took Jane with him next morning, introducing her to the mysteries of getting their daily orders from the operations team at Tower Pier. Today would be a mail distribution run down to Greenwich, pick up some officials from the Royal Docks entrance and run them to Woolwich, then collect some Dutch merchant seamen from their ship to be brought to Tower Pier. By relative standards this was a light and easy day's running, necessary though it all was.

But it got complicated when they found the Dutch ship, lying to buoys in Limehouse Reach. It had a police boat warning other craft away; there was an unexploded parachute mine just feet away. Frustrated, Petty Officer Herbert went alongside the police boat.

"We've got orders to pick up some men from that ship. Can't we get in and collect them?"

"I'm afraid not, sir. That mine is too close to the ship."

"When are the clearance boys coming to deal with it?"

"Divers are on their way. But we're short of boats and if you wanted to help you could speed things up a lot by collecting their gear from their truck at Regent's Canal Dock entrance."

Having collected, *Water Gypsy's* crew found themselves in for a very uncomfortable hour as they were then asked to moor up to the divers' boat and support the operation. Tension was high as the divers got a sling round the mine. *Water Gypsy* was then used to hold one end of the sling while the dive boat hauled the other end and lifted the mine clear of the river bed. Firmly attached right above this highly volatile load the two boats motored cautiously to a quieter spot in mid river. There they lowered it gently onto the riverbed, the divers attached a charge to it and, with all river traffic held back, the mine was detonated. Even some hundreds of yards away, the explosion and water column rocked *Water Gypsy* fiercely, rolling her onto her beam ends and drenching everyone on board. Her skipper, Jane and Punch took this calmly if less than impressed by it all. Sparrer and Evadne were clearly shaken by it, Evadne muttering, "What have I let myself in for here?"

Jane smiled gently, "You'll see worse than that before we're finished, I promise you."

"Heavens, that's a scary thought."

"I've learnt the hard way not to worry about these things; if you get hit it's curtains anyway and you'll know nothing about it. On a boat the things that miss don't make much difference unless they hit something nearby and the blast spreads to us too. That's how I picked up my injuries at Dunkirk; other ships close by, getting hit. Don't worry, you will soon get used to it."

"I hope you're right but it is still a scary thought."

They returned the divers' gear to the truck at the dock entrance, finally collected and delivered their Dutch seamen, then returned to Lambeth Pier several hours late after what was to prove to a be a fairly typical day on the river in the midst of the Blitz. As *Water Gypsy* approached the pontoon, a Wren could be seen waiting patiently, kitbag at her feet. This one stepped aboard effortlessly and introduced herself.

"Hello, I'm Susannah Brownlow but call me Suki."

Her elegant cut glass accent puzzled Jane, who had been expecting a Wren with some mechanical knowledge to look after the engines.

"I was hoping for a girl able to look after our engines. That surely isn't you, is it?"

"Well actually it is. They asked me if I could use my mechanical knowledge and I was pleased to get the opportunity. You see, before the war I was keen on powerboat racing and that meant looking after my own boat including its engine. From there I got fascinated by engines generally and I think I can probably be useful here."

"So you know engines and boats? That's a really handy combination. Welcome to the first Wren boat crew. We're working for Mr Herbert for a month's trial and if that goes well we will be getting our own boat after that."

Suki looked at Jane with a half smile on her face, as though enjoying a secret thought. "Yes, you're the Dunkirk Wren aren't you? I hope I can live up to your standards."

"Oh, don't worry about that. Come and have supper – I think the hash will extend to one more mouth."

David was late picking up Jane that night, having been held up with dock trials of his ship which was close to being ready for sea again.

"I've got a treat for you tonight. With parents coming up to Town again this weekend we've kept the suite at the Savoy. So I can show you that tonight."

"Wow, David, that would be nice. I'm ever so curious about them."

The suite proved to be better than Jane expected – comfortable rather than ornate but with every little luxury and convenience to hand. Jane bounced on the bed, "that's a very superior mattress. Do you realise this is the first time we've been completely private?"

"The thought had crossed my mind, yes."

Jane smiled at him and said, very softly, "It is an opportunity."

"Jane, don't say things like that. A chap might get ideas."

She got up, walked over to him very slowly then wrapped her arms round his neck.

"What sort of ideas might those be?"

"Jane, please." And he tried to pull away.

"David Daubeney-Fowkes, we love each other and it is quite natural to show that with our bodies too. At least you can kiss me."

With a sob and a puzzled shake of his head, he relented and the teaching he had been quietly getting was put to good use. From there it seemed inevitable to fall onto the bed and for some time the only sound was the occasional whimper. Jane had a strong urge to encourage him to go beyond kissing, but the calm voice at the back of her head said 'That's enough for now. Remember how innocent he is really. Don't lose this one too.' So she disentangled and sat up, smiling at him.

"Let's have supper here tomorrow night. I presume you can get away?"

"I don't see why not but I'll make sure it is clear."

With five girls plus its skipper, *Water Gypsy* lacked sufficient bunks for them all and her skipper took himself off ashore. As Jane settled to lapping river sounds she smiled gently, loving thoughts mingling with a familiar warm glow from her body which she was coming to know, and to understand needed an outlet. Perhaps having Stefan as well was a good way of dealing with urges which might otherwise push her into doing something damaging with the innocent she had acquired. 'But David, it's you I love' was her last drifting away thought.

Suddenly David wasn't there any more. A brief loving note his last contact, hours before going to sea and "back to the convoy routine". But *Water Gypsy* kept them too busy for Jane to feel sad for long. Five crew plus her regular skipper were really too many for a small boat like *Water Gypsy* so she organised a training rota, Evadne doubling up with Punch, and Suki paired with Sparrer in a very unlikely combination. But the differences meant that the elegantly well-spoken and the East London twang had to find out about each other to be able to do the job, and an odd friendship grew up between them – off to the cinema together after their third day working as a team, having discovered a mutual taste for musicals. Suki gave *Water Gypsy's* two little engines, Thorneycroft Handy Billy nine horse power two-cylinder engines, a dismissive glance "Is that all I'm being told to look after?"

"Not for long, Suki. Our own boat will be a bit more of a challenge, I think."

"Well thank goodness for that."

Jane smiled, thinking 'Let's hope you really live up to your own opinion of yourself.'

Sparrer rarely had letters but a scruffy note to her was passed on to Jane. It simply said 'Evening dresses available. Bring your friend to the back room of the '*Waggoners*' on Sunday night to see them. She'll need at least twenty quid.' Suddenly another of her little impulses had propelled Jane into the unknown, and a nervous shiver went through her. "I don't suppose they'd take a cheque, would they?"

Sparrer just laughed "Do me a favour, Jane. These guys hardly trust cash. It will need to be good used notes and nothing higher than a fiver."

So Jane drew thirty pounds in used fivers, halving her bank account in the process. 'Father, I hope you think your money is being put to good use' she thought as she tucked the bank notes away; she rather suspected he wouldn't, not really.

Plunging into the depths of Bermondsey, Jane felt distinctly uneasy despite the cover of being in uniform. These were mean streets, poverty clear in the clothes and attitudes of the people she passed. Sparrer seemed to know most of them, giving cheerful greetings along the way and leaving Jane with a suspicion that it was as well she was with a local. There was a raid going on, and loud explosions were not far away but it seemed to be mostly the North bank of the river that was being targeted. The streets they were in had their share of snaggle-toothed remains of building sticking up and too many empty lots, but by now keeping going while a raid was on – unless you were in the direct line – was normal and the two girls did not hesitate.

Going in to the *Waggoners,* Sparrer gave the barman a friendly wave then passed through and into the back room.

"Hello Dad," Sparrer greeted the largest of the three burly middle-aged men in the room.

"Hello Princess," he responded. "This your friend?"

Sparrer nodded enthusiastically.

"Yes Dad, this is Jane, my boss. She's the real thing."

Sparrer turned to Jane.

"You can trust this lot. They won't cheat you, I promise."

Jane had a strong sense of being in a new world with quite different standards. Sparrer's Dad looked closely at Jane's face.

"You've been in the wars, ain't you?"

Jane had pretty much forgotten the effect her white streak and scarred face could have on people and had to control her sense of surprise. "Yep, got these at Dunkirk."

"Yeah, Princess said something about you'd been at Dunkirk. So you rescued some soldiers?"

"Yes indeed, three thousand-odd."

"Blimey, so you really are the genuine article. That makes a big difference y'know. Now I see why Princess thinks so much of you. Okay, for that we'll give you a good deal. Come over here."

And he led her to a table in the corner which she hadn't noticed. On it were half a dozen white evening dresses.

"Take your pick. How many do you want?"

"That depends on how much you want for them. A couple at least."

"These, let's say a fiver each."

Sparrer butted in, "Jane, that's a good price."

"Is it? I really don't know much about this sort of thing. All right, I'll believe you."

Jane sorted through the pile. As far as she could tell, they were all silk, all well made and modish. There wasn't much to choose between them so she tried them against her length and chose the two which seemed the best fit. With them selected Sparrer's Dad produced another dress with a flourish, holding it out for Jane to see. This was stunning, with the finest of gauzy over-layers on a silk dress with a hint of an emerald sheen to it, gold trim on the deeply plunging neckline and a similar gold trim loose fitting belt. Even Jane's untrained eye could tell this was haute couture, the finish to an exquisite standard she had never seen before.

"This is gorgeous. Where on earth did this one come from?"

Again, Sparrer butted in. "Jane, I told you that was one question you couldn't ask."

Jane sighed. "All right, I know. But how much do you want for this one?" She doing a quick run over her cash and doubting if she had enough.

"As a special favour we'll let you have it for ten quid."

"Ten quid? You're on."

A desperate need to have any garment was new to Jane, but the feeling now was overwhelming. She pulled out her purse and counted out four used fivers. Sparrer's Dad smiled, turned to one of the other men and asked, "That all right with you?"

This man, who had said nothing, nodded, smiled in particularly grim way, and scooped up the cash. He said, "They're all yours and tell you what, we'll throw in some fancy undies as well. Anyone who Princess is happy to call boss deserves real respect. There ain't many of 'em."

Jane turned to Sparrer's Dad.

"Well thank you, Mr Jack. This is a new experience for me and I really appreciate how well you've treated me."

He smiled, a gentle yet hard smile from another world.

"You're welcome me darling. It's been a pleasure doing business with you. Let me know if you want any other clothes – I can probably fix something."

Back at Lambeth Palace Jane carefully hung up her new acquisitions and again got that strange new feeling, almost of love, as she gazed at the Special One. The half dozen pairs of gauzy French knickers might be an attractive addition to her wardrobe, too.

CHAPTER 10

Down river

Picking up the mail next morning Jane found a bulky envelope from a Chief Wren Writer Paterson, saying, 'that she had been instructed to issue the relevant forms for administration of a detached outpost, and these were enclosed'. There were various returns, to be done in triplicate, covering the members of her crew, food and clothing issues, untoward events and a monthly activity report. It had not occurred to Jane that she would very shortly be in charge of not only herself but a whole boat and its crew, and with that the inevitable administration would only be a step behind. She found it a depressing prospect but in fairness to her crew it would have to be done.

There was a smaller formal-looking letter as well. Opening it, Jane found a short letter from Arthur, reminding her that 'he would like her to undertake something extra for him once she had her own boat. Could she drop a short note confirming that Thursday evening would be suitable for a private conversation? If so, he would pick her up from Lambeth pier at 1900, in time for supper.' A quick check showed that evening clear so she confirmed, wondering what on earth this was about.

Arthur proved to be good company over dinner, talking about the Americans, life on a large estate and the nuisance his title could be at times. Anything, in fact, except whatever the purpose of the meeting might be. Over coffee he said, "Jane, we've taken a suite here as parents are coming up to Town again tomorrow. I need to talk to you in private, so can we go up to it please?"

This slightly startled Jane. Wangling into the suite with David had been one thing; going anywhere as private with another, relatively unknown, man seemed a much worse idea. And the 'please' on the end almost had the ring of an order about it. But there was clearly something specific to this, so she followed him up. He poured them both a brandy then finally got to the point.

"I'm going to be telling you some very secret things now. You must keep these to yourself under pain of contravening the official secrets act if you let them out. Do you understand that?"

Jane gulped, nodded, and waited.

"You know me as being in the Foreign Office. This is only partly true. I am also involved with counter-espionage work, keeping tabs on what is going on in various areas. I am one of a team that looks after the East End of London and there is something odd going on there that I'd like you to keep your eyes and ears open for. Every time a valuable cargo is delivered to the Royal Docks the *Luftwaffe* seems to know about it and make an extra effort to bomb it before we can get it moved. This points to some sort of spying going on there. I have arranged for a good deal of your work on your own boat to be around that area and I'd like you to keep your eyes and ears open for anything out of the ordinary that you pick up. Report back to me once a week and also whenever you come across anything that seems relevant. Do I make sense?"

Jane nodded, slowly. "Yes Arthur, I understand what you say but I'm not sure how much I'll hear, running on the river. We only touch briefly at most of the places we call at. And it occurs to me that my two senior crew, with Punch's knowledge of the river people and Sparrer's East End connections will be far more tuned to things going on than I will. I think I'd be more effective if we can include them in this. Would that be all right?"

"You are sure we can trust them?"

"Oh God yes, they are probably more reliable than I am."

"All right but don't mention me. As far as they are concerned it is just a general enquiry."

"Oh, that shouldn't be a problem. I'll see what we can do."

He gave Jane a business card. "That's my flat in Pont Street. You can phone me there and we can use it for private meetings in the evenings too. Just let me know and I'll pick you up."

With this business transacted Arthur stood up. Jane drained her brandy glass and was going to follow when Arthur abruptly sat down next to her, put an arm round her waist and said "Jane, you are the most gorgeous woman. Why do you waste your time with an ignoramus like David? I'd have you any time. You needn't come the little innocent with me, either. I can see you know just what you're doing."

Jane was struggling to escape his arm but he held very firm. "Arthur, really. You just don't seem to understand. I love David and have done since I met him second time round. So no, I'm not going to chuck him to go with you instead. I'm sorry but there's no way I will give David up."

"Well, I suppose I don't mind sharing."

"Oh Arthur, this is too much. No, I won't come the little innocent with you but that also means I fully understand what you mean and the answer is 'no.' Please get it into your head that I am not about to two-time David."

He pulled her round so their faces were inches apart.

"God, you are the sexiest woman. We really could have a good time together."

"Is that what you take me for? A good-time girl? Well thanks, but that's hardly a comment to make a girl change her mind. Now let go of me, Arthur, before I get really angry."

Up to now Jane had been using minimum force to keep him at bay. But it was time to put a stop to this charade and using all her rowing and work developed strength she threw him off. He landed in an untidy heap on the floor, looking utterly startled.

"Good heavens, you're strong." As he got to his feet he laughed.

"D'you know, that makes you even more desirable. I like a bit of danger and it looks like you are all of that."

"Arthur Daubeny-Fowkes, if you don't want me to throw you down the stairs, stop it now. Does this mean you don't want me to spy for you after all?"

"No, no, we must keep the two things separate so do please watch out for me."

"I can keep them separate but I'm not so convinced that you will. I'll be very careful not to get trapped in private with you again."

He walked her back to *Water Gypsy* and very gently took her hand as they parted, kissing it and giving her a lingering look of sheer lust. He was obviously wound up but Jane just thought, 'Too bad, I don't think I did anything to encourage him so he'll have to deal with it.'

She wasn't sorry to get back on board.

Alan Herbert had been letting Jane do the boat handling during the first three weeks under test and it had all gone well. They were doing after dark work as well and feeling their way round on a blackout-darkened river was not easy, especially going through the bridges. But there were marks and buildings to help guide them and Jane managed while feeling distinctly dubious about doing it on her own after dark. With a week to go she said to him, "Alan, how would you feel about letting Punch do the driving this last week? She's ever so good at it."

"Is she now? Well, if you say so I don't mind giving it a try."

So Punch was called aft, handed the controls, and told that she was in charge. This did not seem to bother the big girl much; she simply took the wheel, nodded and looked around. "How long am I doing this for?"

"We thought all week. It's important that we have a reliable first back-up when we go on our own. Nothing's been said yet but I am hoping we can be self-relieving for leave and the likes, and you will be the stand-in skipper. Are you all right with that?"

The question seemed to amuse Punch.

"Yes, Jane, I'm all right with that. We'll have to work out a rota. It will be good to get some regular leave system going. So far it's been 'come on and stay on'. Apart from Christmas I haven't had any leave since last summer."

Their first call – a ship at the buoys in mid-stream – was looming up rapidly, putting a stop to this conversation. Punch spun *Water Gypsy* with practised skill to stem the tide and neatly laid her alongside. Alan Herbert, watching this closely, nodded in approval and visibly relaxed. Although there was nothing like the pre-war levels of traffic, the river was still noisily busy, with lighters and barges and tugs and ships of all sorts going about their business. Immediately below Greenwich they had to dodge a Thames sailing barge which abruptly tacked in front of them. Punch was onto this in a moment, calmly spinning *Water Gypsy* and calling out "Hello Harry," as they went close under the barge's stern. Her skipper, startled to be called by name, peered over the side and bellowed "Punch! Whatever are you doing there?"

"I'm a Wren now, y'know."

He gave her a wave as the distance rapidly widened between them.

"If I know Old Harry he'll be heading up to Hay's Wharf just now. Regular run for him."

Alan Herbert was amused by this.

"Do you know them all like this?"

"All the North side ones, anyway. The Medway lot are a bit different."

Jane looked at the retreating sail with a dreamy eye.

"It must be a wonderful way of life, carrying cargo under sail like that."

"Yes and no Jane. Lovely in decent weather. But get caught in a gale against you and at the least you've lost a week and at worst you could lose your life. It's a pretty harsh way to earn a poor living, believe me."

"Well maybe but there's something very romantic about it."

Punch simply gave her trademark snort and concentrated on coming alongside the wharf which was their next call.

Their orders for the day were for them to tie up at Tower Pier when they had finished. This proved to be so they were ready for an early start the next day. Turning her crew out, with Sparrer as inclined as ever to steal an extra two minute before emerging, Jane was a bit short with them. Six o'clock starts had rather faded from memory with the easier hours of *Water Gypsy*. But they shook themselves awake soon enough and when a large van arrived they were ready. A large consignment of charts, CBs (Confidential Books, the Navy's instructions for every conceivable need) and pilot books, was taken below and by seven they were under way, their destination Southend Pier. This iconic landmark built out from Southend over mudflats to the edge of the deep water in Victorian times for paddle steamers to deliver their loads of pleasure-seeking Londoners having a day out, saw a drastic change in its fortunes with the coming of war.

The Navy took it over, named it *HMS Leigh,* established its convoy control centre there, and used it for gathering and despatching ships from the Thames to the sea; much of the Naval control of the Thames Estuary fell under its sway. It is forty-three miles from Tower Bridge to Southend Pier. At *Water Gypsy's* maximum of five and a half knots, that is about an eight hour trip, so Punch was left in charge on deck while Alan Herbert summoned Jane below to discuss progress.

"Jane, I have been really impressed by you and your crew and have no qualms about recommending that you get your own boat. Even your beginners have shaped up very well and as for Punch, I see now why you said she would have her own boat soon enough. I've got one problem and that won't be going in the report I land tomorrow. All of you – and especially you - seem as keen on your social life as you are on being sailors. I know you're all young but a greater degree of putting the job first would do no harm."

"Good heavens, no-one's said that to me before. Surely we need to have some time off, don't we?"

Alan pulled a face. "It's not just time off, it's the way your social life keeps coming first. You need to think about that a bit."

"Well our personal lives are important to us, you know. We've all got a lot of life still to come. But I'll try to get more focussed if you think that is necessary."

Alan Herbert smiled. "All right Jane, that's good. I spoke to our own people yesterday and the intention is that you'll stay with me till Friday night, then have ten days' leave before you re-assemble on your new boat. Detailed written instructions will come by Friday, I think."

A call from Punch, "We are just passing Gravesend. Do you want to come up?" prompted Jane to say, "I haven't been on the river seaward of Gravesend. Do you mind if I go up and see it all? I really need to know about this bit too."

Alan laughed, picked up a battered old chart and followed Jane out into the fresh air. Suki was steering with casual competence, Punch keeping the watch, Sparrer and Evadne sitting out on the little foredeck enjoying the day, sunny and remarkably warm for late January.

From there Alan gave a running commentary on the places they were passing, and as *Water Gypsy* turned East again to pass Canvey Island and Thameshaven with its tanker berths, they picked up the beginning of the Sea Reach buoys providing a highway out to seaward. Southend Pier could be seen in the distance on the port hand, a white ensign standing out over it in the breeze. As they approached it Punch asked, "Where to, please?"

"See those steps tucked in the corner? They will do us."

Once alongside Alan took Jane – and Punch – with him to show them where to find Naval control where they would get their orders if running from there, support services, and the station for the electric railway than ran the one and a half miles of the pier's length. A working party was organised and half a dozen matelots appeared on the steps, forming a chain to pass the material up. Clearly they had never seen Wrens in bell bottoms before.

"Ere, lads, there's sailor girls here. Get a load of that. The Navy's really looking up. Give us a kiss, Jenny."

To a greater or lesser extent all Jane's crew were used to this low-grade sexism which was built into how the lower deck saw its Wrens and gave as good as they got. Jane was interested to note that Suki was much the quickest at giving them waspish answers, seeing a side to her, which hadn't emerged in the few days she had been aboard. When Jane commented on this Suki just said, "Oh, powerboat racing is every bit as bad and with only a few females in it we have to be able to answer back any time."

With their cargo delivered, and their skipper vanished somewhere deep in the Naval offices, the girls had time to brew up and look around. Anchored nearby were about a dozen merchant ships; some of them coastwise colliers in ballast and waiting to sail north for another load of coal to fuel London, a large tanker which had discharged its vital petrol cargo next door at Thameshaven and was due to take its chances crossing the Atlantic again, and assorted other cargo ships.

* * *

The anchorage off Southend Pier and along the Sea Reach channel, the first spacious area of deep water available to ships outward bound from the Thames, became the primary place for controlling ship movements in and out of the river. Inbound ships dispersed to their discharging berths from there, and outward bound ships were assembled into convoys to be despatched under Naval control. My journalist work at Greenwich where I had first encountered Jane and her story was always only a part of my interests. Pre-war it had included more general reporting of the river and its many differing users. Wartime restrictions seriously hampered my efforts but I kept a close watching brief and even when I could say nothing about it I was able to see what was going on.

It has to be said that traffic on the river was greatly reduced from its pre-war levels. The myriad big ships which used to come in, mainly to the Royal Docks, had all gone to West Coast ports. This in turn had drastically reduced the lightering and transhipment work which had been such a feature of the river; there was still some barge traffic and the river could appear quite busy at times, but it was deceptive. If anything, there was more official traffic than freight work. Ships kept on coming and going and always needed attention but the pressure had gone.

Remarkably, the elegant Spritsail sailing barges just kept plodding on, in and out, throughout the war and many of their skippers found Royal Naval restrictions more of a hamper to their work than was enemy activity. Their biggest enemy was the mine; the wooden hull is sturdily built for what it was intended to do but simply disintegrated into matchwood when half a ton of high explosive went off right underneath it. No few were lost that way as throughout the war the enemy kept on mining the Thames seaward approaches with little interference from the British.

CHAPTER 11:

Getting accepted

Alan Herbert returned to *Water Gypsy* with a broad smile on his face. "Nothing else to do today, so we'll pop round to Holehaven and have a bit of a make and mend. I'll introduce you girls to my favourite pub there later on." So they cast off and headed east along the Sea Reaches, mooring up within the hour. With time in hand Jane decided to go through the pile of forms and paperwork that had been sent, and got thoroughly depressed by the process. But looking through the returns and reports – all in triplicate – she found a list of her crew with personal details including dates of birth. She was startled to discover she was the youngest member of her group, with Punch and Sparrer twenty-three, Evadne twenty-four and Suki positively old at twenty-seven. Somehow this put a different aspect on how she saw her boatmates. 'Really', she thought, 'the only reason I am in charge is because I've done more of it. I think I might keep quiet about this one.'

Holehaven is a convenient, reasonably sheltered creek at the west end of Canvey Island, with an Auxiliary Patrol depot and easy access to fuel. So the skipper got Suki involved in helping him take petrol and do a general check over the engines, then they ate well on casseroled sausages and a large cabbage the skipper had produced from somewhere mysterious. With that done he suggested they smarten up a little – although he didn't do much himself – then led them off to the '*Lobster Smack*' Inn, his favourite refreshment stop in the area. As they walked to it he explained that it wasn't usually a girls' place, being full of seamen, but as they were more or less seamen too he would introduce them to the landlord and they could use it again once they were on their own. Jane had made sure they all had their white lanyards tucked under their collars and stretched across their chests so they presented a uniform appearance. With a little introducing the landlord served them happily, giving an assurance that they'd be welcome back any time. Here were both river men of various sorts and deep-sea seamen off the tankers at Thameshaven, so Jane's crew got a strong sense of being part of a tight-knit exclusive brotherhood, even if only on the edge of it.

They were ushered into the snug and once they all had a drink Alan beckoned them to listen closely to him. He had his usual pink gin and red wine chaser.

"Girls, this last month has been a real eye-opener to me. I will freely admit that I was very dubious about having an all-female crew on board. Jane had been pretty impressive when she came to me before Christmas but it's easy for one person to be exceptional without that meaning a larger number would be as good. But all of you have exceeded my greatest expectation and I have said so in my report. As a result I think I can safely say that you are to be launched on your own directly and I wish you well. Everyone on the river will be holding their breath a bit and watching you closely. I do know there are some serious doubters in the hierarchy on the river but also some who are supporters. Give the well-wishers the ammunition and they should be able to overcome the doubters but which happens is in your own hands. I believe a boat has been selected for you to take over but I don't know which. Good luck."

There was silence after this little speech; the girls looked at each other with expressions varying between worried and bright-eyed. Suki, whose relative maturity was starting to show, looked at Jane and said, "Does this worry you, Jane? Y'know, being on show like this?"

Jane gave that a wry lop-sided smile.

"Suki, I've been on show like that from the start. The only thing new for me now is being responsible for a whole crew and in a new area. It's been one at a time: first me, then Punch and me, and then Sparrer as well, have been doing this for a while. My biggest worry now will be making sure we don't get lost because I still don't know the Thames all that well."

Punch, as always, took this calmly then said, "Don't worry, we are all in this together and I will make sure we don't get lost. Remember I've been running in and out this ditch since I was a little girl."

Evadne then asked, "Does this suggest that if we do well, there will be other Wrens go on the boats?"

"We hope so, Eva. The Navy is so short of men that anything a female can do instead is being handed over. But Wrens in boats is being fiercely argued about right up to their Lordships who are also split over it. It's up to us to show them we can do it, that women are perfectly capable of crewing boats."

Strolling back to the boat, leaving Alan Herbert behind to stay in a room at the pub, Jane asked her crew, "Do we need a strict hierarchy on board? The Navy always has, even on a launch, but then that's the Navy for you. Punch is my obvious number two, but apart from that can we get along on equal terms?"

Again, it was Suki who spoke up. "No reason why not, Jane. We all have our jobs to do so there's no reason why we shouldn't simply get on with them. It will all settle down once we have our own boat, to my mind. Let's see."

The others murmured agreement and the topic didn't come up again.

There was a sparkle in Alan Herbert's eye the next morning when he came on board. "We've got an interesting day today; we're running as the boarding officer's boat, which means taking him from the pier to go on board merchantmen lying in the anchorage and give them their orders. We'll see how you get on in more open waters." It was a bright breezy day and in the open spaces of the Sea Reaches even getting back to the pier had *Water Gypsy* butting into the short steep seas throwing spray overall. This rapidly showed up the difference between the experienced and the less so. In no time Sparrer and Evadne were hanging over the side saying goodbye to their breakfasts. Punch, Suki and Jane took it calmly. Fortunately carrying the Boarding Officer round various outbound ships did not call for much crew activity. Tending him on and off pilot ladders, passing his bag to him and generally looking after things allowed Sparrer to lie down, groaning quietly, while Evadne hung on in the fresh air, determined not to give in. After the first couple of ships Jane was put on the helm and, conscious of the many eyes watching, concentrated hard. The ships, lying to their anchors bow to the weather had the seas running down their sides; nothing to the ships but enough to keep *Water Gypsy* bouncing around so that holding her alongside was challenging but Jane and Punch both worked on it and succeeded. At the end of a long day they tied up again in Holehaven, weatherbeaten but glowing. Sparrer was worried. "Jane, why was I seasick there? I wasn't down at Dover even in bad weather; when we went out to that corvette it was horrible but I was fine. Here I just couldn't stop meself."

"I'd guess it was because we were motoring into the seas. It gives a short harsh motion which knocks you about more." She grinned at the two sufferers, "Don't worry, you soon get over that sort of thing with any luck."

"I hope so." muttered Evadne with a heavy sigh.

Next day saw them running back up-river loaded with unidentified sacks of documents from *HMS Leigh* which they offloaded at Tower Pier and returned to Lambeth. This was the end of their time on *Water Gypsy* and to the girls' surprise their skipper produced a couple of bottles of champagne which made for a cheerful evening. Late on Punch, her natural reserve lowered a bit, asked the great poet, "Mr Herbert, would you look at me poems? Oi know they're nothing much but I do like writing them."

He laughed. "Yes of course, let's see them."

She produced a slightly battered school notebook, each page a poem written in Punch's beautiful copperplate handwriting.

"*The Barrow Deep at Sunset*", "*All Flags Flying*", "*Seagulls Soaring*" and "*Anchored off Lowestoft*" were four among many. A P Herbert glanced at a couple, then stopped and read them much more closely. His silence lengthened as he studied them. Fifteen minutes later he looked up and smiled. "You know, Punch, these are really rather good. Simple and unshowy but the better for that and they catch the essence of your subjects. With a little development you could write very good poetry. If I can find a little time I'll try to show you what I mean. Would you like that?"

Punch blushed, "Ooh yes please, Mr Herbert. I'd love that. Do you really think they're any good?"

"Yes I do. There's real promise there."

Punch sat with a beam on her face, blushing all the while; the others exchanged surprised glances.

Next day some of A P Herbert's own friends turned up as crew and the girls went on leave. A letter had been delivered from Third Officer Baker to Jane the previous day with clear instructions. They were all to take ten days' leave then report to Tough's Yard at Teddington to take over the motor launch *Kittiwake,* take stores, then bring it to Tower Pier where it – and they - would come under the control of Royal Naval Auxiliary Patrol to operate over the full length of the Thames as required from day to day.

Knowing something like this was going to happen, Jane had arranged the weekend with Stefan and they lost themselves in each other. There was no doubt that Stefan was deeply in love with her; by now it was much more than physical enthusiasm – although there was plenty of that - and wonderful though the couple of days had been it left Jane ever deeper in a quandary. Once Stefan had gone back to his squadron she took a night off at their little base at Lambeth Palace before going home, just to try to look a bit less shattered. A large love bite on her neck was going to cause problems if her mother spotted it.

By now the girls had developed the Londoner's capacity to get on with life despite the nightly assault from the air. For two nights in a hotel bedroom Jane and her paramour had ignored the sirens and encouragement to get into the air raid shelter, agreeing that if they were going to die they might as well do so enjoying themselves. This fatalism was fairly widespread and although it produced casualties a surprising number of Londoners stuck to their homes and their own beds throughout the Blitz. Even a resounding crash from a collapsing building nearby didn't put Stefan off his stroke. The raw battered remnants of buildings were a constant reminder of what London was being subjected to, but life went on.

Included in the paper work sent to Jane had been a book of rail travel warrants which apparently she was authorised to sign. It had never occurred to her that being in charge of a detached unit would carry privileges like this, but she now gleefully wrote out warrants to Lowestoft, Bermondsey, Chichester and Plymouth. Evadne was going to stay with an Aunt in Carshalton but every member of the crew invited her to come to their homes next time.

The train to the West Country left Paddington on time and was only an hour late arriving Plymouth so by wartime standards Jane had a good journey, even finding a window seat. She spent the trip staring dreamily out of the window trying without success to sort out her thoughts on her love life and the two men who were so important to her. Her mother had managed enough petrol for a trip into Plymouth and picked up Jane in the Austin Ruby, shoving her kitbag and suitcase into the back beside various purchases. Rufus the giant teddy bear, still around, had been left at Lambeth Palace. Jane had brought her recently acquired evening dresses with her and before they went home she dropped them off with the family dressmaker. They were all distinctive, in particular the special one and an hour was spent working out how to alter them so their appearance changed. Given their dubious origins Jane worried that she might meet their previous owners somewhere which could have been highly embarrassing so some alterations seemed necessary.

A week in the peace of the Old Grange left Jane refreshed but lethargic. It hadn't taken her mother five minutes to spot the love bite; despite a lingering look of disbelief she accepted Jane's cover story that it had been the result of a prank at a party. "You are still being a good girl, aren't you Jane?"

"Yes mummy. David's away at sea anyway so what else could I be?"

"I don't know but one reads such dreadful tales in the papers of wild promiscuity among girls in uniform that I do worry a bit."

"Mummy, the Wrens are notoriously the respectable women's service so at least I'm in the right one."

"D'you know Jane, I saw a dreadful remark by a naval officer in one of the papers. He said that life in a naval base was a case of 'Up with the lark and to bed with a Wren'. I really shuddered when I read that, thinking of how casually dismissive it was, as though every naval officer was entitled to a Wren in his bed at night."

"Mummy, you must know enough about men to know that that sort of boasting is only the way they talk. Real life isn't like that, I assure you."

Reflecting on this conversation, Jane could almost feel her nose growing longer. She hated the duplicity involved. In a year and a half she had had sexual encounters with four different men, had her eye on a fifth and was dodging a sixth. How on earth could she explain that to her strict and in many ways conformist mother? Well, she knew very well that she couldn't and would have to keep silent. Yet it didn't feel to her as though she was being particularly promiscuous. With one exception it was just the result of her wanting to show her feelings to the man involved. 'Too bad about Jamie,' she reflected. 'That was an awful warning about being too open.' And for the three people she was deceiving now, she didn't see any choice but to keep them compartmentalised and try to ensure nothing leaked out. A natural chatterbox, Jane found this guarding her tongue difficult at times but it had to be done, so in one sense the end of her leave was a relief.

PART THREE:

ON THEIR OWN

CHAPTER 12:
Masts and bridges

Jane reported to the yard office at Teddington to find her new command. Sparrer and Suki were on board already, trying to get the paraffin cooker to boil a kettle while workmen were putting finishing touches to the boat. Jane liked what she saw: *Kittiwake* was a substantial and impressive former motor yacht, given an experimental rebuild to suit the job it was now going to be doing. The boat had a wide square transom and an open after deck, big enough to carry a fair bit of cargo, a wheelhouse, open to the rear, at the aft end of the raised hull accommodation. Under the wheelhouse the boat had twin twenty horse power petrol engines so the forty-two feet long boat would have sufficient power for most purposes. Morse controls at the steering position gave Jane the whole boat immediately to hand. On the foredeck was an electric windlass with two useful-looking anchors and a little davit on the bow, mainly to cat the anchors but it would prove to be useful for all sorts of other jobs. The boat's dominant feature, however, was a sturdy mast and one ton derrick mounted at the aft end of the wheelhouse to plumb the open after deck. It was evidently expected that the boat would carry some fairly hefty loads. There was provision for ropes to be led to the windlass in the bow if power was needed on the derrick. Jane and her crew were being given a seriously useful craft: someone in authority had evidently decided that at least the all-Wren experiment should have an excellent tool to demonstrate whether they were up to the job or not.

Jane went back to the yard office to ask about stores, spare gear and the likes.

"D'you like your new command?" Asked a foreman with a shy grin. "This is the best one we've produced for a while."

Jane stood in the office doorway eyeing *Kittiwake.* "She looks lovely and should be a really useful boat. But isn't that mast a bit high for going under the bridges? It looks awfully tall to me."

"No, it shouldn't be. We have standard heights for these things and have built it to those. You'll be all right unless you are trying to sneak into side creeks with low bridges."

"I hope you're right. It would be awfully limiting otherwise."

"Don't worry, lass. You will be fine."

Jane shrugged and took their word for it. During the afternoon Evadne turned up and Punch arrived about six o'clock in the evening after a nightmare journey of nine hours with the train making long stops in the countryside. There was very little food on board so they found a fish and chip shop for supper. The accommodation was nicely laid out, with a foc'sle cabin with four bunks in it, a roomy saloon with hooks for hammocks in the deckhead beams and a small single cabin on the port side aft which Jane claimed for herself. To starboard were the galley, the heads and wash house and a general store. There was electric power throughout the boat from a substantial battery but also a Tilley Lamp on the forward bulkhead and a large paraffin stove for heating so they should be snug on board. *Kittiwake* was really very well set up and Jane felt a surge of excitement at the boat and what being given something like this meant for official estimation. Someone high up wanted the Wren crew to succeed.

Next morning they were up early and got guided tours by the yard hands. Suki and Punch went over the engines with the foreman fitter, Sparrer and Evadne tallied all the stores and spare gear on board and drew up a list of what was still needed while Jane discussed handling the boat and the way the controls worked. She then ran through the stores lists with her crew; a raid on the yard's storehouse produced some further items, given somewhat unwillingly from dwindling stocks, and after lunch they took the boat out for a short trial run. Everything seemed fine and late afternoon Jane ceremonially signed for the boat with her crew watching.

Day three, they were ready to go, no longer a part of the boatyard but a living working part of the river's fleets. With horn blowing and flags flying they set off an hour before high water, looking to get below Putney Bridge and past the shallow part of the tidal Thames before half ebb. It was a cool grey day with a steely glint on the water but Jane and her crew set off in a bright mood, an exciting new world before them. Three miles downstream came Richmond Bridge, the oldest on the tideway and a splendid five-arch stone structure with pretty gas lamps on top.

Punch, standing beside Jane as they approached it, remarked, "It looks awfully low. I hope we clear it all right."

"Well, they assured me in the yard that they knew how high our mast should be. Let's trust them." The bow went under the central arch of the bridge, Punch stepped out to watch the masthead passing under then yelled "Look out" a second before there was an almighty bang, crunch and the mast broke off at wheelhouse level. The whole boat jerked and rocked from the force of the contact. The mast fell over backwards and its ragged lower end charged into the wheelhouse, largely demolishing it and missing Jane by about three inches. It landed with a crash on the afterdeck wrecking the flagpole as it landed. With the boat going at full speed it rushed through the bridge before Jane had time to react; below the bridge Jane stopped the engines. "Punch are you all right?"

Punch emerged from under a tangle of ropes and rigging looking pale. "Unhurt, anyway, but ye Gods what a scare. It missed me by inches. What are we going to do, Jane?"

Jane shook her head in fury. "Go back to the yard, I suppose. We can't go on like this. My God, what a mess."

She turned the boat round and headed back up river. The reception at the yard was distinctly cool. "What have you done to her?" was yelled even as they were mooring up. "Mast was too high" She shouted back. The yard's men swarmed over the boat as soon as she tied up. It was late in the day by now and the senior foreman said "We'll get her sorted out in the morning but it will take a few days to deal with this mess."

They still did not have much food on board so it was fish and chips again. There was a council of war among them as they ate. Jane was still shaking with anger and fright. "You know what the worst thing is about this lot? They'll be blaming us for it and saying women can't cope, can't do the job properly. I can see it coming from a mile off that there will be a big effort to say it's all our fault and I'm not going to have it."

She was right. Next morning the foreman's first question was "How did you manage to do that to her?"

Jane was fired up and ready. "By taking your word for it that the mast would go under the bridge. It's the last time I believe you lot."

"Well I don't know. We measured it and according to our standards it should have gone under."

"Yes, but it didn't so it must mean your standards are wrong. If you look at the mast you'll see it was the top foot or so which struck the bridge. I reckon that thing needs shortened by about three feet for safety going under bridges. What are you going to do now?"

"Luckily we've got another spar in the yard so we'll be able to replace it. But that will take a week or so by the time we shape it, fit it and get it rigged. You'll probably have to varnish it yourselves. The rest of the damage is superficial so we'll get that done at the same time. We could have done without this, we're too damn busy anyway."

"Too bad; if it you'd got it right first time you wouldn't have this problem now. Are you sure you can do it in a week?"

"We're going to have to. There's a big repair job coming in next week and we can't do both at once."

"Anything up to a week we can probably go on living on board. Longer than that and we will get moved out, so you'd better be right."

While this was being discussed the yard men were already stripping the mast remnants, saving what they could for the new one. It was a hefty spar so the yard crane was brought alongside and used to remove the shattered timber.

At lunch time Jane had another discussion with her crew. "It looks like we're here for a week. What can we do in the meantime?"

Suki spoke first "There's a bedplate for a small generator on the port side. If we could come by a suitable set we could get that in. It'd be very useful rather than relying on the main engines and battery for electric all the time."

"Well great, but where do we find one in the middle of a war?"

Suki smiled. "I know of an outfit that supplies them and could probably get something."

"Fine, let's do it, but how are we going to pay for it?"

"I'll pay them now if you can get the money back from their Lordships."

"I can try but I've no idea if I'll succeed. They tend not to like us going off doing our own thing."

"Too bad; I'll get it ordered today." And next day a shiny new generator set was delivered and lowered into place, accompanied by an invoice for fifty pounds. Suki, who seemed to enjoy this sort of work, spent the rest of the week getting it bedded down, plumbed in and wired up and running. Even fitting some new pipework didn't seem to trouble her and she got quite a thing going with the yard's head fitter.

Although *Kittiwake* was a well equipped and solid boat she was a bit spartan down below so Sparrer and Evadne set about making the accommodation a bit more homely. They painted, scrounged and fitted curtains, persuaded the heater and the cooker to work properly, found extra bedding and managed to get a couple of hammocks sent up from Woolwich. Punch meantime was taking herself off into the yard each day to join in the work preparing and fitting the new mast.

On their second day back in the yard a message came through: Commander Coleman required Jane to present herself at his office next day at 1030 to explain herself. She had been half expecting, half dreading a summons like this and took a deep breath when the message got to her.

* * *

Commander Coleman was one of the dominant figures on the Thames. He had been the PLA's (Port of London Authority) Chief Harbourmaster before the war. After being at sea in the merchant navy he had worked his way up the PLA's substantial harbourmaster hierarchy to the top job. Anticipating the war, he had been instrumental in setting up the River Emergency Service in 1938. This PLA organisation consisted of various grades of motor launch (mostly yachts) and also ambulance boats which were adapted pleasure steamers with medical teams on board. The best of the launches proved so useful that they were absorbed into the Royal Naval Auxiliary Patrol when it was set up; the ambulance boats had not found a use and were disbanded. Captain Coleman, as he had been before the war, was called up into the Royal Navy. Already a reservist, he held the naval rank of Commander and was put in command of the Auxiliary Patrol fleet. Throughout the war he was deeply involved in marine matters all along the Thames and was universally known simply as 'The Captain'. Although a genial and outgoing person, he was not one to trifle with.

* * *

Next morning Jane, in best tiddley uniform and black silk stockings, made her way to the PLA head office on Tower Hill for 1015 and waited, feeling distinctly nervous but determined. At 1030 precisely she was summoned into the presence, standing looking out of the window. She came to attention and reported. Slowly he turned round and surveyed her, nodding approvingly as he took in her medal ribbons. "Right Beacon, this is a bit of a disappointment, isn't it?"

"Yes indeed sir."

"Why did you do it?"

Jane struggled to control her rising irritation. The implication that it was her fault was clear. "Sir, I had been assured by the yard that the mast would clear the bridges and I took their word for it. Big mistake."

"But surely you must have seen that the mast was too high as you approached the bridge?"

"And you must be aware, sir, that bridges always look too low as you approach them. This one might have looked particularly low but I was lulled into thinking it would be all right, knowing that appearance is deceptive. I'm sorry sir, but I simply won't have it that it was my fault."

"Is that so, young lady? You did it and captains always have to take responsibility for their vessels and actions no matter who else might be involved."

"Yes sir, I know that, and I am not trying to say I wasn't in charge when it happened. Therefore I have some blame attached to me. But what was I to do? We were stemming the flood tide so at least I had decent control of the boat and I suppose I could have gone astern and stopped short. But what then? If I'd gone back to the yard and said the mast looked too high, I bet they would have simply told me I was being a silly girl and go and try again. The foreman I dealt with seemed convinced they had got the mast's height correct. So now I'm on the carpet for someone else's mistake. Please don't think I'm trying to shirk my responsibility but you must see the dilemma I was in."

"You are a very eloquent young lady, I must say."

Jane had a wry grin. "It's that or sink, sir."

"Mr Tough himself is looking into this; I gather he wasn't involved before because the yard is so busy and I think is acknowledging that they got it wrong. It seems that they used the standard for a mast stepped on the keel when yours is stepped on deck, for which a shorter length would have been correct. That lets you off the hook but I will still require an incident report form – you have got some, haven't you? - and a written report on everything to do with this business."

"Yes, sir, more bureaucracy."

He laughed. "That's the Navy for you. Now, having dealt with the formal bit, what do you think of the boat? We have given quite a lot of thought to her rebuild to be suitable for the job, and right now she is about the best boat we have. Round these parts there are some people who think you lot should sent back to the kitchen immediately and some, like me, who suspect that women can do this job perfectly well. We have tried to give you the best start possible by giving you the best boat and I need hardly tell you that the Jeremiahs are having a field day just now. So please don't bend her again."

"Well, thank you for the vote of confidence, sir. She looks as though she should be very useful and I can see her being busy on the more interesting jobs which will suit us very well. I'll let you know what we find with experience."

"Very good. That will be all." And he nodded dismissal so it was, "Aye aye sir" and another salute. Outside, a keen wind was blowing up the hill but Jane felt nothing but an enormous sense of relief.

CHAPTER 13:

Doing it

It took the full week but *Kittiwake* was re-rigged and looking splendid, if a little foreshortened, in time for her crew to avoid having to go ashore. Mooring up on Lambeth Pier brought a sense of anticipation in Jane and her crew. The run down had been trouble free and suddenly the job they had come to do was in sight. Jane had arranged that their mail would be left in their room in Lambeth Palace so, as well as rescuing her evening dresses from the crush of a suitcase, she picked up the mail and they all settled down to catch up with the news from home, loved ones and friends. All, that is, except Sparrer who as usual had nothing. "Nothing from Lofty?" queried Jane.

"Naw, he's not much of a letter writer anyway and recently he seems to have been posted far away. I think it's the Med but who knows? For sure his last note implied they'd been seeing a lot of action. Not to worry; I'll see him one of these days."

"That must be tough."

"Not really. I trust him an' we know where we're going. He did promise we'd get engaged next time he got home."

Punch gave that her trademark snort and muttered, "Lucky girl."

But Jane looked at Sparrer more closely. "You really trust him that much?"

"Yeah, too right Jane. Me an' Lofty, we know each other, so I know I can trust him."

"You're sure?"

"Yeah, Lofty's an orphan an' the most important thing in the world to him is family. I'm giving him that. You've met me Dad. We're a solid lot and Lofty loved 'em all when he came to visit. And he knows I love him, Jane, more than me own left arm. So I don't worry when he only writes occasionally. It's just not him, and when he does he really struggles. But one of these days, when this bleedin' war is over, me an' Lofty will make a real home and we both know it. Meantime what we hope for is far more important than any casual shag."

"What happened to his parents?"

"His dad was killed at Ypres and his mum got Spanish flu an' died. His gran tried but she died too then it was an orphanage until he went into the Navy as a boy."

Sparrer's black eyes had acquired a glow and power Jane had never seen before. Right beside her one of her crew had developed a love and a life of her own and Jane had barely noticed. 'I really must think about my crew more' she thought 'I know Punch is out of luck but what about Evadne and Suki for that matter?' She knew nothing about their inner personal lives.

For her own heart she read through David's three letters, each a little warmer than the previous one. Stefan's was predictable. Jane then turned to news from Alicia, who was thriving in Liverpool despite the fierce bombing. A letter from Fiona brought surprising news: Dora had been promoted Petty Officer Regulator, the first of Pro Course Two to reach that giddy height. "She must be seriously terrifying to get to that so quickly." mused Punch.

"Probably something to do with nothing to lose." Opined Evadne. "I could never figure her out on pro course. Why anything so mouse-like could have got in, in the first place and then hung on to pass out successfully."

Jane thought for a minute about confidences she really shouldn't let out. "Well, she'd had a pretty hard life which she had to sort out in her mind when she got committed to the Wrens. But once she had done that I found she had a really sharp brain."

Punch held up a letter. "Dad tells me he's getting an engine in the boat, 'cos he's been offered a good contract with a grain firm if he's got one. That'll be better than scratching a living on the open market."

"Oh, that's good. It makes my rescuing the barge at Dunkirk really worth-while after all."

"Yes, you've no idea how pleased my Dad was about that."

Suki looked puzzled. "What's this about rescuing a barge?"

Punch answered. "Dad's barge got left behind at Dunkirk and Jane rescued it with a load of pongoes on board. He'd given up any hope of seeing it ever again so he was more than a little surprised when it turned up in Dover."

"What was it doing at Dunkirk?"

"Quite a few were taken over and because of their shallow draft they were beached to act as kind of jetties for small boats to get alongside and pick up pongoes from. My Dad's was one of them and he was told to leave it and catch a ship back to UK which grieved him 'cos he wasn't insured. The Navy said it would give him compensation but nothing like the barge's worth so he was more than delighted when it was suddenly handed back to him, all thanks to Jane."

Suki eyed Jane. "You really did that?"

"Yep, I was doing a few salvage jobs at the time and when I saw this barge crawling with pongoes but going nowhere I figured it was worth having a go at. It was lifting to the swell so it was nearly afloat anyway some time before high water which meant that pulling it off was just a matter of patience. Once off all I had to do was to teach some of the trench diggers how to sail the boat. Luckily they got a tow later."

Suki looked impressed. "Well well, quite the seaman. Now I start to see where those medals come from."

Jane shrugged and smiled, passing it off as just one of those things.

Next morning she was up bright and early. "Come on, girls, today is *Der Tag*. Let's get to it." There were the usual groans and grumbles but they turned out and cleaning stations followed by breakfast kept them busy till 0730. With the boat looking shiny they headed down to Tower Pier and Jane went for their orders. She came back with half a dozen RAF types and orders to take them to Greenwich, then go to a battery in Long Reach to collect empty ammunition cases for return to St. Katherine's Dock. The RAF were a bit surprised to find they were being taken down river by girls. "I say, this is a bit unusual, isn't it? I've never come across girls on boats before. Who do you belong to?"

"We're Wrens, sir. The first female boat crew to be let loose on our own but you'll find we do actually know what we're doing. Think of us as being a bit like the ATA, sir."

"Well, I hope you do. When will we get to Greenwich?"

"Should take about forty minutes, sir. Have you a fixed timetable?"

"Meeting starts at ten."

"Oh, you'll be fine for that. It's only five minutes' walk from the landing stage to the main building."

An item the girls had managed to acquire was a coffee pot and soon the aromatic smell filled the cabin, gently tranquilising the passengers' doubts. By the time they arrived Suki had a date for that night. The RAF having been delivered with crisp despatch, the rest of the day proved interesting in dealing with the mundane. The ammunition boxes were offloaded in the St Katherine's lock pit, and as it was low water they used their derrick and cargo net for the first time to get the boxes up onto the lock side. With the little generator going and a runner onto the drum end of the windlass the whole job was done with power for the work. The girls were watched closely by several Naval officers standing nearby and it was an excellent opportunity for them to show off their seamanship. With Jane leading them on the cargo deck and Punch on the drum end they did it with quick efficiency, the waiting lorry being loaded in half an hour. By hand it would have taken most of the afternoon. The Naval officers, clearly impressed, came to the lock edge and called, "Have you done this before?"

"Just once or twice, sir."

"Are you regulars here? I didn't know we had any girl crews."

"Well, we've just started here but we have had previous experience in boats. It's a bit experimental yet but the signs are good."

"How interesting. I presume you're part of the RNAP? Does Petty Officer Herbert know about you? We're on the Naval control staff here and use the Auxiliary Patrol boats a lot."

"Yes sir, we started by doing a month with Mr Herbert on *Water Gypsy* and he gave us a good report. So now we're on our own with the Patrol."

"Right: we'll keep our eyes open for you. That derrick looks like a useful bit of kit; what's its safe working load?"

"One ton sir."

"We could have done with that last week to move some machinery down to Gravesend. You could be busy girls."

Jane smiled. "Suits us, sir. We're here to be useful."

"Which boat is this?"

"Called *Kittiwake*. Number M21."

They called round at Tower Pier but there was no more work for them, so it was back to Lambeth and moor up for the night.

Suki, in her best uniform, disappeared ashore for her RAF date and the other three went to a film leaving Jane on her own. She settled down to write a long letter to David full of love and hope then curled up with Conrad's '*Typhoon*'. The movie-goers had all turned in by the time Suki got back; Jane peeped out of her little cabin and noted that her engineer looked distinctly rough, unsteady on her feet and a bit dishevelled. "Interesting' thought Jane. 'That may need watching'.

A grey dawn with light drizzle did nothing to encourage them next morning but necessity pushed them on. Jane looked brighter coming back from the office. "It looks like being an easy day" she remarked. "Four pongoes down to Erith then pick up some kit from a ship on the Greenwich buoys. Back by mid-afternoon."

"That's all? I bet they find us another job late on."

Sparrer was right. Calling in at Tower Pier mid-afternoon for their next day's orders, the Scheduling Officer said, "We've got another little job for you today. They need some spare parts for a tug down at the Royal Docks. They're on the pontoon already. Take 'em down then you can have the rest of the day off."

"Well thanks sir. It'll be after dark before we get back at that rate."

"Yes well, they need the spare parts more than you need a nice easy life. Just think of them working all night to get the bits fitted."

"My heart bleeds, you've no idea."

"Go on young lady, you know you like it really."

She gave that a wordless curl of a lip and headed back down to the pier. There, neatly stacked, were six crates with '*Tug Sun IX*' on them. Grumbling, the girls loaded them and headed down river into the gathering gloom of a damp February evening. "Going to turn foggy later" remarked Punch to no-one in particular.

By the time the crates were landed at the pierhead dark was falling and visibility had shrunk to perhaps half a mile – enough to get on with heading up river but no more. Passing Bow Creek mouth Punch suddenly said, "What's that in the water? Looks a bit odd." Jane swung the boat to look at the lump floating in the river.

"Oh dear, it's a body. What are we supposed to do with them?"

"Collect them and hand them over to the River Police, I think. Can we get the net round it and pull it inboard?"

"Ugh."

"Well Eva, I'm afraid we have to. Let's get on with it."

With the net round the body the five girls struggled to get the still floppy body inboard. Three times they almost got it onto the bulwark and three times one end or the other fell out and they had to start again. So they topped the derrick, hooked the net on and much more easily swung the body inboard. Sparrer looked at it closely, stretched out on the afterdeck, checking if it was anyone she knew. No, but there was certainly something odd about the male cadaver. "Have you noticed he's got full make-up on?" She queried.

"Can't say I had. I wonder why?"

That was explained when they moored up at Wapping Steps and handed the body over to the River Police. The Sergeant they reported to, took one look at the unfortunate man and said, "Oh him. He's one of a bunch of queers who hang about the Royal Docks area. I've known him for years. Looks remarkably undamaged. All right girls, leave him with us and we'll dispose of him."

"Aren't you going to find out how he died?" Queried Jane.

"Well we might but what's one poof more or less. If you saw as many bodies as we do you'd not be bothered either."

"Yes but....." And Jane wandered back to the boat shaking her head in slow puzzlement. Supper that night was a subdued affair.

Jane quietly took Punch aside and said "I wonder if I should tell Arthur about this? I can't see why a dead queer should have anything to do with his spy nonsense but he did say to report anything unusual. Maybe I'll drop him a note."

"Yes, better safe than sorry. There's certainly something odd about it and at least he might know if anything was going on."

CHAPTER 14:
The reality of the Blitz

March came in cold and blustery after a February that had been particularly wet and raw, leaving people equally grey and depressed. The only good thing had been that on many nights the cloud cover was too thick for much flying so the *Luftwaffe* had been limited in how much damage it could do. But whenever the cloud cover thinned the bombers were back dumping large numbers of bombs fairly indiscriminately over the city. Hitler's policy was now to abandon attempts at breaking Britain's morale by mass bombing, recognising that it wasn't working, and concentrate on the means of moving goods in and out of the country in the hope of starving it. This meant that the UK's sea ports became the Blitz's primary targets and many were particularly hard hit. But the bombing was not accurate and cities were blasted over large and indiscriminate areas. Underneath this, life went on and *Kittiwake* with her Wren crew was becoming established as an everyday part of the river scene.

It took Arthur a week to respond to Jane's note about the body they had picked up. When his reply came, it asked Jane to meet him late in the evening of the eighth; he would pick her up in a taxi from Lambeth Pier. After their last encounter Jane was distinctly dubious about this but decided that for the moment she would have to go along with it. So, in her best uniform, at nine o'clock she got into the taxi, carefully sat as far away from Arthur as she could, and asked, "What now?"

"We'll go to the Cafe de Paris and find a table in a secluded corner."

Well, Cafe de Paris sounded fine but a secluded corner? Already alarm bells were ringing in Jane's mind. There was a smattering of small talk until they got there; Arthur was greeted in familiar fashion by the doorman and he had a table reserved on the balcony, well away from the dance floor and the slightly brighter lights. A bottle of champagne was ordered and they eyed each other warily. "Relax, Jane, I'm not about to climb all over you."

"Well, that's a relief but are you seriously suggesting you are not attracted to me any more?"

"No Jane I'm not saying that all. I think you are the sexiest young woman I've ever come across but business comes first so you are quite safe."

'For now' she thought to herself. "All right Arthur, what's the story?"

"Well now Jane, this body you pulled out of the river has proved to be quite interesting. He was a well-known member of a queer community which hangs about a pub called the '*Roundhouse*' near an entrance to the Royal Docks. It's a well-established setup which used to have all the queer stewards from the passenger liners as part of its clientele. They were famous queens –marvellously talented drag artists and the likes – and it was considered one of the most entertaining places in East London by those who knew. But the war has seen all the ships go to west coast ports so the poor old Roundhouse only has a rump of a clientele now with some local queers and the odd visiting sailor. The local ones were – still are – a stable community which operates with the authorities on the basis of 'we won't bother you if you don't bother us.' It's more common in London than you might imagine. So why one of them should be found drowned in the river we don't know. It might be an accident but he had no alcohol in him, and our local contacts think that it is unlikely to be suicide. He was a contented bloke with a loving partner. This partner is reported as being utterly distraught but acting oddly, stonewalling any enquiries about his mate's activities or doings just before he fell in. The partner seems terrified of something but won't say what. The whole lot have clammed up and the normal relaxed relationship with the local bobbies has changed to a blank wall. So there's something going on. I am arranging for your boat to be based there sometimes, so when you are, perhaps you can keep your eyes and ears open."

"Well fine, but what are a bunch of girls going to find out? I don't imagine we could go into a pub like that and they're hardly likely to come to the boat for a confessional."

"That is true but people will sometimes say things to a girl that they wouldn't to a man who was being a bit too interested. You never know what may come up; just keep looking and listening. Combined with our other sources we may find something."

"Is this connected to the spy story you told me last time?"

"We haven't found any connection but one of the things you learn in intelligence is to keep an open mind and think laterally as well as straight down the line. Now, how about another glass of champers?" This with a hand landing on her knee.

"Champers yes, wandering hands no. Behave yourself Arthur. This whole thing will end now if you don't keep your hands to yourself."

He shook his head slowly, sadly. "God, Jane, why do you deny me? We could have such a time together."

"Arthur, we've been over this already and the reasons haven't changed. I love David, not you, and that's something you will just have to come to terms with. And you don't know much about women if you think that casual gropes are going to turn them on."

"All right, but let's dance in the meantime."

Jane was turning to get up when there was an almighty flash and bang from the dance floor and everything went dark. Coming to, she found she was lying on top of Arthur who was groaning and twitching. From below came groans and wails and screams. Struggling upright she found that her limbs seemed to work so she slowly got to her feet, conscious of blood running down her face. 'As if it isn't enough of a mess already' she thought to herself bitterly.

"Arthur, are you all right?" She bent down and felt him; he grabbed her hand fiercely then hoarsely whispered, "What happened?"

"I think we've been bombed."

"But that's not possible, this place is down in a cellar and well protected."

"Tell that to the bomb that found its way in. Come on Arthur, can you get up?"

"I'll try." And he pulled on Jane's hand as he struggled upright. Everything seemed to be working so he slowly got to his feet and shook the thick layer of dust off his suit. "I suppose we should see if we can help."

Jane nodded and cautiously they made their way down to the dance floor. Here there was gruesome chaos. Bodies and bits of bodies lay around. Snakehips Johnson's head lay on the edge of the bandstand, his body not in sight. "No point messing with the corpses. Let's see if there are any live ones we can help." And she bent over a woman crying and holding up the stump of her arm. Blood was pouring from it so Jane pulled a tie off a corpse, wound it round the stump and twisted it tight. The tourniquet did its job and the blood stopped. Arthur was standing in a corner retching and shaking, unable to move. Jane went from person to person, helping where she could, then returned to the lady with the stump. She was conscious and crying gently, moaning to herself, "It hurts, it hurts".

"Yes, I'm sure it does. Does anything else hurt?" The lady shook her head, "I don't think so, it is hard to tell." Her elegant cut-glass speech was at odds with the surroundings, suggesting refinement and comfort. But not much of that here so Jane lifted the victim's bloodied head into her lap and cradled it, crooning quietly which seemed to help the distraught lady. By now the first of the emergency services were arriving and taking over but Jane noticed a furtive shape in the shadows bending over a corpse and doing something to its hand. With a sickening lurch of her stomach Jane realised she was watching a looter sawing a woman's finger off to get at her ring. She rushed over: "Stop that, it's horrible" The man stood up, swung a chair leg and smashed Jane over the head with it.

Coming to had an odd familiarity to it, lying in a bed with a white ceiling overhead. Oh yes, this was Dover Hospital. Hang on, it couldn't be Dover, so where was she? Looking round in the semi-darkness she saw half a dozen other beds, each with a recumbent body in it. She freed a hand and waved at a passing nurse. "Where am I?"

"St Thomas' Hospital, minor injuries ward."

"Only minor injuries, eh? I suppose that's good news. What is wrong with me?"

"Hang on and I'll get Sister."

In the ten minutes before Sister arrived, Jane felt around herself and concluded that basically she was sound.

"Hello, I'm Sister Johnson. I gather you're asking questions." Her strong seasoned face gave nothing away.

"Yes, I only wanted to know what was wrong with me that I've ended up here."

"You have a fair number of cuts and bruises, two of which on your face have needed a stitch or two. But mainly you came in unconscious and it's taken a while for you to come round again. You almost certainly have concussion so should take it easy. We found your Wren ID card but no indication of who to contact about your position. Who can we tell?"

"My boat, *Kittiwake*, lying on Lambeth Pier. She's due to start work at 0730 and they need to know about me so my second in command can take over. When will I get out?"

"You'll be in for twenty-four hours for observation but I would expect you to be discharged after that. We'll know more after the doctor has looked at you in the morning."

When she got up and dressed again next evening, Jane discovered how much of a mess she must have been in. Her lovely tiddley doeskin uniform was covered in cuts and holes and scorch marks, a ruin that certainly had no future in the Wrens. She got a cab and dropped off at the pier, cautiously making her way on board. Her crew eyed her bandaged head and patched up face with some concern. "Jane what happened? Are you all right? All we got was a message that you were in hospital."

"Oh, I got caught in the Cafe de Paris bomb. Luckily away from the blast centre or I wouldn't be here now but got whacked on the head and was out for the count for a while. They think I've probably got concussion but not severely so I've been discharged 'fit for service'. But Punch, I think maybe you should stay in charge for a day or two. I take it you're managing all right without me?"

Punch laughed, "Yes Jane, we're managing fine. We've got a long run down to Tilbury tomorrow so you can relax while your ace seamen point us in the right direction."

The trip down to Tilbury was routine in half a gale and intermittent driving sleet squalls. Jane took the opportunity to get up to date with the Naval form filling and paperwork she was rapidly acquiring a hatred of, but knew had to be done. Their sacks of mail delivered, as instructed they went over to Gravesend and picked up orders to go to West India Dock Pier with only a pouch of correspondence to take. There was a slight holiday air about the trip, except that into the wind and weather it was a slog.

It was early evening by the time they got there, weaving through the tiers of barges lying to buoys in the river to get to the pier head. Jane and Punch went up to the signal station that acted as the local Auxiliary Patrol control office to find a Petty Officer in charge. "Good evening Chief, here's the mail. Do you have any orders for us?"

The Chief looked startled. "I didn't know it was a boat load of girls that were coming. Are you running that boat?"

"Oh yes, that's us. Soon there will be nothing else so get used to us now. Does that bother you?"

"No, no, I just didn't expect you to turn up. I had no idea girls could run a boat."

"Give us half a chance and we'll run the Navy. Now, do you have any orders for us?"

"Go over to Surrey Docks entrance and lie overnight to be available to the harbourmasters there in the morning. I've no idea what they want."

"We're getting used to knowing nothing till the last moment so it's not new. *Kittiwake's* magical mystery tours, that's us."

"Incidentally, girls, it may be quite lively there tonight so keep a watch going overnight just in case."

"That's no problem but why livelier there than anywhere else? We're used to the bombing."

"Look around you when you get there. What do you see? Thousands and thousands of tons of timber. Even the lighters there are full of timber. And what does timber do? It burns. That can make it a very lively place indeed if Gerry bombs it."

"Oh right, we'll keep our eyes open."

Boat moved and watch set, *Kittiwake's* crew settled down to wait. Around 2300 the sirens went. "There goes Wailing Willie again. Tin hats on, I think." Half an hour later the local ack-ack guns opened up and right after that the first bombs fell on the timber. Huge fires were blazing in short order, with thick smoke billowing up. A lot of sparks were drifting about and the first lighter of timber caught fire. Soon another then another were burning. The girls, up in the wheelhouse and watching anxiously, exchanged glances. No orders were necessary; Suki started the engines as the roadsman came along, "Can you shift those burning lighters so they don't set fire to the rest?"

"We can try. C'mon girls, let's go to it."

By now there was someone on one of the burning lighters, waving frantically.

They rushed over and picked him up. "Thanks for that."

"Do you know what you're doing with these things?"

"Yeah, I'm a lighterman; know all about them."

"Right, if we cut out the burning ones where do we take them?"

"Just below entrance here there's a mud bank. Land them there."

"OK, let's do it."

The tide was at full flood so they cut the upstream ropes first, went round and took their downstream mooring ropes on board. "Make them fast round the mast" screamed Jane. The roaring noise from the fires was deafening. Pulling three barges against the tide was slow work for the boat but inch by inch they made progress. The heat from the burning barges was intense. "In there, in there," shouted the lighterman, gesticulating wildly to the river bank. Jane charged the bank and was relieved when she saw the end of the lighters rear up, taking the ground. Hastily they put the mooring ropes ashore with *Kittiwake's* bow hard against the bank, then pulled off to see what else needed doing. The tide carried the boat down onto the next tier of barges and Jane had to swing her rapidly to avoid collision. Some of the other barges now had small fires starting on them. The lighterman called out, "Let's see if we can put those fires out. Follow me." And he jumped onto the first barge. Punch, Eva and Sparrer all followed him and they went round it stamping out little outbreaks.

In the next tier downstream they could see a figure frantically waving. "That 's my mate Tommy. Can we get him off?"

"We can try but he's right in the middle; could be tricky."

Jane ran the boat down and looked carefully. The tide was running hard round the bows and the buoys; getting trapped there could easily be disastrous. Best to go in stern first, she thought and try to keep head to the tide. That way she'd have some control. But right under the lighter's prow, with the water boiling up, it felt very scary. Jane eased back until the lighter overhung their stern then shouted, "Jump." But the lighterman being smarter, dropped a rope and slid down it. The lighter must have been damaged as it sank where it was just a minute later, almost catching the boat's stern as it went.

"Welcome aboard," Jane roared at the latest arrival who shook his head in mute terror.

"Now what?" They headed back towards the lock entrance, almost unrecognisable beneath the fire smoke so thick it was like a searingly hot fog. Above them the flames from the timber stacks towered a hundred feet high, roaring and crackling as though the whole world was being consumed. For Jane the scene brought back bad memories of the Dunkirk Docks. On the dockside they could see firemen tackling the blaze and the *Massey Shaw,* the fire service's famous float, was pumping great arcs of river water over the lock and onto the outer end of the blaze.

Jane laid *Kittiwake* alongside. "Can we help?"

"Yes, get me ashore." A senior officer jumped over and in moments they had landed him on the lock entrance. "Keep handy, I'll want to go back to the tender as soon as I've conferred with my opposite number here." So they lay in the fog, coughing and spluttering and lying as low as they could to keep out of the ferocious heat and smoke. Ten minutes later their fire officer was back, delivered to his boat and they looked around. He said to them, "My men are bringing a couple of hoses to the bank now. Can you bring them off to me here, so we can couple them to our pumps? Then keep handy in case we need you for anything else." With this done the launch was moored up again at the lock entrance and they waited. The all clear had sounded but with the inferno ashore still raging there was no respite.

By five o'clock in the morning it was quietening down and Punch said to their two lightermen, "Would you like a cup of tea?"

"Best idea I've heard all night. Yes please."

They all retired to the cabin, the girls peeling off oilskins and shedding their steel helmets. This caused consternation as the two men looked at the crew's blackened, drawn faces. "Good God, are you girls?"

"Oh yes, we're Wrens running a boat."

"Blimey, I don't know. This is a rum old world we're in, in't it? Girls out all night fighting fires and risking their necks on the water. Tommy, have you ever seen the likes?"

Tommy, an older man who hadn't said a word since he arrived on the boat, finally spoke. "Never seen the likes of it. But by gum, you girls are good at it. 'Ere Jacky, we'll have to tell our people about them. He turned to Jane's crew, quietly enjoying their cups of tea "Are you lot on this boat all the time?"

"Oh yes, we're the first but there will be more, mark my words. We run all up and down the river so maybe we'll see you again sometime."

"Any time you see a lighterman, just tell them that Tommy sent you. We owe you girls a lot now and you can be sure of friendly help anywhere you want it."

Jane noted that he was smartly dressed with collar and tie beneath his battered overcoat, so presumably he was something important among the lightermen. She smiled at him. "Thank you, but really we only did what we had to do. We couldn't leave you to drown, now could we?"

"Don't you believe it. A lot of people would."

In the meantime Punch had pulled her wellington boots off and looked at their soles sadly. They were melted and holey. "Funny, I don't think my feet are burned but look at these. I'll need to indent for new ones."

"We all will, I think."

With the fire damping down the two rescued men went ashore, debating how they were going to get home in the aftermath of the Blitz and the girls all fell asleep where they were.

CHAPTER 15

Command

"*Kittiwake* Ahoy! Anyone there?"

Her crew, sprawled in uncomfy positions about the saloon slowly came to the surface as one of the lock masters looked in on them. "You lot been up all night?" There were groans to go with the nods as they untangled themselves and stretched life into cramped limbs. "Who is in charge here?"

Jane held up a hand. She had never felt less like being in charge of anything.

"Right. Because of last night's fires we won't be needing you this morning anyway, so you can go back to Tower Pier and see what orders they have. We need you off here in ten minutes to let a ship into the lock."

"Well thanks. Your appreciation of our efforts is deeply felt. You don't give much leeway, do you?"

"Don't you know there's a war on? We're all under pressure now." He glanced at his watch. "It's five minutes to scarper now. Come on, lively there."

Jane scowled. "Suki, engines please. Punch would you mind taking her away? I've got a screaming headache and feel dreadful."

"Women, eh? Can't take it when the going gets rough."

Jane wasn't up to arguing but to her surprise Punch drew herself up to her full six feet two and bellowed, "You nasty little prick. We've been up all night fighting fires while you skulked in your bed. You've no idea why she is like that. Why don't you do something useful for a change, instead of hanging about here acting superior? For two pins I'd throw you in the river, then we'd see who can't take it. Piss off while you're still able to."

Punch towering over anyone – male or female – was an impressive sight and the Harbourmaster backed off hastily. "All right, all right, but you've got to go."

"And good riddance to you lot."

They slipped and went in a couple of minutes but the altercation left a sour taste. Punch was still visibly seething, so unusual for this calm young lady.

"Sorry about that, but he got right up my nose. Oi'm finding it more and more difficult to put up with stupid men acting like that."

Jane gave her a gentle pat on the shoulder. "There's plenty of it around, I'm afraid." Looking at Punch in a towering rage, it suddenly struck Jane that if she ever did lose her calm it could be very tricky. There was nothing anyone else on board could do to restrain her, certainly not physically, and the thought of Punch running amok was a terrifying one.

None of them had washed or tidied up so they were still black of face and looking thoroughly scruffy when they berthed at Tower Pier. Jane's head bandage was now a grubby grey with a smudge of dried blood showing through, so when Punch and she presented themselves in the office it was to a concerned greeting. "Been in the wars, then?"

"You could say so. It was pretty lively down at Surrey Docks last night. They don't want us after all, so have you got anything for us?"

"No we don't – didn't expect you back. I suggest you go back to base, take the day off and get cleaned up. See you tomorrow bright and early."

They took it in turns for a bath over at Lambeth Palace then a general lethargy took over. Jane's headache persisted so she lay down and fell asleep. An hour later she frightened everyone by sitting up screaming and wailing. It took some serious shaking to wake her up out of the nightmare. "It's the faces, the heads, the dead bits lying around," She moaned. A cup of tea restored some equanimity but she lay for some time quietly sobbing and muttering under her breath while her worried crew kept an eye on her.

When *Kittiwake* moved off for its day's work the next day, Jane took herself off and lay down in their little room at Lambeth Palace. Her headache was fierce and she felt rough but resting helped. A couple of days of this and the pain had gone; she still felt a bit under the weather but up to working again so, while leaving Punch in charge, she returned on board and helped with mooring lines, handling mail and stores and brewing tea for passengers. Punch seemed completely at ease in charge and Jane noticed that Suki was also taking turns handling the boat and generally acting as number two to Punch. Sparrer and Evadne seemed content to do the deckhand jobs, but it was noticeable how much more confident and certain of their work both were to the point of correcting Jane over how to moor up at a tricky berth.

This led to the next discussion in the cabin of an evening. "Jane, we've been here for more than two months now without a break and without any suggestion of getting time off. Is it up to us to decide who takes leave and when, or do we get told from HQ?"

"You know, I have no idea and hadn't actually thought about that at all. Yes, some leave would be nice, wouldn't it? Maybe I should write to HQ asking for guidance on this."

"Yes, I think you should. We know you never think beyond the next job but the rest of us would like some time off occasionally."

Jane smiled. "I'm not so sure about that. David is due leave shortly and already I'm planning time with him."

"Yes, but you haven't thought about time off for any of the rest of us, have you? As skipper you've got a crew to think about now and the best way of doing that is to have a plan. So yes, you should write and ask what is to be done." A letter to Third Officer Baker was drafted and in the mail that night.

This discussion bothered Jane. It hadn't occurred to her that being appointed cox'n of the boat also brought administrative responsibilities with it, especially acting as a detached unit. She could detect an undercurrent of dissatisfaction from her crew about the way she wasn't really giving much thought to their interests or wellbeing. Being brutally honest with herself, she acknowledged that she had simply seen them as a means of running the boat and furthering the cause. Their welfare being in her hands was a worrying thought.

Knowing David was getting leave, Jane had wangled for the boat to be off for a couple of days with the full intention of escaping to be with him. It didn't quite work that way. They had already decided that after the early morning cleaning session and breakfast, everyone would be free except for taking turns as shipkeeper. Before anyone could get away, there was a call of "*Kittiwake* Ahoy" and Third Officer Baker came on board. The enduring ties from pro course meant that she get an informal friendly welcome from Punch and Evadne; Suki and Sparrer acknowledged her rather more formally. Once the kettle was on she got down to business. "I gather from your letter that you don't know much about organising a crew. I have brought a copy of the WRNS regulations and disciplinary code for the boat, and am here to see that everything is being done properly. Incidentally, there is no complaint about what you are doing with the boat. I have checked and give or take a wrecked mast everyone is very pleased with how you are doing the job. But already you are behind on the paperwork and it seems you do not have much idea of how to organise personnel matters on board. So I've come this morning to see if we can sort that out."

For the next couple of hours they debated leave rotas, getting a complete plan worked out which would give everyone their entitlement while ensuring that the boat was properly crewed at all times. With that in place they discussed victualling arrangements which had been a bit hit and miss, moved on to welfare issues and what arrangements were for contacting authority if need be. Third Officer Baker asked if there were any disciplinary issues. The crew looked at each other and shook their heads. Suki spoke up. "Jane is in charge and none of us have any problems with that. We all get along and there's never any need for strict discipline; we all know what to do and get on with it. These organisational things might have been problematic but with a little encouragement Jane was sensible enough to look for help as soon as she realised they might become an issue. Now here you are dealing with them. Provided what we've arranged this morning works all right, I don't think discipline is likely to be an issue."

"Well, I'm pleased to hear that. I was a bit concerned when the letter arrived that there might have been a hidden agenda but I see now that it was simply a request for guidance."

Punch then asked, "Are we any closer to getting Wrens on boats more generally? Oi hope we're not going to be only ones."

"Difficult to say, Johnson, but slowly the opposition is thawing. I do know Superintendent Carpenter is very pleased with the way you're working on the Thames so far and her views carry weight at a high level. Keep going like you are here and who knows, something magical may happen. Now, I need to speak to Beacon privately, so would you mind leaving us?"

The crew gave a collective shrug and retired to the afterdeck; fortunately it was a good day. There followed half an hour going through paperwork and returns from the boat with some emphasis on ensuring that crew matters were dealt with right away when they arose. With that done Third Officer Baker closed up her attache case and turned to look Jane in the eye.

"Now, Jane. We've had a letter from a Lady Ormond presently a patient in Saint Thomas Hospital, asking us to identify and thank the Wren who saved her life in the Cafe de Paris bombing. From her description it could be you. We heard you'd a few scratches and ended up in hospital yourself so presumably this ministering angel was you?"

"Had she lost part of her left arm? If so I suppose the answer is yes but really I didn't do that much."

"Your modesty is very fine but the letter suggests you did rather a lot. Do you mind if we tell Lady Ormond that it was you?"

"No, I suppose not, not that I was looking for anything back. In conditions like that, one does what one can and if gently soothing an injured person counts at all then one is only happy to help. But I'm not sure it saved her life."

"Don't indulge in mock modesty, Jane. We were interested that you frequented the Cafe de Paris at all; was there a reason for your being there?"

"My boyfriend uses it and I know his family. That night I was meeting his brother. Fortunately we were up on the balcony and away from the main blast area."

"I didn't know you had a boyfriend. Anyone I know?"

"I doubt it - his name is a bit of a mouthful but he is Lieutenant-Commander

Lord David Daubeny-Fowkes. I rescued him at Dunkirk and things have rather grown since."

"Very impressive. I've heard of the family. Was he from that burning destroyer you took survivors from?"

Jane nodded.

"Right: we'll write back to Lady Ormond telling her it was you but will keep it brief. I don't think there will be any medals this time."

"Oh come on, Merle. I didn't do it for medals. The poor woman badly needed help and you don't think of anything but what has to be done at that moment."

When Third Officer Baker left early in the afternoon there was a sense of a cloud on the horizon having been blown away, the girls looking at the master leave plan – now pinned up on the bulkhead – and jotting down their own allotments. First off would be Jane, with David's arrival on leave now imminent. As soon as she got back Suki would go then Sparrer, hoping that Lofty's planned leave would work out. With Sparrer's return Punch would go and finally Evadne who admitted that she had nowhere special to go, the boat was now her home and she wasn't too bothered about leave but maybe a break would be nice.

Jane was in for a disappointment: although *HMS Bowman* had docked, a note from David said he couldn't get away until the next day and he'd see Jane at the Savoy at 1800.

This gave the girls an opportunity that evening. There had been a certain amount of secretive scribbling and giggling going on and after supper Suki said, "Jane, we've been making up a little song for you, based on the old folk song 'The Sloop John B'. It goes like this:

We sail with the Wren Jane B
All of the girls and me,
All round the ports and harbours we have roamed
We're working all day
For very poor pay
I feel so weary, I wanna turn in.

Chorus: So hoist up the Wren Jane's flag,
See how the mainsail sets,
Put down the helm and head right out of the port
Oh let me go home, or let me lie down
I feel so weary, I just wanna turn in.

Our skipper's a driven girl,
Disobey her at your peril.......
She will give any job – any job a whirl
She works us so hard,
we're always off guard
I feel so weary, I just wanna turn in.

Chorus: So hoist up....

But we're so proud of what we do
We're the very best of the few
We Wrens are always out, out in the lead
And our skipper's the one
Who makes it such fun
That sleep doesn't matter to make our name count.

Chorus So hoist up.......

"Well thanks. I don't know whether to be flattered or not. Am I really that bad? "
Punch snorted a laugh. "Let's just say your first focus tends to be the job."
And they sang it again, to make the point.

Next evening came soon enough and as Jane came into the hotel's foyer her heart gave a lurch as there he was, looking a bit thin and strained but otherwise the man she loved. Hugs and kisses over, he took her off into the American Bar, ordered champagne cocktails and they settled to catching up. "David I've wangled five days' leave so really we are free agents. Do you have to go home and for how long?"

"No need to go home. Parents are due in Town in two days' time so I'll see them then. I see you are in your everyday uniform; what happened to the smart one?"

"Oh, of course, you won't have heard. Arthur asked to see me and we went to Cafe de Paris as it was late. Just my luck; it was the night it was bombed. We were both more or less all right but my nice tiddley uniform was cut and torn and burnt so I've sent it home and asked the parental wallet to fund an identical one. My mother was horrified when she saw the state it was in and threatened to send me a suit of armour. But I suggested that armour wasn't the smartest thing on board a boat – just think how quickly you'd sink – so she has relented and a new uniform is on its way."

David laughed. "Jane, you really are amazing. You mean your uniform was cut to pieces and you weren't hurt?"

"Well, you will have noticed I still have a couple of stitches on my forehead and I only got rid of the bandage this evening to see you, but nothing major was damaged so I count myself lucky. The scene down on the dance floor was pretty grizzly. Anyway, how have you been?"

"Oh, it's all been routine lately, convoy after convoy. Boring but necessary, I suppose. Not much more I can say. My ship is running pretty well, we had a little outbreak of Bolshevism from a watch of stokers but I dealt with that as firmly as possible without triggering outright revolt and since then we've got along fine. Constant convoy work can be pretty wearing and patience runs thin. Now, you look beautiful even in uniform but have you anything smarter? We've taken a suite as usual and you can change there if you like."

"I've got a couple of new evening dresses which I can nip back to base and get if you like."

"Yes, let's go together."

An hour later Jane emerged from the suite in one of the recently acquired long white evening gowns. Somehow she felt a bit naked in its thin silky fabric after the reassuring solidity of uniform, but as she was dressed much as the other ladies were in the dining room, she relaxed and even started to enjoy the sense of being on display.

CHAPTER 16:
Docked

The tingling sense of electricity flowing was still there. As they ate, hands kept touching, glances flowed, a little gentle foot pressure kept contact. Dancing followed: the thinness of her gown did nothing to disguise the feel of her body pressed gently against his and she could tell it was having a powerful effect on this gorgeous man. He almost stammered as he tried to be casual about asking, "W-Would you like to come up to the suite for a nightcap?"

'I thought he'd never ask' crossed her mind but she smiled, "Yes David, I would like to." Behind the closed door she wrapped her arms round him, pressed up close; the first kiss lasted a long time. Again, she could feel his urgent need but a deep sense of caution controlled her. Off came his jacket, tie and detached collar and they fell onto the bed. After that there was little conversation but a great deal of physical communing. Greatly daring, he cupped her right breast and fondled it inexpertly. Even this fumble had a powerful effect on Jane, a surge of raw physical urge running from the breast to her lower body. "I must not push this too hard," ran like a refrain through her mind, terror at the thought of a repeat of the Jamie episode acting as a bridle on the physical forces. And it was obvious to her that he knew very little about what he was doing.

Eventually they disentangled, Jane changed back into uniform and he walked her back to the boat. She slipped aboard as quietly as she could, hoping not to alert her crew to the fact that it was 0230, but got an ironic, "Filthy stop out" from Punch in the morning accompanied by a sly smile. She casually mentioned that she probably wouldn't come back to the boat until her leave was up, wished them good luck and got off before they sailed at 0800 sharp for their day's work.

She had arranged to meet David again at 0900 and was waiting in the foyer when he came up from the restaurant. "Jane, I hear that Myra Hess is giving a concert in the National Gallery at lunch time today. Would that appeal?"

"Well yes, but won't it be sold out?"

"Oh you just turn up and take a chance on getting a seat. Costs a shilling each. Do you think we can afford it?"

"Well, that might strain the bank balance a little. Tell you what, I'll treat you." And they laughed into each other's eyes.

They had to sit on the floor but that didn't bother them. The recital was out-standing, listening to a pianist at the height of her powers while Jane gently held

David's hand. Soon to be damed, Myra Hess played a couple of Brahms impromptus then set off along the Beethoven Moonlight Sonata, followed by some French music and then Chopin's raindrop prelude before the concert closed, as ever, with Hess's own transcription of Bach's '*Jesu Joy of Man's Desiring*'. Suitably inspired, they wandered down to the Embankment, found a bench looking out over the river and talked about everything possible for several hours. They then had to split as David had to see someone at the Admiralty. By now, the secrecy inherent in not asking people details of what they were doing had become totally ingrained so Jane simply accepted their going different ways until they met again in the American Bar in the early evening. Jane brought a bag of clothes with her and changed into the other white evening dress. It was equally thin and dancing had, if anything, an even more powerful effect on them.

Once up in the suite preliminaries were dispensed with and physical passion took over. Disentangling herself after a while she remarked, "I'd better take this dress off or it will get ripped to shreds and I can't afford another one."

This startled David. "Jane, would you really undress here with me?"

"Yes David, I want to."

He gasped and looked at her in startled amazement as she shed the dress. In suspenders and a pair of the gauzy French knickers the firm beauty of her body was clear and he obviously didn't know what to say or do. She cuddled up close to him and murmured, "Please kiss me again," so he did. By now he was shaking with the urge inside him so she put a hand down and took hold of his painful erection. "Jane! What are doing?"

"Just feeling your body. Would you like to go further?"

"Oh Jane, don't please. I couldn't despoil you that way."

"You wouldn't be despoiling me David, just loving me."

"You mean you've done this before?"

A great black pit – an elephant trap – yawned in front of her. This was the crucial moment and the result of the next minute would be with her for life; but as with Jamie, somehow she couldn't lie.

"Yes David, I have."

David hugged her fiercely. "Jane, Jane, I had no idea. Oh God, do you really love me or is this something else?" But at least he hadn't let go.

"David, I love you like I have never loved anything or anyone in my life. With both the others I thought it was love but it was nothing like the way I feel for you. Please believe me, I love love love you and this is the only way I have of really showing it." She hung on tight, praying that he would not recoil.

"Well, this changes things but Jane I want you, I want you."

"I can tell that and you can have me. Show me you love me."

A great wave of relief swept over Jane as he embraced her fiercely. "Oh Jane, yes please yes please." His physical urge was now utterly dominant and clothes were ripped off in short order. After the emotional drama the sexual act was brief. He rolled on and in, trembled violently for about thirty seconds and climaxed. Spent, he lay on her sobbing; she wrapped her arms and legs round him tightly and murmured gentle caressing noises in his ear. The thought occurred to her that she had just received an enormous blast of his fluids and they had taken no precautions; the force driving them had been too strong to stop for any fiddling with things like that. But her period was due in a couple of days and with any luck she was past ovulating; she could only hope so.

He stayed on and in her, closely entwined, sobbing gently into her neck as she stroked his back. Jane felt his ribs and could count every one. "You poor man, you are so skinny. Don't you look after yourself?"

"Jane, sometimes I'm on the bridge for a week without a break, snatching a little sleep in my sea cabin when I can. Food is occasional spam sandwiches and my tiger is good at keeping up the flow of coffee. I'd never keep going without that."

"That must be tough. Was the weather bad?"

"Sometimes you get seas sixty feet high and it's all you can do to keep the ship safe and on course. At least the u-boats can't operate either in those sorts of conditions. Then you get five day in port for essential maintenance and you're off again."

"I know you're not supposed to say but I presume this is the Atlantic?"

He gulped and nodded.

"All right my dear, all right; here, in me, you are in your safe harbour. Me wrapped around you is the other face of your life. With me is the calm between the storms and a comfort you can't find out there."

"Oh Jane, Oh Jane," and something let go; the sobs became heartfelt gulping wailing with torrents of tears, running down her neck and soaking the sheet. For five, or ten, or who knows how many minutes they lay like that while his stresses poured out. Jane lay there, letting his light skinny body tremble and shake on top of her, stroking his back and hair, nibbling his ear and crooning gently to him. He had not withdrawn during this close communing and she could feel him slowly stiffening again. She held his buttocks tightly, keeping him in while they lay motionless and silent for a spell. Then he began to tremble again and she murmured encouragement, his movements rising to a frenzied shaking before subsiding again. Jane silently reflected that, like kissing, he had a lot to learn about lovemaking. "You haven't done much of this, have you, dear?"

"No, I'm afraid not. A couple of professional ladies out East, but this is the first time with an ordinary girl."

"Am I ordinary?"

"No, no, you are extra special but what I meant was..."

She interrupted him "Hush, darling, I know what you mean. Welcome to your ordinary girl."

Eventually they came up from the depths and he rolled over. "I'm sorry, I shouldn't have let go like that."

"You silly man, that is one reason why I'm here. Not the only one, but an important one. Maybe you can do the same for me sometime. I get my tough moments too y'know, which is why I understand so well what you are feeling. But for now just let it all go and merge with me."

They lay side by side, in touch but with passion spent for the moment. "This is all new to me, Jane. I knew I was in love with you but something quite new and utterly beautiful has just opened inside me. O God, Jane, please don't go."

A brief flash of Stefan ran cross her mind but then she smiled gently and said "Go? Why should I go? I love you utterly David Daubeny-Fowkes and have just shown it. I hope I'll go on showing it. Welcome to the new world of love."

In the midst of their lovemaking the clear bit of Jane's brain had registered that David had a couple of ridges across his buttocks. Calmer now, she asked, "What are the ridges on your buttocks?"

"Oh, I got caned at Eton and was left with those scars. Hope you don't mind. Please don't laugh."

But Jane rolled over onto her tummy and did laugh, a gentle conspiratorial gurgle. "Laugh? Me laugh? Try my backside David."

"Good heavens, those are awfully strong. Was that a caning too?"

"Yes David, courtesy of the Navy. I got caned for going AWOL with my Frenchman while I was on pro course. Besides those and the mess on my face I have a hole in my left shoulder and two lumpy scars on my left ribs from shrapnel. I hope you don't mind a battlescarred partner."

He laughed and shook his head in gentle amusement. "You haven't noticed the mess on my left thigh, have you? We really are two of a kind, you and I."

He had been gently caressing the stripes across Jane's buttocks while they talked. Now he propped himself up on one elbow, kissed her very gently and asked, "What is this about two other lovers?"

'Oh dear', she thought, 'this was bound to come.'

"Well, I was seduced by a French Naval officer who fortunately proved very skilled and very kind. The affair lasted about three months when I first joined the Wrens but then I discovered he was married and that was the end of that. But I did learn a lot from him."

"And the other one?"

"Oh, he was a mad passionate Polish flyer who I fished out of the sea." She giggled gently. "I seem to make a habit of falling for men I have rescued. But I gave him the elbow when I fell for you."

She could feel her nose growing longer as she said it. 'Damn Pinocchio', she thought.

"How on earth do you appear so pure and perfect when really you are quite experienced?"

"I don't know, David. I don't try to or anything, it's just the way I am."

He laughed, leant over and gently kissed a nipple. "I must say this isn't how I imagined I would take the love of my life to the altar."

"David, nothing would please me more than to be your blushing virgin bride but it's too late for that, I'm afraid. You'll have to take me as I am. And what's this about altars anyway? Isn't that a bit of a jump from where we are now?"

David looked perplexed. "Well surely, after this, we're going to get married?"

"Do you really want to spend your life with me, David? Getting married is about a lot more than a night's passion y'know. And I'm sure your mother wouldn't consider me suitable for a moment."

"Oh damn Mater. It's high time I did something for myself anyway and this is where I start because yes I do want to spend the rest of my life with you more than anything in the world."

"That's all very well but I see some rocks up ahead. It would be such a shame if our love got wrecked on them. Let's keep this to ourselves for now, and see how things work out, shall we?"

He smiled, kissed her again and suddenly fell asleep in her arms. She hitched round a little to get comfy and fell asleep too with his hand on her left breast and a smile on her face.

The Savoy staff were much too professional to show any surprise when Jane came down with David for breakfast and afterwards Jane made sure every trace of her incursion was removed from the suite, ready for his parents' arrival. Dinner that night, *en famille* with the Daubeney-Fowkes clan, still required her to be on her very best behaviour. After some debate with herself she decided to wear the Special One from the dresses she had bought from Sparrer's Dad, figuring that the sooner she impressed the matriarch with her polish and sophistication, the better. It certainly made an impression on the men, even the Marquis visibly starting over it. The Marchioness frowned and said nothing, but Jane suspected she had struck a blow.

Dinner finished, David took Jane onto the dance floor and they relaxed in their little world. Then an 'excuse me' was called and immediately Arthur was there, "My turn now, I think." Like David he was an excellent dancer but he pressed up too close and little suggestive hip movements showed his real interest. "Arthur, calm down and behave yourself."

"Don't worry Jane I shan't make an exhibition of us here. But it is nice, in't it?"

"Not really but I don't suppose I can do much about it here." And she relaxed into his arms for the rest of the number, tolerating more intimacy than she would have liked.

But Arthur apart, the evening passed peaceably. With the hotel suite now occupied David walked her back to Lambeth Palace and its little bed. Next day David was in the Admiralty again so it was early evening before they met. Jane had settled for one of the white dresses this time; the Marchioness greeted Jane frostily. "David has been telling me that you are planning to get engaged. I have to tell you, young lady, that he will do no such thing with you. His position requires that he marries someone of equal rank and you are not that. So you can forget any ideas of that sort now."

But interestingly, she simply joined the family for dinner and there was no visible hostility during the meal. Jane had been half expecting something like this and was not downcast by it, sparkling and being amusing about David's state at Dunkirk while they ate. Walking her back to the Palace he said, "I'm sorry, Jane. Mater was onto something anyway so I decided to tell her what we want to do and, well, you know how she reacted."

"So are you going to be a good little boy and do what you're told, or is what you said to me in bed, real? And does she actually have any hold over you or is it no more than mental bullying?"

David thought for a minute before replying. "No, she doesn't have any hold over me except being my mother and the strong family ties which have always been important to me. But I love you Jane Beacon, more than anything and if I have to lose my family to marry you, I'm willing to do it. I was afraid she'd react like that."

"David, you know I love you utterly and I'm sure I could be a good wife to you. For ninety-nine percent of people that would be enough. Do you know what I think? That we just get on with our lives for now as though your mother hadn't said anything, and we don't bother her with our doings. Let's wait and see. Is she a very stubborn woman?"

"She can dig her heels in but she's always had a soft spot for me as the youngest which I'll play on shamelessly."

By now they were back at the Lambeth Palace gates and she turned to him. "I don't think his Grace will be awfully pleased if I bring you in here so we'd better say good night now. But you will keep the suite on for tomorrow night as well, won't you?"

"Yes, my darling and really look forward to it. Good night."

They met for lunch the next day, wandered around looking at the bomb damage in the West End then retired to the suite with a bottle of champagne to freshen up and change for the evening. Somehow they got very close during changing and Jane found herself on the bed again in no time. He was clearly impatient. "I'm sorry, my love, it's wrong time of the month now. Not much we can do tonight."

"Oh God, Jane, I was looking forward to it so much. Is there nothing we can do?"

"Well," she said thoughtfully, but this time it would be an act of love. Slowly she kissed her way down his body. "Oh Jane! What are doing? Good God, Jane that's wonderful." And he squealed and squirmed. Coming up again with a smirk on her face, Jane washed her mouth out with champagne and looked at him triumphantly. "There you are. I've lots of ways of showing you how I love you and that's another one."

He was still trembling, shaking in the aftermath of what had been done to him. "You really are amazing. Just as well one of us knows what they're doing. I'd never even heard of that being done, is it a common act?"

"Well enough known, I think. Let's get dressed and go downstairs." She was keen not to get into too deep a conversation about how she knew of what she had just done and David seemed happy simply to enjoy it.

Dinner passed in a contented haze. Back in the suite he asked rather tentatively, "You know what you did earlier? Any chance of doing it again?"

She had to laugh at the loosening of inhibitions that were dropping from him. This time she didn't wash her mouth out, but kept his sperm in her mouth. It wasn't exactly a pleasant taste but it was David, her beloved and she drifted off to sleep still savouring it. And next morning there was the same request: 'Have I made a mistake here?' she wondered to herself. 'This could get a bit much.' "Dear me, no stopping you now, is there? Oh all right, sit in the chair." She got down on her knees so he could see exactly what she was doing, looking up and smiling at him with her eyes as she performed. The third time in quick succession took rather longer and he was able to see exactly what was being done. Afterwards she gave her teeth a good cleaning to freshen up; the performance seemed to please him so much that it was worth sore knees. He was positively frisky as they went down for breakfast despite their imminent parting. He was due back on his ship, her leave was up. But somehow being parted seemed like a trivial inconvenience compared with the strength of the bonds they had just established. "Do look after yourself, David. I couldn't bear to lose you now."

"Jane, I could say the same to you. A boat on the Thames just now isn't the safest place in England."

"Oh I'll be all right, better than hacking across oceans."

They hugged, a closeness of affection and caring rather than sexuality, and went their separate ways.

PART FOUR:

GOING DEEP

CHAPTER 17

Dead and alive

By the time *Kittiwake* berthed that evening, Jane had used her day making some interesting enquiries, finding out that old newspapers could be accessed for reading and by paying a fee, copies could be obtained. This was something to follow up. She was still in a contented daze from being with David and it was a bit of a jolt coming back to immediate reality on boarding the boat again. But the welcome from her crew was cheerfully friendly, supper was on the stove and everything on board seemed calmly normal. Suki made the tea and handing a mug to Jane asked, "Did you dock him, then?"

Jane smiled, a gentle reminiscent smile "Oh yes, he's in dock, tied up with double head ropes and the lock gates closed. We'll be getting engaged next time he has leave."

"Taking your time about it, then."

"It seemed pretty quick to me. We decided on that within a couple of days of getting together again."

Punch joined in. "What about your Pole, then?"

"Yes, I'll have to do something about that. David and I got a lot closer this time and I can't go on two-timing him."

"If I know you half as well as I think I do, getting closer means exactly what it says."

Jane laughed. "No comment. What have you been up to?"

And they turned to telling her of their doings since she went ashore. Nothing outstanding, although a trip to Gravesend and back in record time had drawn praise from the office. "We've got some heavy lifting to do over the next couple of days, I gather. Kit for a new gun battery they're building at Tilbury Fort. Pick it up at Woolwich and drop it off at the fort's pier. Should be interesting: I gather it's derrick work. And have you heard? Tilbury landing stage got bombed and there's a lot of damage there. It's still just about working but is in a bit of a mess."

There was mail for her: An excited one from her mother: while Jane had been peacefully wrapped up in her own world, Plymouth had been subjected to a ferocious three night Blitz which destroyed the city centre and changed the place for ever. The Old Grange being on its own in the countryside kept it out of the bombers' sights; they were trying to hit the dockyard but their aim was so indiscriminate that a large part of the city had been affected as well. Her father had a narrow escape trying to get to the hospital but apart from that her family were all well. '*But the biggest change,*' her mother wrote *'is that we are to have evacuees billeted on us. We have agreed to take half a dozen and they can have the servant's rooms which are now free. Your father has managed to arrange to take children from hospital staff which hopefully will make sure that they are decent sorts. They arrive later this week.'*

A note from Alicia reported on life in Liverpool which she was finding quite tolerable despite the bomb damage, having found a few like-minded souls to socialise with and out of the blue a letter came direct from Dora saying that her promotion to Petty Officer was going well and she had been working with local police to break up a prostitution ring which had included a couple of Wrens. 'If anyone can, Dora can,' reflected Jane, thinking of the transformation there must have been from the abused, mouse-quiet girl on their probationer course. The rest of the letter was a hymn of thanks to Jane for rescuing her on pro course. Finally a peremptory note From Louise Joycey, the QAIMNS Sister she had rescued from Dunkirk, reminded Jane that they were due to meet for dinner; Louise had an evening off next week, was in London and could they meet? Jane wrote back right away saying yes.

It was pleasant to be back with her boatmates and the evening flew by with banter about the work they did, but when Jane retired to her little cabin she found her emotions very mixed. Happy thoughts of David were clouded by worry about what to do about Stefan. Her affair with him would have to end, but he deserved better than a "Dear John" letter so what to do? She knew the boat was due for the weekend off so Suki could give the engines an oil change and servicing before going on leave. Perhaps she could meet Stefan somewhere on neutral ground and tell him it was finished?

She was still gently turning thoughts like that over when the alarm went after a poor night's sleep. *Kittiwake* set off in good time and was in the Pool heading east when Punch said, "I'll just check Tower pier in passing." She got the telescope out and surveyed the shore, "Oh look, they're flying our number and someone on the pier is waving at us. Better go and check." This was so much an order that it irritated Jane but she turned the boat and went alongside the pier pontoon. "We've got four people to go to Woolwich. You can take them down."

"All right, are they here and ready?"

"Just finishing a cup of tea; be with you in a minute."

"Well, don't be long, we've got a lot to do today."

Five minutes later four civilians turned up, clutching heavy briefcases. They wobbled as they got on board and sat down in the saloon with an unsteady thump, immediately going into conclave about their own affairs.

It didn't take long to get to Woolwich and the four got off. They had not said a word to the girls or even seem to notice their existence. "I suppose it takes all sorts," remarked Suki to the wide world. The rest of their day was more straightforward. Bits of gun and equipment loaded until *Kittiwake's* stern was deep in the water, a slow run down the river with the stern dragging and setting up an enormous wake, then a relative sprint up river. The second load was on board quite smartly, the crew by now well practised at using the derrick and they set off again in early evening. It was dark by the time they tied up at the Fort pier again and there was no-one around, so they set a watch to tend the mooring lines overnight with Jane taking midnight to 0200. Turning Sparrer out was the usual performance of extracting a limpet from its protective shell but she got there by 0220. Jane was asleep ten minutes later. She had spent her two hours – apart from easing the moorings as the boat dropped on the tide - debating what on earth she should do about Stefan. A dozen different scenarios ran through her mind, including the thought that her time with David might have been deeply satisfying at an emotional level but had left her serious frustrated sexually. At least that wouldn't be a problem with Stefan; might she perhaps keep him on? But no, that wouldn't work and she had to put an end to seeing Stefan. David would have to learn about her needs as well.

Discharge next morning went well and they were under way again by 1030, heading up river for orders. But passing the Royal Docks Suki was on the wheel when she called out, "Something in the river there. I'm taking a look." It proved to be another body. Derrick and cargo net made quick work of getting it on board; this one had been in the water for a few days and was distinctly smelly. If the first one had seemed a little odd, this one was downright peculiar, in a dress and heavily made up but the beard growth made it plain it was another male. They pulled into Wapping steps and reported to the River Police Sergeant. "All right, leave it on the steps and we'll deal with it. Don't worry about it, we know about this and are dealing with it."

"Yes, but what is 'this'?"

"Don't you bother your pretty head about that, dearie, you've done your job and you can leave it to us now."

Jane glared at him, fuming quietly, but clearly wasn't going to get any more. 'Just as well Punch wasn't here' she thought. They extracted the net from under the body and had to give it plus the afterdeck a quick scrub on the short run up to Tower Pier. Jane puzzled over it. Two queers found floating in the river. This wasn't chance and the more she thought about it the more convinced she became that there must be a connection to Arthur's interest in spying in the docks. But what? There wasn't an obvious link between the two. Anyway, she dropped Arthur a note that night about the second body, to keep him informed.

Next day they found themselves mail boat, delivering and collecting from half a dozen merchant ships lying to buoys in the river, then an isolated barrage balloon unit at Cross Ness. Jane asked Suki to do the boat handling, putting *Kittiwake* alongside each ship in turn and was impressed by how neatly and tidily she did it, if perhaps going a bit too fast for comfort. But that, Jane assumed, was a result of years of powerboat racing. Return mail delivered, they were ordered to go down to the outer entrance to the Royal Docks and lie over there. "Apparently you are being assigned to special duties there. Come back here on Friday." Jane suspected Arthur's hand in this somewhere, but to what purpose she didn't know.

Moored up outboard of a craft tug just below the bellmouth, Jane and Punch found the Lockmaster and asked what they were doing. "Search me, lassie. I was only told to expect you. You'll be snug enough where you are for now but the tug will be moving off in the morning."

None the wiser, Jane declared a make and mend for the rest of the day. Around 2200 she was chatting to Punch and Suki in the wheelhouse when there was a yelp and a splash from just up river. They looked out but in the dark there was nothing to see. "I wonder if it might be worth going up close to the bank in case we saw anything."

"Yes, might be a good idea. Suki, engines please."

The Aldis signalling lamp adapts very well as a search light and they eased their way up, scanning the surface. Jane and Punch were exchanging, "Let's give up," looks when suddenly Suki said, "There – over there," pointing close in to the bank. Nosing in cautiously they found another body. Derrick and cargo net were hastily rigged and the body hoisted inboard. As with the other two, Sparrer took a close look just in case she recognised it. She got close to the face then exclaimed, "Hang on, this one's still alive." He might only have been in the water for a few minutes but there was barely any sign of breathing. Jane checked then put her Lifesaving Award of Merit to good use, pushing and pulling to get the water out of his lungs. After a few minutes of this he coughed convulsively, retched and shook. Life was coming back. Satisfied that he was breathing again, they picked him up, took him down into the saloon and stripped his wet outer clothing off. Wrapped in a blanket he started to come back to them. As soon as he opened his eyes, terror spread across his face "Who are you palones?" he asked. Sparrer understood him. "We're the crew of this boat and we've just pulled you out of the water."

"That's dally of you but cod for me. I should be out and gone. Now what do I do?"

This mystified them, even Sparrer not understanding him.

Punch, on the wheel, called down, "Coming alongside, mooring crew please."

By the time they had tied up, their visitor was sitting up and looking a lot livelier. "I'll put the kettle on," volunteered Evadne.

"That's bona." With a cup of tea in hand he seemed to relax a little and Jane tried to get some information out of him. But without success. "I can screech you nada." He said, the look of terror he had when first regaining consciousness, coming back onto his face. What on earth was he scared of?

"If you aren't able to go home you can stay here overnight if you like."

"Thanks. Couldn't go to my latty tonight anyway. Too dangerous."

It seemed to Jane almost as though he had known he was going to die and hadn't yet adjusted to still being alive. "Were you trying to commit suicide?" she asked. Mostly he was speaking normal English but then dropped in words which meant nothing to her. "No, nothing like that but it was my turn and I had to go. I really shouldn't be here."

"But you are, so you might as well make the best of it."

The terrified look was still on his face. "No, really, I can't. "

"Oh well, make yourself comfy on the settee here and we'll feed you breakfast in the morning. Then we'll probably have to go to work."

"What do you do?"

"Oh, fetch and carry up and down the river. We're Wrens and are the crew of this boat."

"Fancy that. Palones crewing a boat like this. You must be really bona for that.

Jane just smiled. They saw him settled and turned in themselves. In the morning Jane had dimly heard voices for a while before she turned-to herself and found their visitor deep in conversation with Sparrer. He appeared to have found a soul mate.

"If you're going anywhere else can I come with you? I really don't want to get off here." Behind his back Sparrer was nodding urgently and mouthed 'yes'.

Having established that there were no orders for them at the Royal Docks, Jane decided to head upstream and report to Tower Pier again. Here their visitor seemed happy to go ashore and merge into the crowd.

Their orders were to go for a jolly with ten minewatching Wrens, up to Putney Bridge and back. These girls and their job were new to Jane and her crew. It turned out that whenever the Hun bombers came over these Wrens occupied little watch huts looking over the river and had to note the position of anything – especially mines - that landed in the river. It was tedious but essential work in keeping the river clear and a day out for them to see what good their careful watch made, was a great morale booster to them. It again reminded Jane of how much went on that she knew nothing about and how privileged she and her crew were with their pioneering action job.

Tied up again at Lambeth, Jane asked Sparrer what she'd been talking about to their rescued queer. "Well, he was talking to me really. He wouldn't say an awful lot but there was something about the Roundhouse people being blackmailed over their trade with some dockers. Seems there are some dockers with a taste for that sort of thing which the Roundhouse crowd are happy to service. Someone – he wouldn't say who - is blackmailing them in some way because of it. I asked him why some of them had ended up in the river and he muttered about discipline which didn't make sense to me. He was obviously terrified of something in the background but wouldn't say what or who. D'you think this is connected to your friend Arthur's concerns?"

"I don't know but perhaps a pattern is starting to emerge. Who would know about valuable ships or goods in warehouses? The dockers. Perhaps they would tell the Roundhouse crowd about it but why? There's nothing in it for any of them for the ships or warehouses to be bombed. So now what? I think I'll ask Arthur to come to the boat and listen to you, Sparrer. He knows more than he has let on to us."

A phone call had Arthur on board the boat later that evening. He listened intently to Sparrer's tale and Jane's theories about what it all meant, smiled and said, "Ladies, you have now filled in a couple of important pieces in a jigsaw. We're not there yet but progress is being made. Why don't you go to the Roundhouse some evening to listen and watch?"

Sparrer chipped in. "Yes, Jem said he could make it all right for us to go there, but not in uniform. Friday's the best night, apparently. He said leave a message at the bar and he'd get it."

Jane suggested Arthur fix it for the boat to be sent to the Royal Dock entrance again. They could walk from there and sure enough, their orders for the next day ended with the boat tied up to the same little tug.

CHAPTER 18:

It gets murky

By the spring of 1941 the immediate threat of invasion of Britain had faded. Precautions were maintained at a high level and there was still a sense of nervous uncertainty in the air, but the massed ranks of German soldiers had gone from North France and already the British people were looking beyond basic survival, towards fighting back and ultimate victory.

But that did not mean the country could relax. The ever-present Blitz was causing massive damage and killings with its nightly visitations. Although Hitler had abandoned his hopes that he could crack British morale with mass bombings, recognising that that was not happening, he still hoped to achieve victory by starving the country into submission. This was to be achieved by the combination of the U-Boat campaign sinking the ships bringing foodstuffs into Britain and the Luftwaffe bombing the ports and communications systems to a halt. These campaigns caused the country a great deal of damage and suffering, but never came near to achieving their object. But it did mean that, although the Baedeker Raids were seriously unpleasant and industrial centres elsewhere were also attacked, above all it was London, Liverpool, Bristol and Hull along with the Welsh ports and even Belfast and Glasgow which got the biggest weight of bombs dropped on them.

British military action was in other theatres, mainly the Mediterranean where the eighth army was having a push-you, pull-me war with the Italians along the North African littoral, in a dance of advance and retreat. This went on until the British looked like winning and Hitler, wanting access to the Suez Canal and Middle East oilfields, sent Rommel and the Afrika Corps to take over. That changed the balance in the area dramatically and he came very close to winning. Meanwhile the Navy had also been busy with convoy work and, at the end of March, the full-scale Battle of Matapan. This was in support of convoys to Tobruk and was that relative rarity, a big-gun fight which the Royal Navy won decisively. The Italian Navy, although big modern and powerful, was suitably chastised and never sortied to sea in strength again. The Royal Navy's capacity for aggressive action no matter what the odds had won again. Churchill's determination that the Mediterranean would remain a British sphere of involvement had many critics but he never wavered from his conviction that protecting Malta, the Suez Canal and the oilfields beyond were vital to Britain's interests.

By the spring of 1941 people had adjusted to their new way of life. Many had gone into the armed forces and enormous numbers, especially women, were being drafted into industry and the myriad of jobs previously done by men. Day to day, people simply got on with their lives to a remarkable extent, in uniform or not.

* * *

Against this background, the concerns of *Kittiwake's* crew were above all to do their work properly and well and to get on with it regardless. An awareness of their pioneer role imbued their actions with an extra dimension and many anxious discussions were about whether they were advancing the cause or not. Beyond that, they pursued their personal lives, each in their own way and wrote home regularly. Running up and down the Thames tideway every day, they were acquiring a deeper understanding of their area of operations and could talk with some confidence about difficult wharves and awkward loads to carry. But always, there was something new as well as the ever-present threat from German aerial warfare.

With *Kittiwake* moored alongside the craft tug again at the entrance to the Royal Docks, Sparrer went to the pub and, as arranged, left a note for Jem saying they would come at half past seven that evening. He was there to meet them. "Hello, my palones, nice to vada you."

He looked at Punch. "You're a fine butch dona. The fruits will love you."

This got a nervous giggle and a worried sideways glance from Punch. "Don't worry dear, we can tell you're not trade but the omi will love you. What lallies!"

He led them into the pub and sat them in a corner. "You sit tight there. We'll bring you a drink so you don't get conspicuous." The girls were conscious that he was trying to speak to them in plain English; all around was conversation in Polari, the queer's cant, which simply confused them. To begin with, the evening was highly entertaining with queens who were obviously well known doing song and dance turns, some in outrageous drag. Around nine thirty a chill seemed to descend on the place. The acts went on but the spontaneous gaiety had gone. The girls looked around to see if there was any obvious reason, and sitting quietly near the bar was a tall thin man, elegantly turned out and looking grim. He looked out of place without standing out and it was noticeable that when any of the regulars spoke to him, it was with deference bordering on cringe, but they seemed to need to say something to him. By ten o'clock he had finished his drink and rose to go. The girls instinctively tried to be as inconspicuous as possible but he took them in in passing, pulling the corners of his mouth down as he did so.

Jem joined them soon after. "Who was that man?" Queried Suki.

Jem knew who they were asking about; he tried to pass of the query casually. "Oh he thinks he's so, but not really. He always comes in on his tod but we don't like him." Then Jem almost pleaded, "Don't ask questions about him."

Walking back to the boat, the girls debated what they had seen. "Strange the way the place went quiet as soon as he came in."

"Yes, there's something odd about him. Well dressed and with an air of command about him. Didn't belong in the Roundhouse."

"But did you notice how a lot of the boys felt they had to speak to him, even if just for a minute."

"There's definitely something fishy there. And I don't know if you noticed it but Jem vanished as soon as that bloke arrived in the pub. Came out again after he'd gone. Jem has been very careful not to tell us how he came to be semi-drowned in the river and I wonder if that bloke is connected some way?"

"Perhaps. Oi felt there was something sinister about him."

Back on board, Jane suddenly said, "I think we'll move back up to Lambeth now. Suki could do with the engines cold before she works on them anyway and I'm not happy about staying here. That bloke clocked us as he went out and for all we know he might have followed us to here. Let's go."

Suki nodded. "Yes, I think you're right Jane. I'll get the engines flashed up."

They were back on their usual berth before midnight and a general sigh of relief went round. Next morning Jane phoned Arthur to report what they had seen. This brought a grunt of recognition to Jane's description. "How very interesting. Keep your eyes open for seeing him again. It's possible we may know this man."

Suki set about servicing the engines and doing an oil change, Punch assisting. With no orders for the boat until Monday, Jane had arranged to meet Stefan in the afternoon with the firm intention of telling him it was finished. But when they met he had already booked a hotel for the night and was as keen as ever. Meeting him again, Jane was reminded of why she was so fond of this refugee: tall, good looking, with a lively dashing wit to go with his elegant courtly manners. Add to that, that by now he was also very skilled in bed and what was not to like about him? So despite her earlier resolution she ended up spending the night with him and was well shattered by Sunday morning. Saying goodbye to him was going to be doubly difficult now.

"Stefan, there's something I have to tell you. I'm afraid we are going to have to stop seeing each other. I've met someone else and it wouldn't be fair to go on seeing you as well."

"But Jane I love you. How can you say good-bye to me like that? Haven't we been loving each other just now?"

"Yes Stefan we have and this is very difficult for me, but I really feel we have to go our different ways. Please understand me that I can't go on with two lovers at the same time."

"So tell him to clear off and we make a lovely pair."

"I'm sorry Stefan I cannot do that."

"Oh Jane, Jane, you are so cruel." And he fell back with great wracking sobs. Eventually he stood up. "All right. I am a proud man and will not beg but this is the worst thing for me in my life. Even Nazis not so cruel. Goodbye." And with that he packed his bag quickly and was gone.

Jane was left with a sense of emptiness, of having lost something precious which she would miss very much. She thought of David but at that moment it was little comfort. But it had to be done. 'David, I just hope you appreciate what I've just done. No, hang on, I can't ever tell you about this.' Jumbling confused thoughts warred with each other in her mind so she packed too and trailed back to the boat.

It was difficult to raise any enthusiasm for work but next morning came all too soon and she took the boat over for orders which proved to be fairly humdrum. Mail boat for a couple of days, some machinery to pick up using the derrick on Wednesday and down to the Royal Docks again on Friday. Arthur's unseen hand was still affecting what they did. It hadn't taken her crew long to realise something was wrong. "You gave him the elbow, then?"

Jane nodded glumly. "It hurt, it really hurt. I didn't realise how fond I'd grown of him until too late. But it had to be done."

"That's what you get for two-timing. I hope your David proves worth it."

"Oh, I'm pretty sure about that. He's well and truly docked and he is the one I want so I've got to go with it."

Punch gave her an ironic lift of an eyebrow and they got on with their day. The boat seemed oddly quiet without Suki on board; although she never made much noise she had developed into a constant and reliable cog in the machine, keeping things going and calmly offering ways of making things happen simply and effectively. But Punch managed to start and stop the engines perfectly well and carry out the daily checks. Jane decided it was time for Sparrer to do a bit more so, under close supervision, Jane had her handle the boat, putting it alongside a couple of the easier berths they called at. With Sparrer, confidence was more of a problem than ability, hesitating to pull on the engine controls even when she could see what was needed. But practise is the best teacher for a skill like this, and over a few days she got more confident, putting *Kittiwake* alongside the little tug at the Royal Docks on Friday night with somewhat of a flourish. " 'Ere, this is quite fun when you get the hang of it, ain't it?"

Then it was into mufti and head to the Roundhouse. Jem was there to meet them. "Hello, my palones. Bona to vada you. Just tuck in the corner again."

It all seemed like a repeat of the previous week, quietly sitting unobtrusively and enjoying the brilliant entertainment. The same tall elegant man came in to dampen the fun and one of the pub's regulars went pale and trembled when he was spoken to. Again, he made it plain that the girls were noticed as he left saying nothing. And as before Jem vanished as the tall man came in only to reappear after he had gone. "You don't like that odd man, do you?"

"I'm scared of him. He does the dirty work for him in the shadows. Got to keep clear of them."

"Who is him in the shadows?"

"We don't know but he pulls the strings. Please don't ask too much; they are not nice people."

It was noticeable that his Polari had gone in this exchange and he was clearly under a lot of stress. But when he saw them off the premises it was "Bona Nochy, my dolly donas. Do take care."

The walk back to the boat took about ten minutes with a massive air raid going on in the area. A couple of times odd movements in the shadows bothered them but there was so much other racket going on, fires and explosions and crashing buildings, that they couldn't be sure. As before, Jane elected to cast off and head back to Lambeth pier right away, and as they were leaving the tall man was standing on the quayside in plain sight, making it obvious that he was watching them. This was deeply disturbing.

Saturday was day off for the boat so Jane phoned Arthur and got him to come to the boat where he was given a briefing. He didn't say a lot in reply but what he did say was troubling enough. "Well, we have used our other means to establish definitely that your tall man is Harry Miles, a local freelance enforcer with a fearsome reputation. Even the police are scared of him and he is totally amoral so it wouldn't be a surprise if the 'him' your man referred to was some local spy. We haven't got all the links yet but there is certainly something going on there. Normally he wouldn't bother with the Roundhouse lot who are harmless and expert at keeping out of sight of the straight world anyway. So he's after something and he does nothing without being paid so there's a drive there from somewhere. If he is following you and not bothering to hide, it means he is trying to scare you off without having to do anything nasty. That may simply be a precaution or he may think you're onto something, we don't know yet. We feel you should avoid going there for a couple of weeks now but go on keeping alert in case you spot anything."

He left a quiet and thoughtful group of Wrens, wondering what they had got themselves into. Without anything coming very close there was sense of threat in the air.

CHAPTER 19:

Head on farewell

Suki rejoined on Sunday night looking cheerful. Yes, leave had been nice, a couple of days in Town with friends then down to the APs near Chichester.

"APs?" Queried Sparrer, "Wot's APs?"

Suki laughed. "Aged Parents, Sparrer. Not a term you use?"

"Naw, can't say I've heard that one."

"Yes well, Dad in particular likes to hear about our doings so I always allow a day or two to go there. You're next for leave Sparrer, any news of Lofty?"

Sparrer beamed. "Yes, he's left his ship and is due back in Blighty in a couple of days. His leave starts next Friday then he goes on a course." She turned to Jane "I'm still OK for my leave, ain't I Jane?"

"Yes of course unless anything terrible happens. Let's try to keep out of trouble this week." The glow in Sparrer's eyes told its own story.

Suki had brought mail on board and for Jane, as well as the usual round robin from her mother, they were coping well with their little evacuees, there was a large brown paper envelope. Curious, Jane opened it and spilled out the contents. On top were the two photographs she had given Stefan, each with a large, ragged red cross painted across it. All her letters to him were tied with a bit of ribbon and there were two other letters. The first was a formal one from his Squadron's Commander. It simply stated that Flight Lieutenant Stefan Oszczorowski was killed in action on Wednesday 30th March and that as he had no next of kin in England this notification was being sent to her as apparently the person next closest to him. Formal condolences were recorded.

The other letter was from the senior Polish officer in his squadron. The handwriting was a foreign style but this gentleman had a fluent command of English. His letter said:

Dear Miss Beacon,

Stefan Oszczorowski was our most talented and successful pilot. He was an ace with nineteen kills to his credit and had everything to live for. He was deeply in love with you and would sing to your picture before going on missions. When he returned last weekend it was clear there was something very wrong with him and when he told us that you had left him we all felt for his pain. For the next few days he was very sad but on Wednesday we were tasked for an operation which seemed to cheer him up.

We were in a dogfight with ME109s when he suddenly flew his aircraft straight at an enemy plane and collided with it head on. Of course, he did not survive this. We believe this was a deliberate act of suicide caused by his misery after you left him and for us you are the cause of his untimely death. This has cast a cloud over the whole squadron and I have been asked to tell you the true story of his death. We will fight again but with a heavy heart.

Yours truly

Andrzej Zuwinski.

As Jane read this she went white, then ghostly pale, her hands shaking so much she had to lay the letter down to read it. As she finished it a dam burst. She howled, wailed, fell back, not sobbing this time but bawling loudly, her whole body wracked with spasms of grief. Her crew looked at her in puzzled dismay. "Jane, Jane, what's wrong? Is it David?"

"No, not David; it's Stefan. Read that" and she gestured to the letter. Suki picked it up, read without comment and passed it to Punch. After they had all read it there was silence except for Jane's noisy crying. "Talk about something coming home to roost," muttered Punch, but other than that *Kittiwake's* crew looked at each other helplessly. Suki broke the silence by going over to Jane and wrapping her arms round the weeping bundle. "I didn't mean him any harm. How could he do that? It's horrible." Jane's mutterings were incoherent. "Maybe I should do the same. I'm so sorry Stefan. That's not what I wanted for us." A huge pain filled her, blotting out all rational thought. Eventually Suki broke the silence by saying, "All right Jane. Take a deep breath and sit up. It's happened and you can't do anything about that now. Don't even think about topping yourself, you've far too much to live for. It's war Jane and it can be a cruel business. We all have to live with its consequences, believe me."

"Do you think I can ever face the world again? I'm a killer now, it would seem."

"Yes you can Jane. It may always be a pain in your heart but you can live with it, believe me."

"Do you know about this, Suki?"

"Come with me."

Suki turned to the others, "Excuse me, but this is a bit private." She gathered Jane up and took her into her little cabin, closing the door. "Maybe my story can help you a little, Jane. Did you know that I was a wife and mother? Not now. I'm a widow and bereaved mother and it's all my fault. Early in the war I was driving ambulances, often at night and I insisted my husband and the baby had to go into our Anderson shelter whenever there was a raid. Well, there was a direct hit on a house round the back from ours and when the rescue services found my husband and baby they were dead, in the shelter. Little George was in his father's arms and they both looked utterly untouched but blast had squeezed the life out of them. They'd still be alive if my husband had followed his instinct and sheltered under the stairs in the house but I insisted on them using the shelter. So I killed them and living with the pain from that is never ending. I think you've noticed me coming back on board a bit the worse for wear a few times? Every now and then the pain gets on top of me so I go off, get drunk, have anonymous rough sex and come back feeling emptied out. I can't say I feel better but at least the pressures are eased for a while."

Jane had sat up and stopped weeping during this tale. The two women were sitting side by side on her bunk with arms round each other and Jane gave Suki a big hug. "Suki, Suki, how terrible. How on earth do you manage to live with that?"

"With difficulty Jane, but one endures. Believe me, you can. The pain won't go away but you have so much to look forward to that makes life worth living. Think of David."

"Right now he seems almost irrelevant. How can I be happy with him again after what it has lead to?"

"That may be true but your love for him is still there and believe me, it will come to the top again. Don't let the one spoil the other. And think of what we're doing here; right out there at the front of the biggest challenge we women have had in this war. You've got to believe those things are worth going on for. Grieve for your Stefan now, but you know the rules: an hour off to have a cry then back to work." Suki pointed at the grimy, tattered white ensign from P36 that Jane had pinned up on the bulkhead, its bullet holes showing sharply. "Look at it, Jane, and think what you had to do to get it. You didn't go through all you did and return alive, just to throw your future away now to appease your guilty conscience."

Jane nodded, slowly calming down. "Thanks, Suki, you're right of course but right now that seems bloody difficult to do."

"Right now, what you're suffering from more than anything is an enormous sense of guilt. That will never go away completely but it loses its edge with time and gets overlaid with brighter and happier things. But here and now you have a boat to drive and a job to do. Focus on them and you'll learn to live with the rest."

"All right, I suppose you're right. I will try to get myself together and I promise I won't jump off the bridge. But it would be awfully easy to do, simply take all the pain away."

"Tempting, isn't it? I nearly did, but my family's military background stiffened my rather limp back and I could see how self-indulgent and feeble that was. Fight it Jane and you'll come out stronger."

"The Hell of it is that there are very few people I can tell about Stefan. My family know nothing about him and I can hardly go crying to David who will expect a bright-eyed lover to greet him next time. Really there's only you lot."

"Yes, but we are here and will go on being here. So you're not entirely alone. Stick with it, Jane."

Jane nodded, a weary resigned gesture. "All right, I'll do my best."

"That's good. Would you like a cup of tea?"

"A bottle of gin might be better but yes please, that would be nice."

They re-emerged into the saloon to a silent and worried crew. "Thanks to Suki here I think I'll be all right but don't expect me to sparkle for a bit."

Punch got up and gave Jane a hug. Even a gentle hug from Punch was a bit breath-squeezing but this one nearly cracked Jane's ribs; even so it was re-assuring this time. "Don't worry, we know you pretty well by now. Take it steady and we'll be right there beside you."

Jane gave her a wan smile. "Thanks Punch, you've no idea how much of a comfort that is."

Punch waved the thought away. "It's the least we can do."

Tea drunk they turned in. Jane, emotion expended, fell into a deep sleep but the nightmares came back, with heads being chopped off by propellers this time, their faces flying into hers. She woke up to find a worried trio of crew mates shaking her. "It's the heads, the faces," she moaned as they comforted her. She fell back against the pillows. "Please don't leave me, I can't bear it." Then dropped to sleep on the instant. Her crew took watch turns, an hour about, to stay with her but Jane slept on, whimpering and moaning all the while.

The morning heralded a new day Jane was dreading, but dropping into the daily routine was oddly comforting and half an hour's brisk scrubbing restored her shattered morale a little. By sailing time she was calm and composed again, on the surface at least.

CHAPTER 20:
It's the contrasts

A couple of days' routine work was a bit of a blessing, requiring little thought and with her crew doing ninety per cent of the work Jane could simply go through the motions. Wednesday brought a new challenge: they were sent up to a wharf near Battersea which required some tricky navigation to get into it. That done, the lump of machinery from a nearby factory which they had been sent to collect was waiting for them on the quayside. Jane eyed it doubtfully. "It looks awfully big for our derrick – what weight is it?"

"We don't know, love, but we think it's about a ton."

"Well, we'll give it a go. We'll have to get the multiple purchase and topping lift span preventer rigged. Give us half an hour to get the derrick ready." This would be the first time their three-fold purchase had been used, so it took them a little while to figure out how to rig it, but with that done, the tail led forward to the windlass for power and the preventer span attached to the derrick head, they topped the derrick, swung it over and hooked on the strops ready attached to the machine. With Punch on the windlass drum end, they heaved away. The machine sat there, *Kittiwake* heeled over. The little generator roared, the boat heeled further and further over and the machine still just sat there. With *Kittiwake* lying over at a dangerous angle, close to putting her gunwale under, Jane called a halt. " I'm sorry, that thing must be a lot more than a ton weight. We're certainly not going to be able to move it." The men on the wharf looked pained.

"Come on, love, one last try."

So they heaved away again, but still nothing happened other than the boat lying right over and coming very close to downflooding. At that moment the span wire and preventer broke off simultaneously, the derrick came down with a crash on top of the machine and the tail jumped off the windlass drum smacking Punch in the ribs. She squealed and fell over "God that hurt". At least the derrick itself was not wrecked but there was a good deal of confusion and shouting.

"That's an end to that, I'm afraid. You need a much bigger rig than ours to move that thing."

"Sorry love, we were only told to get it away."

Evadne, a natural climber with no fear of heights, shinned up the mast and reported, "The ring the span was shackled to has broken off the band round the mast. We can tie something round the mast to attach the span to, to get the derrick back on board."

Half an hour later they had recovered the derrick. Punch was sitting in a corner clutching her ribs and took no part. Jane called to the men on the wharf. "We'd better go back to base and report this. No doubt they'll get something bigger to come but you could do to find out what weight that lump really is."

Jane was fairly rasping with her report to the operations office and arranged for Punch to get her ribs x-rayed just in case. Mercifully, that proved to be no more than heavy bruising but the knowledge didn't seem to lessen the pain much. Effectively, the derrick was out of commission so they were put onto being mail boat again until a welder could come to attach a new ring for the span. At the end of a lively day it dawned on Jane that she hadn't thought about Stefan once all day. Perhaps Suki was right: the answer to the pain that hovered there all the time was to keep busy and do her job.

A couple of days later Commander Coleman came aboard when they arrived for their orders in the morning. Jane was in the office so Punch saluted him on board and invited him into their saloon. He sat down and accepted the offer of a cup of tea, so this was not a formal visit. When Jane returned he said, "Now tell me, Beacon, what happened with your derrick the other day? Did you really break your boat trying to lift that machine?"

"Well, sir, the only broken bit was the ring on the hound band and I called it off before any more damage was done."

"We have investigated further and it turns out that machine weighed three tons. It's not surprising that you couldn't lift it. I think in future you will have to be a bit firmer about what you can handle."

Jane considered this. "There's a war on sir and we feel we have to have a go at everything we're asked to do. We were tasked with lifting the thing so we did try. That isn't bad, is it, sir?"

"No, not at all and we like your willingness to have a go. Just don't overdo it." And with that he smiled and went ashore to the greater problems of his daily routine. Suki said thoughtfully, "He does seem quite happy with us, doesn't he? D'you suppose that means we're doing the job properly?"

"Yes Suki, but you watch what happens the first time we get it wrong. Those bloody Jeremiahs will be down on us like vultures on a corpse. That's the joy of being pioneers being watched the whole time."

As if all this wasn't enough for Jane to cope with, next day there was a letter for her from a Lady Ormond, thanking Jane for saving her life in the Cafe de Paris bombing and inviting her for tea. The address was in Mayfair. "Oh gosh, what do you suppose I should do about this?" the question wafted towards her crew in general.

"Oh go, Jane. A contact like that ain't never going to do you no harm. You know how to behave ladylike, don't you?"

"I suppose so Sparrer but I think she is rather grand."

Suki chipped in. "Jane, she is well disposed towards you so she is likely to forgive the odd lack of polish somewhere, not that I think you have any lack. Go for it."

Jane wrote back saying her next day off was the following Friday and might that be suitable?

Lady Ormond replied saying that was entirely suitable and she would send a car to collect Jane at four o'clock.

Then, to complicate matters even further, a note from Arthur arrived saying he needed to see Jane at his flat the following night. By now Jane was deeply wary of giving Arthur any chance of trapping her on her own with him, but there was a peremptory tone to the message which suggested she ought to go.

So she presented herself at his flat at 2000 as instructed and was relieved to see two other men there, both suitably besuited and unlikely to give her bother. Well, maybe not in Arthur's way, but these two brought worrisome news. "Jane, this is Inspector Carson of the Flying Squad. And a representative from Security, never mind what sort. You can call him Plato. They are both involved, as you are, in the strange business going on at the docks. Your inputs so far have been vitally helpful in getting us closer to the bottom of the whole business and we need your co-operation in bringing the matter to an end. Plato from Security took over. "It was your discovery that Harry Miles the enforcer was involved which opened up a line for us which we've been able to exploit very well. He has led us to who we believe is the person behind the whole business but we have yet to fit in a couple of other bits. Do you suppose that you could persuade your queer contact to open up a bit more? We think that group know a good deal more than they are letting on and if we can get them to talk we should be able to make a good deal of progress. Do you think you might be able to use a carrot and stick approach and get him to open up?"

"We can try but fear has kept his mouth shut so far."

The Inspector now joined the conversation. "You can let him know that they have a choice: co-operate with us or the whole lot will go to gaol. They know very well the terms on which we quietly leave them alone."

"I understand that but I have a feeling that fear of being killed is an even stronger force in their minds. Three of them have now been fished out of the river and our contact more or less implied that he had been a sacrificial body to keep the others alive. But I can give it a go."

"That's good. By the way, from now on whenever we ask you to go there, we won't be far behind and if you need help all you have to do is blow this whistle."

And he handed her a silver whistle.

"Well thanks. What's its range?"

"Half a mile or so, a bit less upwind."

The Security spoke again. "Right young lady. Next week we will arrange for you to be sent to the same place outside the Royal Docks. Go in and try to get your man to speak to you privately. See what you can get out of him and let us know. And remember, we'll never be far away."

With that both other men stood up and left, leaving Jane alone with Arthur.

He didn't waste any time about coming to the point. "Jane, please, do stop this devotion to David and come to me instead. Try a real man."

"What makes you think David isn't a real man? I must say your version of brotherly love is pretty horrid. No, Arthur, I am not going to give up David for you and the sooner you can understand that the easier it will be for us both."

Jane had stayed standing with a clear access to the front door but his sudden bound and grab left her trapped in his arms. "Arthur, stop it! What bit of no don't you understand? Let me go now or I'll get violent." This had no effect so she jerked fiercely, spun on her heels and managed to break free. Standing by the open door she snarled, "Don't you realise you are jeopardising the whole operation down at the docks? I'll pull us out of it now and have no hesitation about saying why unless you stop this nonsense."

"Jane, if I give orders for you and your boat to be in it, you will be in it whether you like it or not. Stop messing about."

"Me messing about? I like that. If you think you're going to bully your way into a relationship with me you are very much mistaken. For the sake of this operation and for your family relations get a grip of yourself now, Arthur Daubeny-Fowkes."

And with that she slammed the door and ran down the corridor, only stopping once she was out in the street. The tube was as crammed as ever but the security of its numbers was a comfort. Jane was more angry than frightened but this business with Arthur was becoming ever more of an obstacle to ordinary life.

A day on the water was pleasantly soothing and allowed Jane to shut out the tumbling thoughts and worries in her mind. Concentrating on berthing in a tricky corner had a clean simple pleasure to it well away from the complications of personal matters.

Friday was a bright but breezy day blowing the best part of a gale and Jane wasn't sorry that *Kittiwake* was tied up snug on the pier. Sparrer went on leave in a great tizzy, all keyed up excitement and nervous anticipation.

"Give my best wishes to Lofty and your father."

"Yes Jane I will, I will." And off she went to catch a bus.

Punch got Evadne to help her splicing up some new mooring lines while Suki did routine checking of the boat's machinery, reporting that their battery wasn't very good and could they indent for a new one. Just the week before, Suki had finally been repaid her fifty pounds from an unwilling Admiralty for the little generator she had bought out of her own pocket. As it had proved one of the most useful things on board, Jane had given the request for re-imbursement as much of a push has she could, learning a good deal about the Navy's spare gear and payment systems in the process. With this activity going on around her Jane spent Friday morning battling with the forms and paperwork of being a Naval detached unit and so far as she could tell, more or less had her returns up to date. After lunch, she turned her mind to getting ready to call on Lady Ormond. It would have to be uniform, of course, so the new best tiddley one was given a sponge down, her shoes a polish and her lanyard a whitening scrub. With new silk stockings and her medal ribbons polished she was about as ready as possible, even giving her unruly mane a thorough brushing. The car was at the pier at four o'clock sharp, the chauffeur apologising that it was only the Rover but "Getting enough petrol for the Rolls was very difficult these days". Jane would have hopped into the front seat beside him but he opened a back door with a flourish so Jane travelled in solitary silence. Lady Ormond's home was officially a flat but spread as it was over two floors with marble pillars in the entrance and a seemingly endless vista across the main reception area, describing it as a flat seemed a bit inadequate. The butler met Jane at the front door and had evidently been primed on who to expect, as he bowed ever so slightly and said, "Good afternoon, Miss Beacon. An honour to have you call."

Lady Ormond was sitting by the window, the remains of her left arm in a sling; she gestured to Jane to sit beside her. "Miss Beacon, it is such a pleasure to have you call on me. You are unmistakeably the girl who saved my life in the Cafe de Paris so it is my privilege to thank you in person."

"That is very kind of you Lady Ormond but really I only did what had to be done."

"Yes my dear, but you kept your head and did the right thing while all around people were screaming and panicking."

"A lot of them were also injured or affected by blast. I was lucky in being upstairs so out of the main blast and fairly unaffected."

"I seem to remember blood streaming down your face. Was that scar from there?"

"You mean this one?" Jane pointed at the big scar up her face. It had calmed down and the livid red had gone but it remained a very marked feature. Lady Ormond nodded.

"No ma'am, this one was acquired at Dunkirk, along with my medals."

"Ah, yes, I heard something about exploits at Dunkirk. Tell me more."

There was a pause while a maid served tea and cakes. This dispensed, Jane launched into the by now well-polished twenty-minute tale, finishing up back in Dover. Lady Ormond listened intently, smiling or frowning at points along the way. She particularly liked the tale of the Emperor.

"I can see why you were able to keep your head at the Cafe de Paris after experiences like that. Now tell me, my dear, do you have a boyfriend?"

"Oh yes ma'am, a Naval officer I rescued at Dunkirk. It's quite a romantic story really. We met again at the investiture at Buckingham Palace."

"A Naval officer, eh? Would he be anyone I would know?"

"Well you probably know his family, ma'am. The Daubeny-Fowkes."

"Oh good heavens yes. Is this a serious affair?"

Jane was getting a little uneasy about this close personal probing but felt she had to go along with it. "Yes ma'am, we hope to get engaged next time he has leave. Unfortunately his mother doesn't approve but we hope to overcome that."

"Is yours the Earl?"

"No ma'am, the Earl is in the Army. Mine is David, the youngest of them. He doesn't see why his mother should be so obsessed with breeding when he isn't expected to produce the next heir to the title."

"She is obsessed with breeding is she? Well well, how times change. That dreadful *parvenu* has a lot to be obsessed about. Did you know she is the daughter of a greengrocer? She was a Tiller girl and the outstanding beauty of her age. Give her her due, she really was exceptionally lovely but even so it was the talking point of the season when the old Marquis, a crusty old bachelor, suddenly upped and married her."

"Had he got her pregnant?"

"No, she was too smart for that but certainly had him on a string. Nine months and three weeks after the wedding she produced the Earl. She really has a nerve, going on about other people's breeding. I presume yours is respectable?"

Jane had sat through this exposé open-mouthed, totally stunned by what she was hearing and struggled to find her tongue again. "Yes ma'am, my father is a successful doctor with roots in a farming family in north-east Scotland and my mother comes from a solid Devon family. I suppose you would just about call us upper middle class. But I'm stunned by what you say about the Marchioness. She's more regal than the royal family."

"Yes well, she always was a good actress."

"So it would seem." Jane shook her head, bewildered by the sudden turn of events; but already her mind was running ahead to what this might mean for prospects with David. "Ma'am, you know more about this sort of thing. In a family like the

Daubeny-Fowkes, is it true that the younger siblings have more freedom to choose their own lives and partners?"

Lady Ormond considered this for a minute. "To some extent yes, although some do take off and please themselves anyway. Others are more comfortable with partners who have a similar background and there is some social pressure to keep matters in the same circle. But no hard and fast rules."

"This is all very interesting ma'am and I am sure I don't have to tell you how important it might be to me. Assuming it all works, can I invite you to my wedding?"

"My dear girl, that would be a pleasure. Which moves me on a bit. Meeting you today has been a great joy to me, not only to say 'thank you' but to get to know you a little. I understand you are leading the way for Wrens to operate boats?"

"Yes ma'am, I have been the pioneer boat crew Wren for working on Naval craft. So far it has gone well and we do see some glimmers of hope that the top brass will relent and allow us Wrens to run boats on a wider scale. Getting the Navy to change its ways can be a slow grinding process."

Lady Ormond smiled. "I know that very well. My family have had many Naval types among them so I understand what you are saying. But you personally have been the leader in this?"

"I was the first so I suppose the answer is yes."

"Hmm. How old are you?"

"Twenty, with my birthday due shortly. Then I'll be an adult at last."

Lady Ormond snorted a laugh. "You are remarkably adult already. And so young to have such a responsibility on your shoulders."

"That's been helped by the way I'm doing something which I simply love doing and had a good deal of background experience in."

"Your modesty is becoming but I suspect covers a much more powerful story. Now what I want to tell you is that I like you. I live here on my own without any children and I would like you to start treating this place as your own. With six bedrooms available and a staff eating away for nothing, it would give me great pleasure if you would treat this place as your other home. Where do your parents live?"

"That is incredibly generous of you, although I'd be very nervous of treating this grand place as a second home. My family home is on the Yealm, down in Devon so it's quite a trek to see them."

"All the more reason to have a place in Town. It's six o'clock now and I eat early. Would you care to dine with me?"

"That would be very kind, ma'am."

Lady Ormond rang a bell and the butler appeared. "Johnson, Miss Beacon will be staying for dinner. See her to a room so she can freshen up."

"Very good m'lady."

So Jane, feeling rather bemused by this turn of fortunes, was shown to a large luxurious bedroom with its own facilities. She lay down and was asleep on the instant. A sharp rap on the bedhead awoke her to find a maid bending over her. "It's dinner time, ma'am. Can I get you anything before you go down?"

"No, I don't think so. Hang on a minute while I sort myself out. Jane dragged up to full consciousness, splashed her face and pulled a comb through her mop. One great advantage of uniform was the way it did away with the need to change for dinner, so she smiled at the maid "What's your name?"

"Edith, ma'am." Jane was finding being ma'am–ed rather disconcerting. "Right Edith, lead me to the dining room."

Dinner proved to be entirely formal, with cook bringing in the dishes, the butler supervising and pouring and a maid serving table. Jane was acutely conscious of the need to be on her very best table manners, but fortunately there were no peculiarities and she managed to negotiate the various courses and drinks ending with a rather pleasant port. Eating finished, Lady Ormond enquired "Would you care to stay the night my dear?"

Jane demurred. "That is very kind but I have to start work at six thirty in the morning and that's going to be a lot easier if I am back on board already. I can take a cab home tonight."

"No need, my dear. The chauffeur will run you back."

"It's a bit late to expect him to turn out isn't it?"

"Not at all. He has much too easy a life as it is." As Lady Ormond escorted Jane to the front door she said, "The servants here have been with me for years. They have been told about you and believe they will be looking after an outstanding war heroine. You can be sure of a warm welcome here any time."

"That is so kind and thank you for everything. Good night, Lady Ormond."

"Good night........... Jane."

CHAPTER 21:

Be prepared

Scrubbing the boat next morning brought Jane back down to reality with a bump, but again there was a comfort in the familiar routine. Boat nicely shined up, they got their orders for the day, plus a warning that the Admiral in command of the Thames had selected them to act as his barge the following week for a trip down to Southend Pier and back. This caused some consternation among the boat's newer recruits but Jane and Punch shrugged, having become well accustomed to Admirals on board down at Dover.

This day they took some stores and three soldiers to a gun battery on Long Reach, then called on a Dutch merchant ship on Halfway Reach buoys to take her captain ashore at Tower Pier. By now there was little comment about their presence on the tideway, but the Dutch captain was a bit startled to find he was being conducted ashore by girls and commented "If all English women are like you, we are bound to beat the Germans." All Jane could do was laugh.

Captain delivered, they were sent to find a lighter called *Argonaut* somewhere in the river off Barking Creek. Their orders were to take it in tow to Woolwich Arsenal and put it alongside the naval pier. But when they got there they could find no sign of any such lighter. There were a few on a trot immediately below Barking with men on them, so they went there to ask. "*Argonaut*, you say? Yeah, she's actually lying up Barking Creek so you'll have an interesting job towing her down. Good luck."

"Thanks for that. Are you lightermen?" They were smartly dressed with collar and tie in true lighterman style.

"Yes ducks, we are. Hey, are you the girls who rescued Tommy Smith?"

"If it was off Surrey Docks, yes we are."

"That's interesting. Word is out to do anything we can to help you girls; Tommy reckons he would have been a-gonner without you. What are you doing with *Argonaut*?"

"We have orders to take it to the Naval pier at Woolwich. Do you know which that is?"

"Yes of course we do. Tell you what, ducks, we're not doing a lot just now. Why don't we come with you and help?"

"Well fine if you can. Hang on." Jane put *Kittiwake* alongside and the three lightermen came on board. The kettle was put on and the boat directed up the creek. With the lightermens' huge knowledge of the river they found the lighter, which was half hidden round the back of a jetty. Towing it out was a bit of a challenge but with the eldest of the lightermen – "just call me Danny" – guiding Jane they extracted it from its berth and down the narrow, bendy creek. Hitting the river, the tide sent them skidding sideways but again with a little sage advice, Jane managed to keep the tow under control. Punch and Suki stood close by watching very closely; Evadne was stationed on the afterdeck to make sure the towrope did not foul anything. All of them were learning interesting new wrinkles on dealing with the river. Passing the Royal Docks entrance, Jane looked at the tiers of lighters lying to buoys in the river and remarked to Danny, "Plenty of work for you there."

Danny nodded. "Yes, they keep us busy. But you see that one on its own at the end? That's very odd. We don't know who it belongs to, it never moves yet we see people moving around it at night sometimes. We've been warned off asking about it so we just leave it alone."

Jane smiled "Yes, that does seem a bit odd. With the war on you'd think they wanted everything they could lay their hands on for work." With their lighter close behind them and a flood tide to cope with Jane was too engrossed to ask further, but tucked the comment away. With the lightermen to help and advise, coming alongside the right place at Woolwich proved straightforward and with some sense of relief they saw the *Argonaut* tied up. "Do you gentlemen want a lift to anywhere? Jane asked.

"We could go back to where we were if that's all right."

Jane checked her watch. "Yes, I think so. It's after four now and we won't be given another job today so why not? You've been very helpful to us."

Coming down the river Jane deliberately passed close by the solitary lighter to take a close look at it, but to her untutored eye it seems remarkably nondescript. Danny pointed to its aft end. "See the hatch there? It lets into the little cabin these things all have. Usually they are closed to keep the rain out but that one is always just a little open. You could wonder why."

Jane shrugged but again tucked this morsel away in her mind. Lightermen delivered, a quick council of war decided they had done enough for the day, but kept an eye Tower Pier as they passed in case they were being flagged in. But nothing and Lambeth pier felt very much like home.

Settled for the night, Jane wrote her bread and butter letter to Lady Ormond, asking at its end if her offer of using her flat would require Jane to write in advance. In her own world Jane was accustomed to simply turning up but clearly an establishment like Lady Ormond's needed more notice. To her delight the reply was that a day's notice would be helpful but not to be put off and if she did just turn up the staff would always know what to do.

In the operations office at Tower Pier next morning Jane asked, "Do we know yet which day the admiral is going down the river?"

"Yes Beacon. It's been delayed a bit but this morning he's confirmed that it will be a week on Tuesday. Be on your best behaviour."

Jane grinned. "We'll try. Could the boat have Monday off so we can get her really smart and tiddley? And any chance of a couple of pots of varnish and some Pusser's grey paint? We could do to sharpen up some of the brightwork."

That seemed possible so she pushed it a little further. "And how about some more brass polishing kit? Ours is pretty run down now."

The Operations Officer raised his eyebrows to a remarkable height but it was all arranged and on the Monday they really got the boat gleaming.

This was after a quite different week. While *Kittiwake* and her crew had gone about their business, the Blitz had continued to rain bombs on London. By now this was simply the backdrop to life and they got on with their lives with little disruption. By mutual agreement they lived and slept on board, Jane's experience leading to the conclusion that they were as safe on board as anywhere. Only a direct hit or the nearest of misses was going to harm them and although they moved off to the Savoy moorings a couple of times, mostly they simply took their chances and stayed berthed on Lambeth Pier.

The week was spent doing a few minor runs with mail or stores but mostly they were assigned to mine watching in the Pool of London. Every time the German bombers came over, whether by design or accident bombs and parachute mines fell in the river. By April 1941 it was clear that an organised operation was needed to note where things landed in the river during raids. A good deal of the organising of this system would be carried out in conjunction with Petty Officer A P Herbert and when *Kittiwake* was experimentally assigned to the duty he tied up *Water Gypsy* alongside them to tutor and explain what had to be done. Jane and her crew were delighted to see him again; for the past couple of months the best they had done was to wave to him in passing. The job entailed sitting at anchor in the middle of the river watching the spectacular destruction going on round them and keeping a close eye on the water for things landing in it. On Thursday night their vigilance was rewarded – if that is the right word – by noting a large splash close to London Bridge which they took some pleasure in reporting.

Being anchored in mid-river gave Jane a chance to quiz A P Herbert about Lady Ormond, who – perhaps inevitably – he knew. "Oh yes, a pillar of respectable society now although she did have a racier time back in the '20s. Quite a flapper in her day. No, she has never married and although there are distant family members she has no close relatives. What is your interest?"

"Well, apparently I saved her life in the Cafe de Paris bombing by clapping a tourniquet on what was left of her left arm. She found out it was me, invited me to tea to say thank you and seems inclined to kind of adopt me. Her place is a bit grand for comfort but I don't really see how I can say no."

"She's a kind-hearted soul beneath the heavy formality so you could do worse than let yourself be taken over. But be under no illusions, she will take you over if she's allowed to. Mind you, she is very well connected so if you ever needed that kind of usefulness there's a lot there to be tapped into. I dine with her occasionally myself." Jane tucked all this away in memory.

After a week of what was in effect night duty, they had to adjust rapidly to their more normal routine at the weekend with runs to Greenwich and to Tilbury. They were having supper on Sunday evening when the boat rocked and a very tall Leading Seaman ducked into their saloon. "Lofty! How lovely to see you."

He was closely followed by Sparrer. "Jane, You had to be first to be told. Look!" And she held up her left hand with a rather nice diamond engagement ring on it. "Oh Sparrer, how wonderful for you: it's all worked out."

The glow in Sparrer's eyes told its own story.

Lofty had said nothing during this girls' chat, standing in the middle of the saloon looking a bit awkward. Suki took charge. "Hello Lofty, you don't know me but I'm Suki and now a member of the crew here. Do come and sit down."

He relaxed in the enfolding nautical atmosphere of the saloon but left the talking to the girls. An hour later he said, "Phemie, we're going to have to go for now. When did you say your leave was up?"

"Tomorrow morning, I'm afraid. What is the boat doing tomorrow, Jane?"

"Actually, just sitting here. We are acting as Admiral's barge on Tuesday and we're getting the boat really spotless and shiny tomorrow."

"Blimey, Admiral's Barge, eh? Do we know what to do?"

"More or less. Let's face it we got plenty of practice down at Dover and his Flag Lieutenant is calling on us tomorrow for a briefing. I think we'll survive."

Lofty spoke, more or less for the first time since coming aboard. "Tell you what, I'm not due to go on course till the middle of the week. I will come tomorrow and give you a hand getting her ready if you like."

"Lofty. That would lovely. Are you staying on board tonight then? You can doss in the saloon here, sling a hammock if you like."

"Yes, why not? When do you start in the morning?"

"Oh, six thirty but you needn't be in such a rush."

"No problem. I'll turn to when you do."

Sometime in the middle of the night Jane had to nip to the heads and wasn't surprised to see a female leg hanging out the side of the hammock. Smiling gently to herself she closed her cabin door again silently.

By eight in the morning breakfast was over and the whole crew were hard at it scrubbing and polishing and making sure everything was as smart and tiddley as possible. Lofty and Evadne had an entertaining hour scrubbing and polishing the mast which was not used to such special treatment. Some touching up of its varnish had it looking very smart.

Around nine thirty the Flag Lieutenant turned up with a Chief Wren. He proved to be a sensible career Naval officer dealing with practicalities for the following day. "We will want you on Tower Pier for 0745. The Admiral's party will come on board at 0830 sharp. There will be six people in the party including me; they will bring their own food with them which will have been put on board beforehand. The Admiral will board five minutes later. Do you have a piper?"

Jane looked round her crew. "Well, we did it on probationer course but I don't think any of us will be particularly good at it."

"All right, we'll have a Chief Yeoman signaller with us and he can do it. Just a still and carry on."

Suki spoke up "Oh, I can do that. But I don't think we have a pipe on board, do we?" Shakes of heads all round.

"I'll make sure one is put aboard with the stores. His flag will also come on board with the stores, as will a new white ensign. Be ready to hoist his flag as soon as he steps onto the boat. On the run down he will probably want to sit out on the afterdeck if the weather is good and the forecast is promising. I presume you don't have chairs?"

Again, shakes of the head all round. "Right, I'll send half a dozen down. Your fenders are very scruffy. Can you clean them up a bit?"

"Don't worry, I indented for a new set and much to my surprise we got them without any argument. Somebody must have told stores the Admiral was coming."

The Flag Lieutenant looked amused. "Can't think who that would be. Now, anything else?"

"I don't think so sir. We should be ready."

The Chief Wren had sat in a corner saying nothing but now started. "You are all very scruffy looking. I presume you will be looking a bit better tomorrow? Half of you could do with a haircut and your uniforms are a disgrace."

Jane by now was unaccustomed to the carping of senior rates and bridled a bit at this. "Well Chief, these are our working kit for cleaning and the likes. Yes of course we have proper tiddley uniforms for best and will be wearing them tomorrow."

"I find that hard to believe. Go and put them on for inspection now."

Jane was all set to argue that they had more to do than prance about being inspected but Punch put a restraining hand on her arm. "Let's go and do it Jane." So they changed, tucked hair under hats, cleaned hands and pulled on best uniform leather shoes. The Chief Wren was unimpressed. "Your jackets could all do with pressing and mostly you are still showing too much hair. Your shoes are a disgrace and several collars are none too clean. This must all be remedied by tomorrow morning."

"Yes Chief."

The Flag Lieutenant had watched this with gentle amusement. "All right, time for me to go for now. See you at 0745 tomorrow morning."

With him gone, Jane turned to other practicalities. "Once we've got the gear on board and the party have arrived, we'll go to Admiral stations. I think if Punch takes the foredeck, hoists the Admiral's flag then lets go forr'd, Sparrer can take the aft end, Suki can be at the boarding point to help people on board then pipe the Admiral and Evadne can be in charge of fenders. I'll be waiting on the aft deck to give him the salute and welcome him. We'll be singled up to short breast slip lines fore and aft so we can just throw them off when we're ready. Punch, can you lead the boathook drill as we pull away. Let's try to be smart about it: no shouted orders. I'll give hand signals to let go so let's practise those. Remember the Admiral will always be last on and first off. It will be ebb tide so I will knuckle her bow off initially, cast of aft then bear off with the boathooks. I'll take a swing into the Pool and we're on our way. Sparrer and Eva, once we're away I'd like you to keep handy to the Admiral's party for whatever they may want and Punch and Suki can take turns with me on the helm, half an hour about."

With a little debate they got the hand signals sorted out and as far as they could be, they were ready for the Admiral.

* * *

Apart from the never-ending battering of the Blitz, Britain's main battle activity in the first half of 1941 was still in the Mediterranean theatre. The recent Battle of Matapan had strengthened the Navy's position but it still operated under constant threat from the air and from U-boats which had penetrated the Mediterranean. On land, the German Army swept south through the Balkans and Greece to replace Italian forces collapsing and failing to hold their ground. Airborne forces parachuted into Crete and rapidly pushed the British out of there too. In North Africa the arrival of Erwin Rommel and the Afrika Korps drastically changed the balance of power there, regaining control just when the British looked like pushing the Italian armies out of Africa altogether.

In North Europe it was generally accepted by spring 1941 that any imminent threat of invasion of Britain by the Wehrmacht had faded although it never entirely went away. Britain firmly retained control of the air around its perimeter which allowed the Navy to operate much more freely and the Army had recovered from the Dunkirk disaster to be a fighting force once more. With the withdrawal of German assault troops from Northern France it was felt that Hitler was up to something else but exactly what was less clear. Only a modest portion of his army was engaged in the battles round the Mediterranean but they were making a major nuisance of themselves as they attempted to close a pincer movement round the Sea's Eastern end which would seize the Suez Canal and open up the path to the Gulf oil fields.

Within Britain the established order had settled down and nowhere more so than on the River Thames. Because of the threats from seaward big ships were not routinely routed into it any more, but a substantial coastwise traffic, especially of colliers bringing coal from the North-East of England to London, continued to flow in. Large ocean-going tankers still came to Thameshaven with their vital cargoes of oil and there was some limited traffic of foodstuffs in deep-sea ships. Which meant that the Thames remained busy enough, even if at a much reduced volume from its pre-war levels.

In charge of the Thames was Rear-Admiral E C Boyle, Victoria Cross. A distinguished submarine commander, he had earned his VC for daring deeds in the Sea of Marmara in command of the submarine E14 during the Gallipoli campaign in 1915. His entire boat's company were decorated. Retired in 1932, he was recalled to active service in 1939 and appointed in command of the Thames area under the C-in-C, the Nore. Like many of these old and bold seamen he had a bluff manner which disguised acute perception and understanding of humans, especially the Navy's ratings. Coming on board a launch he would expect everything to be tautly drawn and proper Navy but would be generous in praise when it was so.

PART FIVE:

STEADY, LADIES, STEADY

CHAPTER 22:
The Admiral

Kittiwake was alongside Tower Pier by 0730, looking very smart. Her gleaming new white fenders were arrayed down her side which itself was showing the benefit of a coat of paint. Her crew were all spruced up, even having clean white collars on their shirts and hair well tucked under hats. Ten minutes later a small group of matelots turned up pulling a barrow loaded with supplies. They made short work of getting them onboard and stowed away. The remarkably large new white ensign flew bravely in a stiffish breeze and the Admiral's own flag was bent on ready to be broken out as soon as he stepped aboard. Suki had a few test blows on her bosun's call and one of the matelots listening to her efforts, said "Lift your pinkie a bit more, dearie and it will sound much better," and just had to get close to show her how. But he was right: it did sound better.

At 0830 a group was seen heading down and one by one they came on board. To Jane's delight Petty Officer Herbert was first on board, shaking Jane's hand warmly and greeting her in cheerful mood. Three Wren representatives came including the same Chief Wren who had been stiff with them the day before; surprise of surprises, a familiar Third Officer and an unknown Second Officer. Jane smile broadly. "Good morning, Third Officer Baker. How nice to see you."

"Good morning, Leading Wren Beacon, I see everything is ready."

Jane's smile broadened even more. "I think so, ma'am."

The Second Officer looked at the two closely. "Do you two know each other?"

"Yes ma'am, same pro course."

This conversation was cut short by a call of, "Admiral approaching."

The party retreated below apart from the Flag Lieutenant, Jane's crew flew to their stations and as the Admiral stepped onto the bulwark Suki sounded the still. Jane came rigidly to attention and saluted and his pennant was broken out at the masthead. The Admiral stepped aboard, returned the salute half turned to the flag and came to Jane. Suki sounded the carry on, the Admiral shook Jane's hand warmly and asked "Ready to go?"

"Yes indeed sir, as soon as you say the word."

"Good." His Flag Lieutenant called the party up from below and introductions were made. The Admiral clearly knew A P Herbert well already. As well as the Wren party and the Flag Officer, there was a Chief Petty Officer signalman who had brought a large walkie-talkie radio with him and a steward who had promptly started unloading stores and did not re-appear on deck. The Admiral looked around "Right young lady, we can go."

Engines were already running and everyone was at their station so Jane gave the signal to let go forward, watched the bow drop out on the tide, signalled to let go aft then bear off fore and aft and as the boat came clear she put both engines ahead and signalled ahead to her bow and stern hands. Their boat hook drill was immaculate as the boat swung round and headed downstream under Tower Bridge. All this took place in complete silence. The Admiral smiled and asked, "Been practising then?"

"Just a bit sir."

The Signals Chief set about getting his radio working in the wheelhouse, made contact with his base and listened to messages coming over the ether. Once through Tower Bridge the assembly took on a steady rhythm. Tea was produced, the chairs put out and people settled on the afterdeck in the mild spring sunshine. The Admiral requested a tour of inspection so Jane called Punch to the wheel and showed him round below decks. In her little cabin he looked at the P36 white ensign. "Hmm. Where did you acquire this?"

"It was my ensign on the launch I took to Dunkirk, sir. It came back with the boat when I returned to Dover. The staff there rescued it and presented it to me later."

"I see. So you were really in the thick of the action; now your medal ribbons make sense. Not what I'd expect from a woman but plainly you did it."

"I rather think that non-expectation was why their Lordships had problems deciding what do about me, sir."

The Admiral laughed gently, then turned to looking round the rest of below decks. "All very impressive. I was dubious when it was suggested we give our best boat to you Wrens but it seems to be working very well. I must say she is very well cared for."

"Well we did polish the brass for you, sir."

The Admiral laughed, a cheerful guffaw that sent a message to relax to the others, still watching a bit anxiously. "Now introduce your crew to me." Jane called them up one by one. He was most interested in them all, spending several minutes talking to each one and listening to East End twang, Rhodesian clipped vowels and Suki's elegant drawl. Jane sent Suki to take the helm and Punch came into the saloon, towering over everyone else as usual. "By Jove, you're a prime specimen. What's your background?"

"Me dad owns a spritsail barge sir. Oi've been in and out of the Thames since I was a baby."

"Ah, so you'll know the river then. Keep handy, I need bits pointed out to me as we go along."

"Aye aye sir."

Which meant that Jane and Suki had to do most of the steering, apart from a spell when a very nervous Sparrer took a turn.

Somewhat of a party atmosphere brewed up. The Admiral had not chosen to sit but stood in the wheelhouse looking around all the time. He had taken in Jane's rows of medal ribbons when he boarded but now asked more about them. Jane decided to be frank. "They came from my time at Dunkirk, sir. No doubt you know that the Navy was not entirely happy about my getting them but the Army put a lot of pressure on, as did the French and Belgians. Mostly the opposition seems to have died away now but I am under strict orders to keep a low profile here."

"Yes, I heard about that. Not my business but I must say I am with you after seeing the efficiency your crew are showing this morning. It's a changed war this time and having women like you fully involved gives the country a tremendous extra strength. You and your crew could win the war single-handed, I've no doubt."

Jane smiled at that. "It has been suggested that we could crew a warship entirely with Wrens but their Lordships did seem to feel that was a step too far. But it does show that we women can do a lot more than has traditionally been expected of us."

"No doubt." The Admiral did not seem entirely happy with that thought but let it go. He went aft, settled next to Alan Herbert and chatted with him.

Suki was on the wheel as they came round into Gallions Reach to find the river blocked by a very large cargo ship canting to enter the Royal Docks, tugs straining on both its ends. Round its bow, busily leaving the entrance lock came a craft tug towing a string of lighters so Suki shaped to go under the ship's stern when an up-bound sailing barge materialised there, completely blocking the river. It tacked close to the south shore and headed across *Kittiwake's* bow. Jane jumped up, "*Bloody Hell, full astern Suki! Helm up, helm up!*" *Kittiwake* spun on her heel engines roaring and with much splash coming in over the stern she ducked under the barge's stern by the narrowest of margins. Punch, sitting with the Admiral, stood up and bellowed, "Billy Jago, what are you playing at? Call yourself a sailorman? A cow could do better."

Billy Jago, at the wheel of his barge, looked startled at being shouted at by name then recognised Punch. "Sorry, Punch, couldn't stop."

Jane had pushed Suki out of the way and put the port engine ahead to give more power to the boat's swing, then with both engines going ahead again, aimed to pass under the stern of the ship which had carried on with its own manoeuvre indifferent to the small boat drama going on round it.

Back in clear river with the crisis past, Sparrer passed towels round the wetted party and everyone relaxed again. The Admiral had stayed calm throughout but closely noted everything that had gone on. He nodded and remarked to A P Herbert

"These girls know their stuff, don't they?"

Petty Officer Herbert smiled a reminiscent smile. "Yes sir, I was very impressed by them during their time with me. I wonder if other girls can be as good?"

The Admiral frowned at this. "That's something we need to handle quite carefully but if they are, it would certainly ease the manpower crisis." Jane had quietly watched this exchange and could see the old Admiral's conflicted face. One of the old school but an honest man, it was plain that he still had traditional views on women's place but the mixture of serious manpower shortages and women clearly demonstrating that they could do so much more perfectly competently, was pressing home a realisation that they were coming whether he liked it or not. And he was rather enjoying watching this particular crew going about their business. Jane had handed the helm back to Suki, quietly apologising for pushing her out of the way, but Suki just said, "That's all right Jane; you're in charge so it's you that carries the can."

As *Kittiwake* made her way down the river there were frequent salutes and flags dipped in honour of the Admiral's flag, but also many signs of the damage the Blitz was inflicting on the riverside. There were often green buoys and flags, each marking a sunken wreck or underwater obstruction and *Kittiwake's* crew had to be careful to pass each one on the correct side. A tug lay beached on the south bank in Long Reach, its bows missing. Off Beckton a full scale salvage operation was in progress, with salvage vessels, barges and dive boats crowded round a sunken freighter with its upperworks still above water. The Admiral was very interested in that one. Several battered, listing colliers lay to buoys while emergency repairs were made to bits missing from enemy action. As they passed Purfleet oil terminal a tank was still burning, black oil smoke towering into the sky. Passing Tilbury the damage to the terminal was clear; although it was still just about functioning much of it had been destroyed, as had the nearby hotel. There were sunken tugs at Gravesend on the other bank but the town itself seemed to have survived unscathed allowing it to continue with its critical role as the seaward end of the Port Authority's service. Passing Thameshaven with the open water of the sea reaches in front of them, the gaunt and fractured remains of the tanker *Lunula* were being broken up. This unfortunate ship had been arriving from America with a cargo of petrol, actually tying up on the berth when a mine went off underneath it. The ship burned for five days, spreading chaos around it. A tug attending it had been drenched in petrol and burned so fiercely that it glowed red hot before sinking.

Southend Pier, *HMS Leigh,* was reached a little before 1400. With due ceremonial the Admiral went ashore followed by his Flag Lieutenant, the Second Officer Wren and Petty Officer Herbert. The Radio Chief then went ashore, leaving Third Officer Baker, the Chief Wren and the steward behind. This gave Merle a chance to adopt her divisional officer's role and an opportunity to talk to the crew about any personal concerns. First she dropped a piece of news into the group. "We Wrens have a lot to thank our Admirals for. The other two women's services have recently come under military law which makes their lives much more draconian. The Admirals refused to let us be taken in so we remain, technically, civilians although it certainly doesn't feel like it. But Naval law will be operating a lot closer to us from now on so watch your step all the time." She then talked to each crew member alone but with nothing major to consider she relaxed and chatted, reminiscing gently with Punch and Evadne about pro course and the joys of Whale Island in January. Jane meantime got on with a particular return form which apparently she had made a mess of the previous month, struggling with increasing irritation to get it right until Merle intervened and showed her what was wrong. "You're not very good at this routine stuff, are you?"

"I hate it. I mean, any sensible person ought to be able to do it but it is a complete pain in the backside. Why does it all have to be done in triplicate? And why won't stores give me an adequate supply of carbon paper? Even that would make it easier."

The Chief Wren, who had said very little, snorted with amusement at this. "That's the joy of being in the Navy. The bureaucracy is only ever one step behind you. "

Kittiwake lay alongside the pier all afternoon with nothing much happening. The steward obligingly kept them supplied with tea and titbits from the supplies shipped that morning and someone had to stay on deck tending the fenders and mooring lines as the boat rose then fell on the tide. But otherwise it was peaceful and rather pleasant sitting out on the afterdeck with a gentle sun in a blue sky, wavelets lapping against the boat and a light wind giving a sense of fresh sea breeze. For Jane and her crew this was normal. For Merle, the Chief Wren (whose name they never did discover) and the steward it made a pleasant change and a sense of being close to the sea that lay as a background to their daily work. By 1830 their cheeks were glowing then a messenger came down the steps. "The Admiral advises that he won't be finished today. You are to go to Holehaven overnight and be back here by 1200 tomorrow."

The steward enquired "Ere, is there accommodation here? I'll need somewhere to doss overnight."

The messenger nodded. "Yeah, come with me and I'll fix you up. Nothing for ladies though."

It was Jane's turn. "Oh, that's all right. We can put ladies up on board if they don't mind a settee or a hammock here in the saloon."

Merle laughed. "It will make a change."

Jane stood up. "Right, let's get cracking. The sooner we get there the sooner we can be in the *Lobster Smack*." And ten minutes later they were under way. On the trip round the Admiral's stores were raided and an excellent supper of cold meats and salads emerged, luxuries compared with the restricted diet Deptford victualling supplied them with. Once tied up a bottle of red wine from the stores was opened and even the Chief Wren relaxed and was seen to smile. From there they trekked to the *Lobster Smack* where the publican recognised them and saw them settled in the snug. For Jane and her crew this was a bit of a homecoming. For Merle and the Chief this sudden incursion into a heavily maritime world, surrounded by sailors and sailor talk was a whole new experience which quite visibly they loved despite the occasional colouring of cheeks as wafts of serious bad language drifted their way. By closing time they were very cheerful.

They were back on the pier as instructed for 1200. The steward and radio Chief joined again right away, but there was no sign of anyone else. It was a colder, grey day with occasional drizzle so there was little of yesterday's pleasure in being outside. Shortly after 1600 A P Herbert and the Second Officer Wren came down. "The Admiral will be here in ten minutes. Be ready."

So the engines were started and the mooring lines singled up. Twenty minutes later the Flag Lieutenant came on board. "Admiral coming."

They went to their stations and as he stepped on board due ceremonial greeted him. Jane's signals saw them cast off and heading back up river within minutes, flags flying. It was an uneventful trip in the gathering gloaming until Halfway Reach, where a burning lighter was being tended by a fire float. They were hailed by it. "Can you give this thing a tow over to the North Bank? It's got old car bits in it and Ford's people can deal with it."

"Oh dear, we've got the Admiral on board and shouldn't really be doing hazardous things."

"But there's no-one else."

The Admiral and his Flag Lieutenant had appeared beside Jane. "I think it will be very interesting to see you deal with a burning lighter. Don't let us stop you."

Jane puffed her cheeks. "Well, sir, if that's all right with you I can do it but it might be dangerous."

The Admiral laughed and pointed to his VC medal ribbon. "See that? I didn't get it for being put off because something might be hazardous. Go ahead please."

"All right sir, as you say." She shouted into the saloon, "Crew on deck at the double." Her people tumbled up. "See that thing? We're going to tow it over to the Ford berth on the North side."

Punch did a double take. "Lucky it's loaded; we can get a towrope on it fairly easily."

Jane backed her boat close under the lighter's bow; the heat was intense. Punch and Evadne hauled themselves onto the lighter taking the tail of the towrope with them. A quick make fast and they dropped back into the launch. Jane had been continuously juggling the throttles to keep the boat close under the bow and as soon as her crew were back on board she pulled ahead, giving the towline about thirty feet of slack before screaming, "Make fast at that". The firefloat went round and cast off the lighter's moorings. Free of its restraints it tried to charge *Kittiwake* but Jane knew the tide was behind them so this was likely to happen and she sheared off to starboard, the towline coming taut and tugging the lighter round. Skidding on the tide, Jane hauled the tow round to stem the tide and dodged across it until close alongside the wharf. The firemen on the float were brave people: two of them climbed onto the lighter and threw mooring lines ashore where Ford's own firefighting crew were waiting. As soon as the lighter was secured the shore crew opened up with a foam hose; this was basically an oil fire. Punch called to the float fireman, "Can you let go our towrope please?" and coiled it down. Jane eased the launch away from the wharf and the heat and turned upstream again; the incident had taken just twenty-five minutes.

All her passengers had crowded into the wheelhouse and fore end of the aftdeck to watch. There was silence until they were comfortably away and safe, then not much said as they went below again. But the Admiral stayed beside Jane. "That was exceptional seamanship. I doubt if a man could have done any better."

'Well thanks,' thought Jane, 'why should a bloke be any better?' but she was smart enough to recognise that the old Admiral, a product of a previous age, had intended that to be as high a compliment as he could give to a woman.

"I've been well trained sir. I've had tutoring from lightermen and they really know their business."

"Have you had to deal with burning lighters before?"

"Once before sir, in a big raid on the Surrey Docks where lighters of timber were set on fire. That was a pretty tough night."

"So things like this are only part of the job? I don't think I realised that."

"Well, there is a war on sir, and that makes everything a bit different."

"Quite so. I think I am going to have to re-think my approach to this business."

Which business was not made clear but Jane gave him a smile and concentrated on her navigation. Punch came up and took over the helm. With the Admiral still standing beside her she asked "Sir, do you think there's any chance Oi could get a new tiddley uniform out of the Navy? This one's a bit singed – it wasn't really meant for stuff like we've just done."

"It's Leading Wren Johnson, isn't it?"

Punch nodded.

"Yes of course – send a requisition in to me, marked for my attention, and I'll make sure you get it. And the other girl: Wren Smith is it? she can have one too. That was extreme bravery."

Punch looked rueful. "We do a lot of things like that sir. The only difference is that it got noticed this time."

They were passing under Tower Bridge by now and Punch called down "Coming alongside. Stand by." Jane came up, quite deliberately left Punch on the controls and went aft to pass the stern line. Punch put the boat alongside so gently an egg would not have been broken between boat and pontoon, Suki stepped ashore and took the lines and in two minutes they were all fast. The Admiral noted the change in cox'n.

Engines off and the rest of his party disembarked, the Admiral called *Kittiwake's* crew into the saloon. "Well, young ladies, I cannot find words for my admiration. Like a lot of people, I was doubtful about this whole business of Wrens on boats. But after the last two days I am a convert and will not hesitate to say so. Your bravery, skill and toughness are a revelation to me. Well done. No need for ceremonial to see me off."

Jane went with him and he shook her hand by the bulwark. Then a salute saw him ashore.

Back on Lambeth Pier there was a sudden slump; not in morale, which was sky high, but in simple physical – and emotional - weariness. "Do you think we really did as much good as he suggests?"

This time it was Sparrer who spoke. "Yeah, too right Suki. Wot a trip."

Jane simply nodded.

CHAPTER 23

Another year gone

Another day, another job. Jane had happily signed Punch's travel warrant to Lowestoft. "Doing anything interesting, then?"

"Probably helping me dad install his engine."

"Oh Punch, you need a break. Tell him you're going to bed for a week."

"Well, that's not really how we work, but I'll try."

And Punch went on her way, cheerful enough.

The boat seemed empty without Punch's presence but with mail bags collected and a list of half a dozen barrage balloon barges to deliver to pinned up in the wheelhouse, they set off down river. Suki took over the wheel from Jane and trying to be casual asked, "Jane, you know those evening dresses of yours. I couldn't borrow one for next Saturday night, could I? I've got a hot date."

Jane laughed. "Yes, of course you can borrow one. Won't they be a bit long on you? They're full length on me. And who is the hot date?"

"I'll fix the length, you wait and see." Suki smiled, a sly mischievous smirk. "Actually, the hot date is the Admiral's Flag Lieutenant. I fixed it up with him yesterday and we're going dancing at some club."

"Don't waste any time, do you?"

"There's a war on Jane; we can't afford to hang about and really I've nothing to lose."

"What's his name?"

"Actually, it's Algernon but he is happy to be Algie. I've already found he gets cross if you call him Algebra."

Sparrer emerging with tea broke up this conversation; Jane couldn't help smiling to herself. But her conversation with Suki suddenly brought back memories of Stefan and pain went right through her. Mostly, she was managing to keep him out of her consciousness and to focus on the job in hand, but every now and them something would trigger the memories and they were deeply painful when they came flooding back.

Calling for orders on Friday morning Jane wasn't surprised to find they were listed to stay at the Royal Docks entrance again that night. She knew what that would mean and as they were lying by on Tower Pier at lunchtime she phoned Arthur to see if there was anything new. The answer was no, just be sure to lean on their contact Jem and try to get more out of him.

As before, Evadne opted out of this one, admitting to a horror of homosexuality so Jane picked up the police whistle and with Sparrer and Suki found Jem who settled them in the same corner of the Roundhouse. As ever, the entertainment was outrageous fun and not for innocent ears, but the girls enjoyed it. After doing an early turn, Jem joined them in full makeup and an elegant blue evening dress. "Hope you liked it, Dahlings" he trilled.

"Jem, you're a star with a dirty mind. Listen, we need to talk to you. Can we go where you go when you disappear?"

Jem looked scared. "I don't want to talk to you, it's too dangerous."

"But that's why we want to talk to you, Jem. Maybe to take that danger away. Honest, we think we can."

It was Sparrer who broke the deadlock. "C'mon Jem, we saved you once. Maybe we can do it again."

"Oh all right, go round the bar and down the passage. There's a little side room at the end. But do it quietly and don't draw attention."

"Okay, we'll go one at a time. Suki, you go first."

As inconspicuously as possible they slipped past the bar. They waited five, then ten minutes and were beginning to wonder if they had been stood up when Jem eased silently into the room, now dressed in his ordinary street clothes. "All right palones, what is it?"

"Jem, you know that Harry Miles who comes into the pub? What is it about him that makes you so scared?"

"He's a nasty man who we all hate."

"Yes Jem, but why? He never does anything except talk to you."

"He wants things from us and threatens us horribly if we don't give him what he wants. He's killed two of us already."

"What is it he wants?"

"Please, dahlings, please. This is too risky."

"C'mon Jem, we need to know. And maybe we can take the threat away. Is he blackmailing you?

"Yes, he is" And to the girls' consternation he started to cry, slow rolling tears over trembling cheeks. His makeup smudged rapidly.

"That can't just be because you're a group of poofs, surely?"

"Yes, in part. Oh, what's the use? I'll probably get killed for telling you this but what he wants is information. There are some dockers who like to be serviced by us queers. Instead of charging them ten bob like we used to, they tell us what's in the warehouses and on the ships coming in. That's what Harry Miles wants to know. And no, I don't know why."

"So if Harry Miles was taken out of the reckoning you'd be safe?"

"I'm not sure about that. He's only a local bad man, nothing else special about him. We think he's working for someone in the background but we don't know who or why. Whoever they are, they remain and could get nasty with us. And please, I really don't know any more so do stop quizzing me."

"All right Jem, we'll leave it at that. We'll make enquiries and try to make sure he doesn't cause you any more trouble. Is there a back way out of here?"

"Yes, at the end of the passage. Bona Nochy, my palones. Do take care."

They did take care and sailed as soon as they got back to the boat. But there, standing at the lock head as they moved off, was Harry Miles calmly watching them.

It had been a disturbing evening which they debated as they ran back up to Lambeth Pier. At least they now knew the chain and why the quietly self-effacing community based on the Roundhouse pub were involved - and scared. But where did the trail lead on from Harry Miles?

Moored up, Jane wrote a letter to Arthur with this latest information and how it fitted together. Was there anything else for them to do now, or had they done their bit? Arthur's reply a couple of days later suggested they might be needed at least once more, which did nothing for their peace of mind.

With the same mail delivery came a note from Lady Ormond, inviting Jane to join her and a few guests for dinner the following Saturday night. The car would pick her up at seven o'clock. The slightly peremptory tone of this invitation bothered Jane, A P Herbert's comment that the Lady would take her over if allowed to, surging to the front of her mind. But there was no reason to say no so she sent a brief note back confirming her presence and asking if she could change when she arrived at Lady O's flat, as getting on and off boats in long skirts was very difficult. Lady O's reply by return was, of course Jane could change there and leave clothes there if it helped her.

Suki was amused by this. "Sublime to the Oh Gor Blimey in one week. Say one thing about this war, you get to be a great deal more flexible about your social life. I've met all sorts of people I wouldn't have come close to otherwise." Sparrer gave that one a wry smile.

But in the meantime daily life and work went on. After a long day with extensive use of their derrick to deliver stores and ammunition to remote gun batteries, they were heading back up river and passing one of the Police launches when the Coppers waved them to come over. Curious, Jane came-to a few feet off the Police boat but they hailed "Come alongside, we want you to look at a cadaver, see if you recognise him."

The girls all pulled unhappy faces but knew what had to be done. Jane and

Sparrer hopped over onto the Police boat's after deck, then recoiled in horror. "Oh no, it's Jem. So Harry Miles has got him. What a tragedy." They both went pale and burst into tears. The boat's sergeant regarded them coolly. "Can't take it, eh?"

"Oh we've seen corpses enough but it's different when it is someone you know."

Sparrer had a quiet retch over the side before they took control of themselves. The sergeant had picked up their reaction right away. "You know this poof, then?"

"A bit. He was helping us with some investigative work and we'd already rescued him once."

"What sort of investigative work? Not what you are on the river for, surely?"

"No Sergeant, but we have been helping with other enquiries which I'm afraid we can't say anything about."

Jane hoped that this would put him off but no such luck. "I'm afraid we will have to ask you more about how you come to know this character. Come to the station with us."

"But Sergeant we're not allowed to tell you any more. There's a war on, remember? I promise you we're both on the same side but I can't say more."

Jane called across to Suki, "Go back to base. We're being taken in by this lot. See you later."

Which is how Jane and Sparrer found themselves at the Wapping Police Station and being eyed frostily by an Inspector who wanted to know all about it.

"I can say nothing without clearance. You must let me phone my superiors."

Grudgingly they handed her a phone and she got through to Arthur. "Listen, the River Police have taken us in because the body of our informer has been pulled out of the river and they're demanding to be told how we know him. I won't say anything and they're getting suspicious. Do you think you can call them off?"

"Leave it with me Jane. They're actually much more involved with this investigation than the guys in the station may realise."

The Inspector's cold eye kept them on the spot for fifteen minutes while nothing happened. Then the Inspector took a call, went red in the face and grunted "All right, sir." He turned to Jane and Sparrer; "Apparently you girls are also involved in this investigation down at the Roundhouse. Why didn't you say so? Could have saved us a lot of bother. OK, you are free to go but you can tell our people on the boats what the score is next time without security problems. It's a strange old world when young girls like you are involved in dirty work like this."

"There's a war on, Inspector, hadn't you noticed? We women have been doing a lot of things we'd never have dreamt of before the war and it looks like going on that way. Any chance of a lift back to our boat at Lambeth Pier?"

The Inspector relaxed and gave them a quizzical laugh. "Yes, I suppose we can take a turn up the river." The Police crew appreciated the cup of tea given to them when they tied up alongside *Kittiwake.*

Jane had wangled the weekend off for the boat, claiming essential maintenance. Sunday fourth of May might otherwise have been a big day for Jane, being her twenty-first birthday, but duty came first. Despite this, her crew had noticed the surge of letters and parcels. "Got a birthday, then?" asked Suki. "Yes, I suppose so. Makes me feel very old."

"Can we ask how old, Jane?" Jane sensed a trap here, having to admit to being the youngest person on board but decided there was no point in trying to deny it. "Actually, it's my twenty-first. I'm an adult at last!"

There was a stunned silence from her crew. "You're only twenty-one? Wow."

Suki nodded, "Well, well, that explains your little bits of naivety from time to time. Good Lord, Jane, you have come a long way in a short life. You could easily pass for ten years older."

"Really? I'm not sure that's an accolade I wanted but the last couple of years have crammed an awful lot in. After the war, it is going to feel very strange, so experienced yet relatively still quite young."

But she happily put up the cards round the saloon, keeping only David's to go in her little cabin.

That evening, she went with Suki to select one of her evening dresses for her hot date to appreciate. Jane packed the special one then relaxed back in Lady O's Rover as she was whisked off to the West End. There she was greeted by the butler and shown straight to her room to change. Looking as spectacular as ever, Jane headed to the dining room, expecting to be with a crowd of the old and fusty. It was more than a little of a surprise when Lady Ormond greeted her and introduced her to a group of young people, the men mostly in officer's uniforms. Startlingly, Flag Lieutenant Algernon was there. Jane was puzzled. "But I thought you were on a date with one of my crew tonight?"

He laughed and waved behind himself. From behind a large urn stepped Suki, now resplendent in Jane's evening dress. "Suki, what on earth are you doing here? I thought you and Algie were out dancing somewhere!"

"We will be later, Jane. We knew you had a birthday coming up so decided to help you celebrate it in style. We didn't know it was your twenty-first which makes it even better. And my family have known Lady Ormond for a long time so it wasn't difficult to arrange this. Happy birthday, Jane."

A cheer went up. This group were not likely to burst into 'happy birthday' but champagne glasses were clinked. Then Lady O produced a large orchid for her corsage "Sent by your parents, dear Jane. They are in on the act too."

It proved to be a lively evening with Jane placed next to an army lieutenant whose face seemed faintly familiar. "You don't remember me, do you?" He teased.

"I have seen you before somewhere but can't place it. Do tell."

"Dunkirk? A long line of guardsmen you took off to the ships? Remember the lieutenant keeping the column under control? I promised I'd see you in London and here I am. Thanks for the lift."

"You're welcome; glad to be of service."

Later they said their thank yous and went dancing at the Jacaranda Club which had a hot new group playing. Jane happily lost herself in twirling round the dance floor for several hours and was introduced to the American dancing craze of jitterbugging. She had heard of it but never been with people who could do it and thoroughly enjoyed its energetic style. Some time in the early hours of Sunday morning Suki wandered over and said, "I'm thinking of going soon. Shall we share a fast black?"

"You, Suki? You mean you're not taking this one up a back alley somewhere?"

"No Jane, believe it or not I think this one might be worth a bit more developing."

"Oh well, good luck. But yes, let's get transport organised and go home."

CHAPTER 24:
Only just

Punch rejoined at midday on Sunday, finding both Jane and Suki nursing hangovers. Yes, she had had a good time on leave, teaching her father how to handle a barge with an engine. After a lifetime under sail he was having difficulty adjusting to what could be done with a propeller to drive the boat. "Bit of a busman's holiday, then."

"Well yes, but it was fun and good to work with me dad again. He really is a sailorman."

Punch had been under orders to call by Wren headquarters on her return and brought a pile of mail with her. She had also been given a rather odd grilling by Superintendent Carpenter and Lady Cholmondley, now a full four-ringer, asking about how things were run on *Kittiwake*. Punch had struggled a bit to explain that everyone knew their job so well and were so willing that little overt discipline was needed. "When Leading Wren Beacon gives an order we all do it immediately, knowing that it will be necessary and correct." She had said. For the rest it was all done with little need for orders. Everyone else knew their job and was content with it. This seemed to satisfy the two ladies but it struck Punch as odd, knowing how well the boat ran.

There was a note from Merle, addressed to Leading Wren Beacon so it was formal. Attached to it was a short report from Second Officer Priddy who had been on the boat for the Admiral's trip. 'While the internal running of the boat was not strictly her business, she had been concerned by the lack of visible discipline in the boat and the way the whole crew interacted with each other in a very casual way. This is not the way a uniformed service should be conducting itself,' she wrote, 'and there was a general feeling of slackness in the crew's approach. Something should be done about this'.

"Well, I like that!" Exclaimed Jane, the red mist rising. 'How could this stupid busybody have so missed the point of how I run the boat?'

The note from Merle accompanying this report said that there was no intention of imposing stricter ways on the boat at this stage but it would be a good idea for Jane to be more visibly in command. Apparently their silent signals for letting go and tying up had been particularly disapproved of. "This stupid woman has no seamanship and no idea what is involved in running a boat." grumbled Jane, passing the report round her crew who were inclined to agree with her.

There might have been trouble from this report had not a letter from Admiral Boyle, VC, come into the Director's hands at the same time. This gave fulsome praise for the Wren crews' abilities and smartness during the two days of their acting as Admiral's barge. *"You can always tell when a ship is being well run by the lack of bawling and shouting to get things done and in this respect their silent boat handling had been particularly impressive. And their bravery, discipline and toughness in dealing with the burning lighter had been quite outstanding. He would have no hesitation in recommending Wrens more widely for operating boats. He hoped to have them as his barge crew again in the not too distant future."*

Not for the first time in her Wren career, Jane was finding the contradictions the most difficult part to deal with. There was also a sharp little memo from a stores officer about her returns, which were still haphazard and inaccurate. "These stupid things" she shouted. "Who cares how many sausages we've eaten in the last month?" But some form-filling clerk somewhere obviously did.

Monday morning they were back at work, taking a group of squaddies down to Tilbury Fort, running on down to Hole Haven and a pleasant evening in the *Lobster Smack*, then back up the river next day via the *Worcester*, the imitation wooden wall training ship at Greenhithe now being used as a depot for the patrol and accommodation for many stray bodies. Here they collected a particularly hard-faced group of marines who were affable enough but said little while cleaning their weapons. Unexpectedly, the boat got Wednesday off so finally it was Evadne's turn to go on leave and she set off for her Aunt's home with some little regret at not simply staying on board.

On Friday it was no surprise to be given orders to lay over at the Royal Docks entrance that night. Jane had phoned Arthur to see what he was looking for, and got very specific orders. "Leave two of your people on board looking after the boat, the other two to come ashore about 1930 and walk to the Roundhouse; wait inside until I turn up. Ignore any men you see around the route, as they are likely to be my people watching and waiting. Do not leave the Roundhouse until you have spoken with me and got further instructions."

Their day's work was too busy for Jane to have time to brood about the evening, so it was around 1830 before she could brief her crew and get organised. Suki and Sparrer would remain on board while Punch went ashore with Jane. Was it their imagination working overtime or was there a tense air about? Looking around carefully as they went ashore, Jane and Punch set off leaving a very nervous pair behind. "D'you think we're doing the right thing, Jane?"

"Oh God, I hope so Punch. I hate leaving them so unprotected. But Arthur did say his men would be about so with any luck they'll look after them."

As they walked up the road, there were odd scuffling noises from doorways and several times men showed briefly in the distance before vanishing. The Roundhouse almost seemed like sanctuary by the time they got there; they looked around and tucked in a corner trying to be inconspicuous was Arthur. Although the usual crowd were there the atmosphere was flat and silent. No-one was performing or even chatting loudly in Polari. The girls' arrival seemed to make it worse; the low buzz of conversation died away and they were watched intently as they went up to the bar and ordered half pint shandies each. The two waited patiently until the concentrated gaze on them eased and then sidled over to Arthur, waiting quietly in a corner.

"Hello you two. Did anyone try to get to you on the way here?"

"No Arthur, we saw a couple of blokes acting a bit furtively but I suspect they were your men keeping an eye on us. What on earth is going on?"

"Let's just say we are trying to get our targets to show themselves. We believe your friend Harry Miles is under orders to take you girls out of the set-up. He can't do that on his own so with any luck his accomplices will also have to join in. We will wait here quietly while my men stand by to collar them."

An hour can seem like a lifetime when waiting, tense and on edge, for something – anything – to happen. Arthur shrugged. "Looks like we are going to have to flush them out. I want you two to walk slowly back to your boat not bothering to look behind you."

"Why? Will we be turned to salt?"

Arthur laughed gently at the allusion. "No, I hope not but we need these rogues to feel confident enough to try to get you. Don't worry, we will be in close attendance."

With deep misgivings they set off, strolling gently. The tension in the air was physical, but nothing happened until they came onto the quayside to go on board *Kittiwake*. Suddenly there were running footsteps and both were grabbed from behind. Harry Miles was a seasoned fighter but hadn't bargained on Punch's sheer physical strength. She threw him over her shoulder and as he tried to pick himself up she gave an almighty kick in the chin, knocking him out cold. Jane meantime had been grabbed by two people; she was struggling to get out of their grasp when Punch stepped over and gave each in turn her best uppercut. The two girls were standing there panting and surveying their unconscious attackers, Punch licking her knuckles, when half a dozen policemen came running up. "All right, girls, we're here, you're safe now."

"Bit late aren't you," said Jane with an acid edge to her tongue.

"Blimey, did you knock them out?"

Jane looked at the policemen coolly. "There are advantages to having a heavyweight champion in your team."

By now Arthur had joined in. "Well done, you two. We've got them at last." Arthur was looking as delighted as his sophisticated cynical style would allow. "This is a real feather in our cap."

The Police meantime were collecting the unconscious bodies and were startled to discover that one of them was a woman. "Take them to the incident van, tie 'em up and bring them round. I want to talk to them before we put them away."

Jane had got her breath back. "Right, let's pop on board and see how the other two are."

A minute later she was screaming up to the quayside. "Arthur, they've gone. There's no-one on board. Where are they?"

Arthur looked equally horrified. "I've no idea. We have had the quayside under surveillance all along so how your girls have been spirited away is beyond me." A check with the Police on the quayside confirmed that neither they nor the River Boat Police had seen anything untoward.

"The sooner we get these three conscious again the better. They're bound to know where the girls are and we know how to get information out of people." The incident van had pulled up onto the quayside. Beckoning the girls to follow him Arthur settled to wait for the spies to recover consciousness.

With the three conscious again but firmly tied to chairs, Arthur wasted no time. "All right, where are the two boat girls? We want them back right away."

The female spy snarled, "Save your breath copper. They are our hostages and you'll only get them back when you put us on a boat to Germany."

Arthur grimaced. "We've no time to waste. Tell us now or we will be using methods to make you talk."

The male spy opened up. "We have nothing to say. Good luck to you in trying to find your girls."

"You do realise you have two choices: co-operate now or face execution. Which is it going to be?"

"You don't scare us. Come on now, a boat over the Channel for us and get your silly girls back, or their dead bodies long before you do away with us."

Arthur sighed.

"Have it your own way. Inspector, take these reprobates to Pentonville and get to work on them. And initiate house to house searches for the missing Wrens."

With the spies removed there was nothing for Jane and Punch to do. Arthur gave them a nod and a perfunctory, "Well done." Then went off in a Police car. Feeling abandoned the girls trailed back to the boat, put the kettle on and sat looking at each other. Gnawing anxiety meant that sleep was impossible although they probably dozed a little near dawn.

A Police Sergeant came aboard mid-morning. "We've not got anything out of the spies yet but we are working on them. My men have been combing the area round here and the River Police are keeping a close eye open in case your two have been dumped in the river. So nothing so far, I'm afraid but we'll keep trying."

Rather than sit around feeling desperately worried Jane went ashore and walked all round the area, looking for some sort of inspiration but nothing came. Early evening the same Sergeant came aboard but still had no news. They thought perhaps the spy group were close to cracking and had been handed over to expert interrogators so he hoped for news by next morning but that did nothing to lighten Jane's mood. Punch sat quietly staring into space which in itself showed how worried she was.

Another bad night followed, with both of them sitting in the saloon knowing that Suki and Sparrer had to be nearby but having no idea where. The whole area was subject to a fierce Blitz that night with enormous fires set off nearby but the girls were so focussed on their own worries that they cared little for the noise and heat going on round them. They weren't to know it but this was the last night of continuous Blitz and the *Luftwaffe* signing off in spectacular style.

The sergeant's report next morning was another blank so rather than sit there doing nothing they went ashore again and were standing at the entrance lock bullnose looking out over the tiers of lighters lying to buoys in the river. Jane suddenly looked at Punch, a wild light in her eyes. "Tiers of lighters. Tiers of lighters. Of course, why didn't we think of that? Remember that odd one the lightermen pointed out to us? It's still there, on its own. I'll bet that's where they are. I can just feel it in my belly."

There was a Police launch alongside as well and Jane ran over to it. "We've had a brainwave and think we might know where the missing girls are. See that odd lighter out there on its own? That's the place. Come on, come with us and look."

"Now just a minute, young lady. What makes you think that is where they are?"

"Because it never moves but has strange people around its deck at night. We suspect it may be something to do with the spy ring that's just been cracked. Come on, let's give it a try."

"Well, there's nothing else to do so I suppose we might as well."

"Fine. We'll go in our own boat and you can follow. See you over there." Within minutes the two boats came along side the lighter; Jane and a policeman scrambled on board. "The cabin's the obvious place to start."

"Right, I'll take a look." And he moved aft, pulling up the slightly open hatch. There was an almighty explosion, the unfortunate policeman went flying through the air into the river and his boatmate set off after him. Jane picked herself up from the sidedeck, feeling a lot of pain down her right side but apparently able to move. She looked down into the cabin but no living thing could survive down there. She pulled up the boards over the ladder into the hold, climbed down slowly and called "Anyone there?" A faint thin thread of a voice came back. "Yes, up here at the fore end." Even in these extreme conditions Suki's well modulated vowels were unmistakable. It was pitch dark inside the hold so Jane felt her way forward, wincing from sharp pain in her right shoulder as she did so. Against the forward bulkhead she felt around and found first an arm, then a head. "Suki?" she asked.

"No, you've got Sparrer there. She passed out a couple of hours ago. Our arms are tied up above our heads. Can you let us go?"

Jane pulled out her pusser's clasp knife, sharp as ever, and felt for the ropes to cut. Suki squealed at one point when Jane got her instead of the rope but it didn't take long to cut her free. The unconscious Sparrer was next to her and was also cut free. "Right, now we need to get you out of here smartish." There were ominous water sloshing sounds from the aft end of the hold. "Can you walk?"

"With help perhaps yes but what about Sparrer?"

"Oh, I can carry her." But Jane was dismayed to find that she was more injured than she had realised. She managed to help Suki to the aft end and called for help from Punch. "Bring some rope."

Punch arrived and went into the hold, found Sparrer and heaved her slight frame over a shoulder effortlessly. Punch went straight up the ladder, over the side and lowered Sparrer into the launch. Suki was standing looking helpless at the bottom of the ladder, her arms hanging limply by her sides. Water was rising fast. Punch lowered the rope down. "Tie that around her, I'll heave. There was no time for niceties so a quick bowline had to do. "Heave away," and with Jane pushing from below Punch got Suki up, on deck and over the side into the launch. Now there was just an injured Jane to get out. The water was now up to her chest and vivid memories of being stuck in the mud off Tower Bridge came back to her. Abruptly the lighter dropped its stern under the water. Punch, seeing the danger, raced to throw off the lines tying *Kittiwake* to the lighter. This was just done when the lighter reared up vertically and disappeared below the surface throwing Punch into the water. She swam back to the launch spluttering and spitting river water and managed to climb on board using the trailing mooring rope as an impromptu scrambling line. It was a struggle but with the extra strength of desperation she heaved herself up over the bulwark. Standing on the aft deck she called "Jane, are you there?" and was enormously relieved to hear a weak reply. "Over here but the tide's got me. Come quickly." Luckily they had left the engines running so Punch was able to set the boat moving right away, using their little Aldis lamp to shine over the water. It was a profound relief to see Jane floating nearby. Punch stopped engines and allowed the launch to drop down onto Jane, leaning over the side and grabbing her as they came together. With one almighty heave Punch pulled Jane out of the water and into the launch. By now Jane was semi-conscious and rambling a bit. "Get to hospital, got to get to hospital."

Punch ran the boat into the lock entrance, leapt out shouting at the lock-keepers who had been brought to the lockhead by the explosion. As soon as they grasped the urgency of what was needed they moved very fast indeed and ten minutes later two ambulances were collecting the injured. With them gone Punch figured she might as well go back to Lambeth, so told the lock-keepers where she was off to and was relieved to get tied up there. Lambeth Pier had never looked more like home.

CHAPTER 25:

Coming round again

Consciousness came slowly but with it a terrible familiarity. This was a hospital and her first thought was, 'Oh no, not again.' Looking around she recognised the hospital bed, the clean white surroundings and vaguely in the distance sounds of people moving around. Where was she and how long had she been lying there? She tried to sit up but a sharp pain in her right shoulder stopped the attempt. She waved an arm at a passing nurse who informed Jane that she was in Guy's Hospital and had been unconscious for the best part of two days. "Stay still for a minute while I call the doctor."

This gentleman looked her over, consulted her chart and asked "How do you feel?"

"Well fine I think, apart from a sore shoulder. What's wrong with me?"

"A couple of shrapnel wounds; we've removed metal from your right shoulder and right thigh but fortunately nothing important has been hit and you should be mobile again pretty quickly. Oh, and we had to pump out your stomach. We gather you went swimming and Thames river water isn't nice stuff for your gastric system."

"Dear old Father Thames has some nasty bugs, then?"

"Oh yes, it is standard practise here to stomach pump anyone who has been in the river. It is less trouble in the long run."

"Can I sit up?"

"No reason why not. I'll get a nurse to give you a hand."

Eased up the bed by the nurse, Jane looked around. There, in the next bed, was a gently grinning Suki and beyond her was Sparrer.

"Good heavens, what are you doing here?"

"Much the same as you, Jane; recovering from our injuries. My arms are just about right now apart from chafe and my ribs are recovering rapidly from your rope. Y'know, the one you and Punch used to pull me out of the hold. That made a raw old mess of my ribs and breasts. Sparrer's recovering much the same and we think we'll be discharged in a couple of days' time."

Sparrer gave Jane a wave. Both girls were sporting vivid black eyes and Suki had a bandage round her head. "Why the black eyes?" queried Jane.

"Oh, our friend Harry Miles tried roughing us up a bit, convinced that we would have some vital information we could give him. But we told him we were only obeying orders and knew nothing about where they came from, which is just about true. I can't say I like being punched in the face but I suspect that by relative standards we got off lightly."

"Well, I never. How did you come to be in the lighter in the first place?"

"We were sitting in the boat's saloon quietly worrying when three people came aboard. We recognised our friend Harry Miles so we knew this was not a friendly visit which they emphasised by pulling out pistols and threatening to shoot us. One of them slapped a cloth over our faces which must have had chloroform or something on it as next thing we knew we were in that lighter's hold. They had dumped us against the forward bulkhead and tied us up with our arms strung up over our heads. Bloody uncomfy position for any length of time, I can tell you. After knocking us about a bit they seemed to lose interest and cleared off. We were abandoned there and I have to admit I had visions of us dying of thirst until you turned up. I'm not sure how long we were there, it seemed like an eternity, but I guess maybe two days?"

"That's about right actually. Has anything else been explained to you yet?"

"Not really. Your precious Arthur called in this morning but only seemed to want to speak to you so went away again silently. I believe Third Officer Baker is coming in to see us in the morning so perhaps we'll know a bit more after that. My Dad is popping in this evening."

All this was a bit much and a great wave of lassitude swept over Jane. Evening meal woke her up again and feeling better for some food Jane was sitting up taking things in when a large General swept into the room, escorted by a fluttering ward sister. He laid his cap and baton down and gave Suki a big hug. To Jane there was something naggingly familiar about him. Having checked that his daughter was recovering rapidly he turned to Jane and said, "Nice to see you again, young lady."

Jane sat up straight "Well yes sir, but again? Have I met you before?"

Suki burst into this with a whoop of laughter.

"Oh Jane, really. You just never twigged, did you? My name – Brownlow? What was the General called that you rescued at Dunkirk and who did so much to keep you in the service?"

"He was – he was – no I don't believe it. Oh my goodness me. You're General Brownlow's daughter? Why didn't you say? This changes everything."

Suki and her father were both roaring with laughter. "I said nothing precisely because it would have changed everything. You've no idea how intrigued Dad has been to hear of your exploits, confirming his sense that you were something special. It really has been extremely useful to your career to have the Army onside."

Jane turned to the General. "Well sir, I suppose I have to thank you for saving me. The Navy was certainly feeling pretty vengeful after I got back from Dunkirk. Would you really have taken me into the ATS?"

"Still will young lady, any day. But I suspect you're best staying where you are. I have asked if you could be seconded for a bit to train some ATS in boatwork but have been told that it will be next year at the earliest as they want you for training Wrens before then."

"Do they now? Maybe we are going to see Wren boats crews, then. I wonder what that means?"

"I can't say any more now but I think you will find that your work since the turn of the year has been very well received in high places. I'm only delighted that my daughter has been part of it. You have no idea how important it has been to her recovery to find her place again, to be part of a dynamic team and to be doing her bit for something huge."

"But it was only little us working our boat."

"Indeed. And causing a revolution in the process." With that he turned back to his daughter and started to chat about news from home.

He wasn't long gone when a very tall leading seaman ducked into the room. Sparrer, who had been sitting quietly while the chat went on round her, lit up. "Lofty! Oh, Lofty!" She squealed. He gave the others a wave and swept Sparrer up into his arms. Suki and Jane politely looked the other way. "I got a forty-eight because you'd been hospitalised. What on earth have they been doing to you?"

"Some of it is hush-hush but we was all doin' a special investigation." Somehow further words weren't needed for some time. The Ward Sister pushed him out eventually with a smile on her face. "I'm staying with your folks. We'll be back tomorrow to see you again."

Third Officer Merle Baker arrived on the dot of nine o'clock the next morning, clutching her attaché case from which she produced some mail. "Right, listen in because this affects all of you. Medical advice is that you will be discharged tomorrow but that you all need a convalescent period before you are fit for duties again, especially Beacon. We knew you were doing some hush-hush work as well but hadn't expected you to get into quite such trouble; this does change our plans for you. Leading Wren Johnson has also had to go on sick leave as she strained her back badly pulling Beacon out of the river. As a result we don't have a Wren crew for *Kittiwake* and the boat is too valuable an asset to leave lying around locked up so they are putting some patrol service men onto her meantime. But once Johnson and you two" – she pointed at Suki and Sparrer – "Are fit again we intend to put Wrens back onto her under Johnson's command. Evadne Smith we're sending on a signals course until she rejoins."

Jane started at this: "But .... but..."

"Don't worry Beacon we have plans for you which I'll discuss with you privately.

We then intend to go on with a Wren crew on your boat until other and bigger decisions are made. You will gather from this that the past five months you have put in on the launch have been very well received at the highest levels and the Director herself has asked me to pass on her appreciation of what you have done. I can only say well done to you all. Now are you able to get about yet?"

"I should think so; do we need sister's permission?"

Permission given, Third Officer Baker took each of them into a side room in turn, doing her divisional officer duties.

While this was going on, Jane scooped up her mail. There was a telegram from David, dated three days ago. *"Have forty-eight hours leave stop Will be waiting at Savoy stop. Meet me there love David.* " 'Oh dear' thought Jane, 'that was just as we got into trouble down at the Roundhouse.'

There was a letter from David from the day before. It was an angry, anguished note. *"Jane, I waited for you and you didn't come. So I went to the boat and found it locked up. Where are you and how could you disappear like this without telling me? It really is too much. As I nursed my sick and struggling ship, watching her lift her stern to each huge roller and just about managing to keep going, I saw your face over each crest, empathising with my poor battered boat's straining efforts. My care of her and your care for me merged into one force keeping my ship and I going against the odds. Having made it I longed to tell you how we had done it because I knew you would understand but you weren't there.*

Now she is in dock and likely to be there for some time. I desperately wanted your tender ministrations to me to go alongside my boat's deliverance into dockyard hands but you weren't there. How could you do this to me? I have to go back to her for about a week to see everything settled then will be at Hemel Towers. Please Jane get in touch and let me know where you are. Your loving but distraught David."

Jane sat there stunned, staring blankly at the letter and wondering what to do. She was still vaguely pondering this when Third Officer Baker appeared in front of her. "Your turn, Beacon, I've a lot to discuss with you."

Jane jerked out of here reverie. "Aye Aye Ma'am" she muttered and trailed into the private room. "Right Jane, what on earth is the matter with you? You've gone white and totally distracted and I've important things to tell you. Please pay attention."

"I'm sorry Merle. I've just had an angry note from David who has been trying to reach me and failing. I really must answer him right away."

"That's all very well but for the moment affairs of the heart will have to wait as we've your future to discuss. Regard me as the messenger; the decisions have been made at a much higher level."

"Don't I get say in what happens to me?"

"Not in a uniformed service you don't. Let me explain: We have concluded that your talents lie in special projects, in making things happen and in pioneering, rather than in simply running a boat. What you have done with *Kittiwake* has been outstanding and is recognised as such. But your admin is dreadful and your attitude at times downright unhelpful. Therefore we have asked ourselves what else you can do which makes best use of your talents. We have a couple of special projects we want you to do once you are fit. It is looking more likely all the time that we will be able to have a first batch of Wrens trained as boat crew this Autumn. We want you to be part of the training staff, probably down at Plymouth which presumably will suit you. There's likely to be a gap between the special projects and starting the training course so you will take some leave then do a signals course. Our records don't show you doing any signals training at all and you could do to have some. Do you know any signals?"

"Well, a bit as we did Morse and semaphore in the Sea Rangers at School. Flags I don't know."

"Right, we will send you on a concentrated signals course, probably in August. Now, have you any questions?"

"The medical people here seem to think I need a convalescent period but I don't feel bad at all. Can't I go back on a boat meantime?"

"No, Jane, it is high time you took a break and we want to see those wounds healed up properly before we let you lose again. Just relax; why not go and visit your family for a change? They haven't seen you in a long time."

"I'd need to sort out David first as his boat is in dock for major repairs."

"Yes, so I gather. Sinking a U-boat singlehanded has been a real feather in his cap."

"Good heavens, did he ram it or something?"

"I believe so."

"Well, well. How splendidly old fashioned. And you say we're getting a first boat crew training course this Autumn? That's wonderful."

"It is looking quite likely now. The ramparts of antagonism have more or less been demolished and provided nothing goes wrong in the next month or so the answer is yes. We really are delighted but you have a duty to keep your mouth shut and your nose clean for a bit yet. Please, please, remember that."

Jane smiled gently at that. As soon as Third Officer Baker had left she wrote to David, explaining that she had been on a special mission then unconscious in hospital for a couple of days. She was expecting to be discharged the next day and could see him as soon as he was free. Hoping that that would pacify him she had it posted in the lunch time mail and then snoozed for a bit.

Arthur turned up in mid-afternoon. He took Jane off into the side room and they spent some time analysing what had been done and especially the last bit. "All three of our captives are singing like Canaries now. Miles, of course, will do anything to save his skin so he's settling for being put away for the duration of the war and the other two have agreed to be turned, in exchange for not being hanged after all. That means they'll be sending absolute baloney from their radio at intervals, just to deceive Hitler. And we're busy right now salvaging the lighter as we think it may have important evidence on it."

"Now, do I have it right that you were using us as bait all along?"

"Only towards the end. Before that you got some very useful intelligence and helped to open up what was going on. Your friends at the Roundhouse have been told that they can return to their usual way of living provided they remain discreet about it."

"Two of my crew very nearly died for this. Can we get them some recognition?"

"Possibly a Mentioned in Despatches but these undercover operations tend to stay that way without recognition other than being noted in the right places. We debated what to do for you as you're plastered in medals already but we think we can quietly upgrade your MBE to an OBE as some sort of recognition."

"Well thanks but I'd rather see my crew recognised."

"Oh, we'll fix something."

Jane had one more visitor that day when Lady Ormond swept into the ward. "Jane!" She exclaimed, "Why wasn't I told you were in hospital? I could have arranged a private room for you."

"Well thanks Lady Ormond, but it really is important for me to stay with my crew." And Jane gestured to the adjacent beds.

Lady Ormond peered at them then exclaimed, "Suki Brownlow, I didn't see you there. I hope your family are looking after you."

"Oh yes, Lady Ormond, my Dad comes in each day and that keeps the hospital on its toes."

"Yes, I can imagine it will. And who is the other girl?"

Jane introduced Sparrer to her Ladyship, getting Sparrer's usual "Pleasedter-meechya" in reply.

"And you are a member of Jane's crew?"

"Oh yeah, have been since last year down at Dover."

"How interesting." She turned to Jane again. "You have a mixed bunch on the boat then?"

"Well yes, but it's not just us, y'know. This mixing is going on throughout the services and the world is going to be a very different place socially after the war. Sparrer's an important part of my crew."

"Indeed. Jane, you must come and stay when you are discharged from here. My people will be very pleased to look after you. And congratulations on the OBE, incidentally. I was pleased to be able to help a little."

"Well thank you, Lady Ormond, but I am digging my heels in about my crew getting recognition too. If they don't, I don't."

"Yes, so I hear and I think something may be done. It's always a bit tricky with these undercover operations."

By the time the General and Lofty plus Sparrer's family had been through as well, Jane was feeling distinctly weary, which was some measure of how far from full fitness she still was. Perhaps some quiet convalescence might not be such a bad idea after all.

CHAPTER 26:

Sorted

The three invalids were discharged from hospital in the middle of May, to find the world changed around them. Suddenly, the *Luftwaffe* had stopped raining bombs every night and the relative calm felt odd. But the battered and gap-toothed architecture of London was its own testament to the power of the Blitz and it was debatable how much longer its citizens could have gone on enduring the pounding they had received. The ending of the nightly attacks might have come as enormous relief but sporadic bombing continued and the wailing of the air raid sirens remained an inevitable part of life in the capital throughout the war.

Without their boat as a home and a central unifying presence, the girls simply dispersed. Jane had not received a reply to her explanation to David and was beginning to feel rather worried. Was she to lose both the men she had given her heart to? She certainly did not want to bury herself deep in the West Country until she did hear from him so the logical option was to take up Lady Ormond's invitation to stay. This seemed to please the lady so Jane relaxed a bit. Exceeding her welcome had bothered Jane but it seemed that this problem was only in her own mind, so she settled in. She commissioned the Rover to take her down to Lambeth where she packed up her belongings from *Kittiwake,* collected her evening dresses from the Palace and settled everything into her room at the flat. She felt a bit silly carting Rufus in, a giant teddy bear hardly seemed like the right sort of sophistication to be projecting but the staff treated his arrival calmly and even arranged a low seat for him by the window in her bedroom. There was a message for her, too: Lieutenant-Commander Daubeny-Fowkes would be at the Savoy the next night and could she join him there for dinner, please? Relief flooded through her; at least they were communicating again. But she had no doubt what David would be expecting and that posed a nice diplomatic problem. She would be out all night. With just her boatmates giving her a knowing grin that was not a problem but in Lady O's more rarefied atmosphere things felt different. But she was not about to lose David over this so decided the only satisfactory action was to be honest with the Lady and hope for the best.

Dinner that night presented a good opportunity, with both butler and maid in the background which meant the whole household would be primed. "Lady Ormond, you know I'm seeing David tomorrow night? That will probably mean that I won't come back. I hope you don't mind."

The Lady laughed gently, almost ruefully. "My dear, you must be free to live your life as you see it and my place here is a support to it, not a prison. May I take it this is the only person you'll be staying out for?"

"Oh good heavens yes, Lady Ormond. I'm not a tart, just very in love with this wonderful man and it's wartime. We may all be dead next week and that changes how one sees relationships. He's been at sea for four months more or less without a break and has evidently had some major adventures. Now it's rest time and a chance for some emotional succour. Do you understand?"

The Lady laughed again, the same rueful chuckle. "My dear, I was young once myself, y'know, so I know how you feel. The first war took away my chance of happiness like yours but the pressures and temptations were exactly the same. Yes, I do understand so don't worry about it."

Jane felt deeply relieved at this, one more possible obstacle passed. She smiled her thanks and they moved on to other topics.

She elected to stay in the following day and catch up on correspondence. Changing to go out in the evening she decided on the petrol blue velvet as there was a sense of starting again, of treading carefully over bumpy ground. She packed a bag with a white evening dress, her tiddley uniform and some civvie day clothes. She still had a dressing over the stitches in the wound in her right shoulder so put a scarf over it. Lady Ormond took one look at this arrangement and said "My dear, that won't do. Haven't you got a stole?"

Jane shook her head mutely.

"Well, I have half a dozen so come and chose. You really must have one."

Choosing something from the array of fur in her Ladyship's wardrobe was less easy but under direction she took a white mink number. As she was leaving Lady Ormond said, "My dear, do bring your David here for dinner sometime. I would like to meet him."

"Well thank you. I don't know what his leave position is yet but once I do I'll see what can be arranged."

"Any time. It doesn't have to be arranged in advance."

Jane smiled her thanks and took the lift down to the waiting Rover. Settling in the back seat she reflected that one could get quite fond of this sort of life but a memory of cold wet and windy nights on the water was a reminder of another world just two steps behind her which she would be going back to. It would be a mistake to get too attached to present comforts.

Coming into the foyer of the Savoy she saw David hovering by the desk, looking tense and angry. But when he saw her his face relaxed and a hungry pleading passed over it. "Hello David, it's lovely to see you again." Somehow this trite banality seemed completely inadequate for the churning in her stomach, the weakness in her knees and the lurch in her heart. He looked at her, close but not touching, with despair in his eyes. "Yes it is, isn't it?"

Then somehow they were wrapped round each other, hugging and kissing and ignoring the busy movement round them. "Come on, let's have a drink." Settled in the American bar with champagne cocktails they looked at each other again. "You didn't really think I had run away, did you?"

"Well, I didn't know what to think. With the boat locked up and no sign of any of you I couldn't help thinking the worst. I was so desperate to see you again that the disappointment sort of obliterated more rational thought."

She teased him gently. "Silly man, did you really think that I'd just disappear?"

"That's what it seemed like."

"If you ever get into this sort of state again call Third Officer Merle Baker at Wren Headquarters. She has a kind of D/O responsibility for me and will almost certainly know where to find me. "

"Oh, right; I'll keep that in mind. Does she know you're with me tonight?"

"Not entirely but she does know you are around and has no illusions about my proclivities."

He laughed and shook his head slowly. He pulled her stole back to reveal the dressing on her right shoulder. "Tell me about that."

"To some extent it is hush-hush but we had been carrying out surveillance work on the river which led to two of my girls getting kidnapped. It just came to me that they were being held on a lighter in the stream and when we went aboard the thing the cabin hatch was booby trapped. I got a bit of shrapnel in my shoulder from the explosion, and got knocked about by the blast. I managed to keep going at the time but the blast effect took its toll and I conked out a little later. It took me two days to come round again."

"But your hunch about your crewmates was right, was it?"

"Yes indeed. Suddenly I absolutely knew where they were and went to get them. The River Policeman who lifted the hatch got blown into the river and was badly injured but Punch and I managed to rescue the girls before the bloody thing sank. I'm not sure how much of this I can tell you but your dear brother Arthur was pulling the strings in the background."

"Oh was he now? How very interesting. I knew he did more than wrangle with the Americans from the Foreign Office but he always stays very secretive about what else he is involved in."

"Sounds like I know more than you do now. Tell me about your ship and the U-boat."

"That was an exciting few minutes in the middle of the night. We were on the starboard side of the convoy when we spotted a U-boat, would you believe, on the surface in the middle of the convoy. It was a bit rough at the time so I decided the best way of dealing with him was to ram. I called for maximum power, went charging into the convoy and deceived him by going parallel with his course until the last moment when I went hard-a-port and rammed him immediately forward of his conning tower. That sank him; nearly chopped in two. My poor old boat got badly mangled too, with the bow all buckled and broken and shock damage everywhere. Going maximum power did our dodgy condenser no favours either; it just about held together until we got in but it is a write-off and the boilers none too happy either."

"Wow, that was what you were getting at with your letter. It can't have been easy nursing your damaged ship in after that."

"No, we skulked in the middle of the convoy for the rest of the trip with pumps running the whole time. I wasn't sorry to see her into the dock."

"Does something like this get any recognition?"

"There's talk of something but I don't know what yet. How about you?"

"Your dear brother is talking about upgrading my MBE to an OBE, but doing it very quietly 'cos hush-hush operations are not supposed to be announced publicly."

Dinner passed in a haze and getting re-acquainted later was pure pleasure. As before the stress drained out of David with physical relief and any lingering doubts had evaporated long before dawn. Reconciled again, they then had three of the happiest days of their lives, going to a lunchtime concert at the art gallery, dancing in the evenings and sometimes simply drifting along the Embankment hand in hand.

By the end of it he was starting to get some idea of how to make love and had been reduced to a happy, if exhausted, daze. They considered themselves very firmly engaged and the discussion was about the practicalities of that.

"The dockyard staff seemed to think my ship will be ready for sea again about the end of September. They're cutting the bow off completely and building a new one but it looks like the poor old thing will need new boilers as well as a new condenser and that takes time. How about we get married in mid-September?"

"What a lovely idea, David. I'm not at all sure what I'll be doing as they are taking me away from *Kittiwake* for special projects, whatever those might be. I am to do a signals course then there are hints that we might be going to get Wrens in boats more generally and they want me as a trainer for a first course in the Autumn. But none of it is clear yet and at some stage I really must visit my family down in Devon. So I suspect we'll have to take things as they come. Next time I see Merle I'll try to get a bit more from her and tell her about our wedding plans. But yes, let's set a date for mid-September then take our chances on being able to make it."

"You do realise who you'll be getting for a mother-in-law, don't you? I think she is still pretty opposed to the idea."

"That's too bad, David. If need be we'll hide in a garret out of her reach and love each other all to ourselves. And besides, I think I may be able to tame her a bit if I can only have a private chat with her. Can you arrange that?"

"I can try but she's not the most deliverable of people, y'know. I'll arrange for you to come to Hemel Towers next week and we'll take it from there. Meantime I have to go back to my ship until the weekend so it's good-bye for now."

David's letter on Saturday confirmed that they were expecting her on Monday and he would pick her up at 1600 from the local station; his mother had not reacted well to the news. In the interlude Jane had done a good deal more research in 1910 newspapers and when she caught the train on Monday morning it was with a file well-filled with Newspaper copies.

The first night at Hemel Towers was rather sticky. The Marquis was full of *bonhomie* and really rather pleased that his youngest son should be the first to get hitched. But the Marchioness at the other end of the table was positively frosty, saying virtually nothing and glaring at Jane.

When she arrived a very elderly servant had come to Jane's bedroom and introduced herself as Jane's lady's maid for the visit. It turned out that the maid was, in fact, the children's nanny, allowed to stay on at Hemel Towers after the children had grown up and doing odd jobs about the place. She would care for Jane while at Hemel. "David was always my favourite, y'know. Perhaps because he was the youngest I was more protective of him and he did struggle a bit with his brothers always putting him down. He was such a gentle little soul."

"So he wasn't always up to mischief or anything?"

"He would have liked to be but was too scared of the reaction from his brothers to do anything about it."

Jane tucked away this little window into her fiancé's youth, reflecting on how much the Navy had matured him to be the successful captain he was now.

Jane was at breakfast the next morning when the Marchioness came in, glared at her and said "I understand you want to talk to me. You have good reason to be wanting that. I will be in my boudoir until 1030; come and see me there."

Jane had a sudden tightening of the throat and an urge to tremble all over which she struggled with. Thirty minutes later, newspaper clippings in hand, she presented herself to find the Marchioness being massaged. "All right, child, what have you to say for yourself?"

Jane took a deep breath and said, "I would very much like for you to be reconciled to David and I getting married. We are determined that we will marry, but it would be so much better if you could bless this and accept it as giving David happiness for the rest of his life."

"I wanted David to marry someone of equal social standing, not some service provider's ambitious gold digging daughter."

Jane held on to her temper and rode over the insult to her eminent physician father.

"Ma'am, we are not that lowly a family, y'know. We come of highly successful farming stock and my father is one of the best physicians in his speciality in Britain. As for gold digging, we are perfectly well off already thank you and I have no need to go chasing money."

"Yes, but you lack breeding, for all of your dainty manners. We blue bloods do try to keep contamination from the masses out of our bloodlines."

'One last try before I drop the depth charges' thought Jane. "Have you ever noticed how the mongrels are often the strongest and smartest dogs? And David is the farthest down the line in dynastic terms so who he marries is much less important than would be the Earl's choice. Surely he should be free to chose his own partner in life?"

"I repeat that it is not what I wanted for him. I know of several eminently suitable girls who would be much more appropriate for someone of his social standing."

"Are they aware of your hopes?"

"Not yet, but they are accustomed to the idea of taking their place in married society through a choice made by their parents. A wilful miss like you would never understand the need to observe your place in a hierarchy. To be able to understand that you have to have the breeding in the first place."

"Like you did, ma'am?"

"And what do you mean by that?"

"I looked up the papers recording your marriage back in 1910. The reports make interesting reading" And Jane pulled out several of the copies in her folder. "*Tiller girl marries the Marquis of Hemel*" read the headline. "*Greengrocer's daughter captivates the Marquis of Hemel.*" read another. The Marchioness had gone white, then very red in the face before bursting into tears. "How dare you! How dare you! You will put those things away now and I never want to hear about them again."

"Well, ma'am, I will be happy to do so as soon as you agree to David and I marrying."

The Marchioness glared fiercely at Jane who simply looked back, struggling to stay calm but steeled by what was at stake. It was the Marchioness who looked away.

"I have tried so hard to live up to a standard," she wailed, "Then along comes someone like you to spoil it all."

"But ma'am, I'm not spoiling anything. Look at your progeny, strong healthy successful adults. Where's the harm in repeating that, especially with the youngest of your line?"

"But they'll never be accepted into polite society."

"Well, David doesn't seem to think there will be a problem there. First and foremost I'll be a Naval wife as David is certainly planning on staying in the Service after the war. With the experience I'm accumulating I think I can make a very good Naval officer's wife. I know my protocol and how to behave. What more do you need when it's not up to us to carry on the family line?"

The Marchioness took a firm grip of herself. "Everything I've tried to stand for is being taken away."

Jane couldn't help laughing gently. "You sound exactly like my mother, ma'am. I suspect she has already noted some nice doctor for me to settle down with. I suppose it's this thing about moving out of one's own immediate circle which bothers the older generation but I rather feel social structures are going to be much more fluid anyway after this blasted war is over."

"So it would seem but I can't say I like it."

"Ma'am, David and I are going to marry anyway. But you would make him a much happier man if you gave him your blessing. It's ironic; my mother doesn't trust the aristocracy one bit and I'm expecting a good deal of opposition from her for sort of the reverse of your objections. But we'll manage given half a chance."

"All right child, I will give in to your blackmail but with deep misgivings. What more do you want?"

"Tell David yourself that you are relenting. It's important to him and it will come better direct from you than my relaying it to him."

"Very well, I will do that. But don't think for a minute that I have suddenly acquired an affection for you."

"More or less word for word, that was said to me about their Lordships of the Admiralty after my Dunkirk exploits. They were not best pleased but I survived. My anchor now is my love for David and that transcends everything else."

That night the engagement was formally announced at dinner.

* * *

In the wider world the war went on with its mix of disasters and triumphs. The final 11th May Blitz was the most ferocious ever carried out by the Luftwaffe, but Londoners had become so inured to the bombs dropping on them that very largely they simply got on with their lives. The Houses of Parliament were burnt out and the Docklands areas severely damaged but London continued to function.

Out in the Atlantic the Navy had its greatest disaster and revenge for it when HMS Hood was totally destroyed by the third shell from the Bismark, or possibly Prinz Eugen, when they met in the Denmark Strait. By doing so Bismark sealed its fate with an angry vengeful Royal Navy's determination to get it, giving extra drive to the strategic imperative. In the chase across the Atlantic a torpedo from a Swordfish aircraft, flying from HMS Ark Royal, wrecked Bismarck's steering allowing the pursuing fleet to catch up with it. The next day the giant sixteen inch guns of HMS Rodney pounded the magnificent but crippled beast to a blazing wreck unable to fend off the torpedoes which finally sank it.

Down in the Eastern Mediterranean the battle for Crete was coming to an unhappy end with the British kicked out of yet another outpost, this time by German paratroopers. Once again the Navy rescued a large part of the British force trapped on the Island, as before with significant loss of ships in the process.

* * *

This particular battle had a deeply personal sadness for Jane: her Godfather, as ever up close to the action directing ship movements, failed to return. It was thought likely that he had taken to a boat to get ashore and the boat had been hit by German aircraft but this was never certain and he was posted missing, presumed killed. His loss cast a shadow over her happiness at the time but the accepted response to loss throughout the war was to have a good weep then get on with the job so she sent a letter of condolence to Mrs Rodmayne and put his demise into a mental pocket of sad memories. It was an ever-growing pocket.

Jane's attention had been very close to her own affairs and there was a slightly claustrophobic air to life at Hemel Towers, but even there the outside world could not be ignored. David was deeply affected by the chase to sink the *Bismark* and he paced around full of impotent frustration. He and Jane sat close to the radio following the bulletins, their emotions fluctuating between stark disbelief, horrified dismay and ultimately a sense of satisfaction. But his longing to be there overwhelmed other attentions and Jane took note of this. Being a Naval officer's wife was clearly going to mean taking second place to his loyalty to the white ensign. In the meantime, however, there was a war to be fought. As she thought about this, Jane's refrain came to the front of her mind: 'I will not be defeated. My commitment is just as strong as yours, David, and marrying you will not stop me fulfilling my destiny'.

BIBLIOGRAPHY

TITLE	AUTHOR	PUBLISHER
WOMEN'S ROYAL NAVAL SERVICE (WRNS)		
Blue Tapestry	Vera Laughton Mathews	Hollis & Carter
Britannia's Daughters	Ursula Stuart Mason	Pen & Sword
The Wrens 1917 – 77	Ursula Stuart Mason	Educational Explorers Ltd
The WRNS	M H Fletcher	B T Batsford Ltd
The Story of the W R N S	Eileen Bigland	Nicholson & Watson
Never at Sea	Vonla McBride	Educational Explorers Ltd
Blue for a Girl	John D Drummond	W H Allen
WRNS The Women's Royal Naval Service	Neil RT Storey	Bloomsbury Shire
Women and the Royal Navy	Dr Jo Stanley	I B Tauris
The WRNS in Wartime	Hannah Roberts	I B Tauris
ALL SERVICES		
Women in Uniform	D Collett Wadge	Sampson Low, Marston
World War 2 British Women's Uniforms	Martin Brayley & Richard Ingram	The Crowood Press Ltd
Service Slang	J L Hunt & A G Pringle	Faber & Faber
The Girls who went to War	Duncan Barrett & Nuala Calvi	Harper Collins
Queen and Country	Emma Vickers	Manchester University Press
BOAT CREW WRENS		
I only joined for the Hat	Christian Lamb	Bern Factum Publishing
Entertaining Eric	Maureen Wells	Imperial War Museum
Maid Matelot	Rozelle Raynes	Nautical Publishing Co.
Ten Degrees below Seaweed	Paddy Gregson	Merlin Books Ltd
An intriguing Life	Cynthia Helms	Bowman & Littlefield Inc.
Sea Change	Yvonne Downer	Dreamstar Books
Land Girl to Leading Wren	Lucia Hobson	Hobson Books
WRENS		
Services Wrendered	Sonia Snodgrass AKA Jack Broome	Sampson Low, Marston
Changing Course	Roxane Houston	Grub Street
Wrens in Camera	Lee Miller	Hollis & Carter
WRNS in Camera	Lesley Thomas & Chris Howard Bailey	RN Museum
Love and War in the WRNS	Vicky Unwin	The History Press

TITLE	AUTHOR	PUBLISHER
WRENS continued		
Thank You – Nelson	Nancy Spain	Arrow –Hutchinson Authors
Dancing on the Waves	Angela Mack	Benchmark Press
The War Years	'One small Wren' –Lillian Pickering	Athena Press
From Little Ships to Comets	Audrey Iliffe	Self-published
Bellbottoms and Blackouts	Louisa M Jenkins	Universe Inc
Hostilities Only	Brian Lavery	National Maritime Museum
Wren's Eye View	Stephanie Batstone	Parapress Ltd
Secret duties of a Signals Interceptor	Jenny Nater	Pen & Sword
Brave Faces	Mary Arden	Matador
The Women's Royal Naval Service	Brenda Birney	Hazel Dakers
ROYAL NAVY		
Steam Picket Boats	N B J Stapleton	Terence Dalton Ltd
A Seaman's Pocket Book	Lords Commissioners of the Admiralty	
Jackspeak	Rick Jolly	Palamanando Publishing
Not Enough Room to Swing a Cat	Martin Robson	Conway Maritime
The Royal Navy Day by Day	A B Sainsbury	Ian Allen Publishing
Coasters go to War	John de S Winser	Ships in Focus Publications
The Battle of the Narrow Seas	Peter Scott	Seaforth Publishing
True Glory	Warren Tute	Harper & Row Publishing
German Kreigsmarine in WW II	Chris McNab	Amber Books Ltd
The War at Sea 1939 – 1945	Stuart Robertson & Stephen Dent	Conway Maritime
Naval Life & Customs part 1 & 2	John Irvine	Web site
Hold the Narrow Seas	Peter C Smith	Moorland Publishing Co.
Nelson the Commander	Geoffrey Bennett	Pen & Sword
Men Dressed as Seamen	S Gorley Putt	Christophers
On going to the Wars	Godfrey Winn	Collins
The Hour before Dawn	Godfrey Winn	Collins
Home from Sea	Godfrey Winn	Hutchinson & Co.
One Eye on the Clock	Geoffrey Willans	MacMillan & Co
The British Sailor	Kenneth Poolman	Arms & Armour Press
The Lower Deck of the Royal Navy	Brian Lavery	Conway
Dunkirk Revisited	John Richards	Website off-print
The Evacuation from Dunkirk	W J R Gardner	Routledge/Taylor & Francis
Sunk by Stukas Survived at Salerno	Tony McCrum	Pen & Sword

TITLE	AUTHOR	PUBLISHER
ROYAL NAVY continued		
War at Sea 1939 – 45	Edward Smithies with Colin John	Bruce Constable and Co
Churchill and the Admirals	Stephen Roskill	Pen & Sword
WOMEN IN WARTIME		
Sisters in Arms	Helena Page Schrader	Pen & Sword
Debs at War	Anne de Courcy	Weidenfeld & Nicolson
Jane: A pinup at War	Andy Saunders	Pen & Sword
As Green as Grass	Emma Smith	Bloomsbury
Corsets to Camouflage	Kate Adie	Hodder & Stoughton
Women in Wartime	Jane Waller & Michael Vaughan-Rees	MacDonald & Co
Our Wonderful Women	Cecil Hunt	Raphael Tuck & Sons Ltd
Sisters in Arms	Nicola Tyrer	Weidenfeld & Nicolson
Love Lessons and Love is Blue	Joan Wyndham	Mandarin
The Secret Ministry of Ag. & Fish	Noreen Riols	MacMillan
Britain's Secret War	Chris McNab	Pitkin Guides
What did you do in the War, Mummy?	Mavis Nicholson	Pimlico – Random House
Women in War	Celia Lee & Paul Edward Strong	Pen & Sword
Priscilla	Nicholas Shakespeare	Harvill Secker
Forties Fashion	Jonathan Walford	Thames & Hudson
The WAAF at War	John Frayn Turner	Pen & Sword
A Writer at War	Iris Murdoch	Short Books
The Girl from Station X	Elisa Segrave	Union Books/Aurum Press
Wartime Women	Dorothy Sheridan	William Heinemann Ltd
Whisper of Truth	Mary Vaudoyer	Memoirs Publishing
Unsung Heroines	Vera Lynn with Robin Cross and Jenny de Ge	Sidgwick & Jackson
WAR		
The Second World War 1939 – 1942	Martin Gilbert	The Folio Society
The Second World War 1943 – 1945	Martin Gilbert	The Folio Society
The War within World War II	Thomas Fleming	The Perseus Press
A Muse of Fire	A D Harvey	The Hambledon Press
Love, Sex & War	John Costello	Collins
What Britain Has Done	Ministry of Information	Atlantic Books
The Battle of Britain	Richard Overy	W W Norton & Co

TITLE	AUTHOR	PUBLISHER
WAR continued		
Battle of Britain	Len Deighton	Book Club Associates
The Great Crusade	H P Willmott	Potomac Books Inc
Moral Combat	Michael Burleigh	Harper Press
Lightning War	The Editors of Time-Life Books	
The Second World War in Photographs	Richard Holmes	Carlton Books
All Hell let Loose	Max Hastings	Harper Collins
Blitz Spirit	Jacqueline Mitchell	Osprey Publishing
Home Front	Juliet Gardiner	Andre Deutsch
Britain at War	Maureen Hill	Atlantic World
The Spirit of Wartime	None	Index/Orbis Publishing
The Blitz	Gavin Mortimer	Osprey Publishing
Greasepaint & Cordite	Andy Merrimam	Aurum Press Ltd
Wartime Britain 1939 – 1945	Juliet Gardiner	Headline Book Publishing
We shall never Surrender	P Middleboe, D Fry, C Grace	Pan Books
Cheer up, Mate !	Alan Weeks	The History Press
Millions Like Us?	Nick Hayes & Jeff Hill	Liverpool University Press
Never Surrender	Robert Kershaw	Hodder & Stoughton
Careless Talk	Stuart Hylton	The History Press
Listening to Britain	Paul Addison & Jeremy A Crang	The Bodley Head
Human Smoke	Nicholson Baker	Simon & Schuster
Home from Dunkirk	J B Priestley	British Red Cross
Forgotten Voices of Dunkirk	Joshua Levine	Ebury Press/Random House
Secret Forces of World War II	Philip Warner	Pen & Sword
Churchill and The King	Kenneth Weisbrode	Viking
West End Front	Matthew Sweet	Faber and Fabe
Which People's War?	Sonya O Rose	Oxford University Press
The Secret History of the Blitz	Joshua Levine	Simon & Schuster
Meet Me at the Savoy	Jean Nicol	Museum Press Ltd
Blitz Kids	Sean Longden	Constable
Rationing	Stewart Ross	Evans Brothers Ltd
W W II Remembered	Richard Overy	Andre Deutsch
The Experience of World War II	John Campbell	Oxford University Press

TITLE	AUTHOR	PUBLISHER
RIVER THAMES		
London's Docklands`	Fiona Rule	Ian Allen
The Thames	A P Herbert	Weidenfeld & Nicholson
Independent Member	A P Herbert	Howard Baker
The Thames on Fire	L M Bates	Terence Dalton Ltd
Thames Triumphant	Sydney R Jones	The Studio Publications
Criminal River	Stephen Wade	Robert Hale
Men of the Tideway	Dick Fagan & Eric Burgess	Robert Hale
Coasting Bargemaster	Bob Roberts	Mallard Reprints
London's Changing Riverscape	Charles Craig, Graham Diprose, Mike Seaborne	Francis Lincoln Ltd
An Artist's Journey down the Thames	John Doyle	Pavilion – Michael Joseph
PLACES		
Dover at War 1939 – 1945	Roy Humphreys	Alan Sutton
Hellfire Corner	J G Coad	English Heritage
Life in 1940's London	Mike Hutton	Amberley
The Beaulieu River goes to War	Cyril Cunningham	Montagu Ventures Ltd
Dark City	Simon Reid	Ian Allen
FICTION		
The Cruel Sea	Nicholas Monsarrat	Cassell
The Seafarers	Nevil Shute	The Paper Tiger Inc
Requiem for a Wren	Nevil Shute	William Heinemann Ltd
A Wren called Smith	Alexander Fullerton	Peter Davies
H M S Marlborough Will enter Harbour	Nicholas Monsarrat	Cassell
Not so quiet....Stepdaughters of War	Helen Zenna Smith	The Feminist Press
Trouble on the Thames	Victor Bridges	The British Library
MISCELLANEOUS		
Etiquette for Women	Irene Davison	Chancellor Press
Etiquette in Everyday Life	F R Ings	W Foulsham & Co., Ltd
Table & Domestic Etiquette	Mary Woodman	W Foulsham & Co Lrd
Gypsy Afloat	Ella K Maillart	William Heinemann Ltd
Since Records Began	Paul Simons	Harper Collins

About the Author

Douglas J Lindsay was born to the sea. His parents both came from sailor families and when his father went back to sea for the duration of the Second World War, his mother followed the ship to its new base at Scrabster on the Pentland Firth, Scotland where the author was born in 1941. His father sailed on the small coaster *Drumlough*, which the family owned. It ran as a supply ship for the fleet at Scapa Flow, operating up and down the east coast of the United Kingdom. Remarkably, from 1939 to 1945 it was never touched by enemy action. The family lived in a wooden shack on the Scrabster harbour wall and the author's playground was the harbour and ships berthed there until 1945.

Douglas J Lindsay left his public school in Edinburgh soon after his fifteenth birthday and attended the T/S Dolphin at Leith Nautical College before going deep sea in 1957 as a cadet with the Clan Line – a major cargo liner company – operated to Africa, India and Australia. He settled into a merchant shipping career of which the highpoint was being appointed Captain at the young age of 28, on the large ro-ro freight ships of the Tor Line. Later, he worked in the family shipping office before setting up his own ship management business. In 1985, this business went bankrupt and the author and his wife lost everything. They moved to Berkshire where his wife found work as a housekeeper, a position which provided a roof over their heads.

Very new Captain

The author then took up shipping consultancy and with an interest in square-riggers started sailing them intermittently between consultancy jobs. Working on big sailing ships, mostly as captain, became a major part of his life until 2008 when he retired. In the 1990s, work as a ship repossession superintendent produced some adventurous moments. The author has had vignettes from his own life published in *The Marine Quarterly* drawing on his life in the maritime world.

As well as his time in commercial shipping, the author was for many years a reserve officer in the Royal Navy, sailing as watch officer and/or navigator and gaining a thorough understanding of the Navy's ways and mores. It is with his depth of marine knowledge combined with naval understanding that the idea was born for the *Wren Jane Beacon* and *War* series of well-researched books about the boat crew Wrens during the war years. He knew there was a wonderful story to be told about them.

He has had a lifelong passion for writing. His first published piece, in 1965, was titled rather grandly *Improvement of Navigation Lights and Signals* published in the Journal of the Institute of Navigation. In the 1980s he attended creative writing classes run by John Fairfax and Sue Stewart, who founded the Arvon Foundation. He has written essays, short stories and poetry and many reports.

.

30892817R00122

Printed in Poland
by Amazon Fulfillment
Poland Sp. z o.o., Wrocław